THEIR
BURNING
GRAVES

BOOKS BY HELEN PHIFER

DETECTIVE MORGAN BROOKES SERIES

One Left Alive

The Killer's Girl

The Hiding Place

First Girl to Die

Find the Girl

Sleeping Dolls

Silent Angel

BETH ADAMS SERIES

The Girl in the Grave

The Girls in the Lake

DETECTIVE LUCY HARWIN SERIES

Dark House

Dying Breath

Last Light

STANDALONES

Lakeview House

To Tina,
Merry Christmas!

THEIR
BURNING
GRAVES

HELEN PHIFER

Love,
Helen Phifer
xxx

bookouture

Published by Bookouture in 2022

An imprint of Storyfire Ltd.
Carmelite House
50 Victoria Embankment
London EC4Y 0DZ

www.bookouture.com

ISBN: 978-1-80314-729-1
eBook ISBN: 978-1-80314-728-4

For Emily Gowers, thank you from the bottom of my heart for everything. I'm going to miss you so much xx

PROLOGUE

1991

The rugby club was bouncing, the DJ had the music cranked up so loud that if you pressed your hands against the walls, they vibrated. That was how Erica James knew that she'd drunk far too much. She was in the queue for the loos, her legs feeling like jelly and with the worst case of room spin she had ever had in her life. Leaning against the grubby white wall, she pressed her forehead against it to try and cool herself down and stop the floor from spinning underneath her feet. That green pint was what had tipped her over the edge; it was tradition that at your eighteenth you had to drink a green pint. What was precisely in it, she couldn't tell you, but she knew for certain it had Vodka, gin, Pernod, blue bols – her stomach lurched just thinking about it. She had giggled as she'd passed Beth hers, and they'd crowded round the birthday girl watching her drink it whilst clapping and cheering her on. Then Beth had insisted that they all drink one too and, well, this was the result of that stupid decision. Everyone else was out there dancing and having a great time whilst all she could think about was not being sick or passing out. Three girls came out of the loos giggling, and she gave them the Vs. Silly cows, no idea what they were giggling at. Lurching into the toilets Erica barely made it to the empty stall before she threw her guts up, splashing bright green liquid over the toilet bowl, seat and floor. She felt herself sliding to her knees and wished to God that for once she'd not been a sheep and followed everyone else. Someone was knocking on the door; she buried her face in her hands and growled, 'Sod off.'

Her white jeans were ruined; she could see splotches of the vile green alcohol all over them. She sat there and pushed her head back against the cubicle wall, closing her eyes and willing the room to stop spinning. Erica needed to go home; but she couldn't drive now, she was going to have to get a taxi, if they'd let her in. She stank of puke and stale alcohol. Maybe Jason could drive her; he had a rugby match in the morning, so had told her he wasn't drinking tonight. She'd left him sitting in a corner with his teammates whilst she got drunk and danced. Pulling herself up she stumbled out of the cubicle to the row of sinks and ran the cold tap, splashing water over her face, cupping handfuls of it into her mouth to try and get rid of the horrible taste lingering on her tongue. Finally able to look at herself in the mirror she was mortified: her freshly straightened hair was now a frizzy mess, her eyeliner and smoky eyeshadow were smudged, and she no longer looked like a blonde version of her favourite singer, Dolores O'Riordan, from The Cranberries. She'd toyed once with chopping her long blonde hair short and dyeing it black but had chickened out at her appointment. The music was thudding inside her head, but she felt a little better now that she'd thrown up. Blotting her face dry on a rough green paper towel, she pushed her way out of the toilets to go and find Jason.

The dance floor was pulsating with bodies all pushed close to each other and trying to move to the music. When she reached the corner where she'd left Jason, his friends were there but he wasn't. She scanned the long line at the bar but couldn't see him in the line. Turning back to his friends, she shouted, 'Where's Jason?'

They shrugged, and she rolled her eyes. Lucy saw her looking and pointed to the door mouthing *he went outside*. What Lucy failed to tell her was who he had gone outside with. Oblivious that he might not be alone, she pushed her way through the crowds to get to the front door. She felt like crap and wanted to go home to bed.

The cool evening air hit her hard, and she found herself wobbling a bit more, but the breeze felt wonderful. She looked around. Jason wasn't out here, and she didn't know why he would be out here on his own anyway. Then she heard a high-pitched giggle from around the side of the building, a narrow alley leading to the back of the clubhouse where the bins were kept. She stumbled towards it hoping to ask whoever it was if they'd seen Jason. The voices stopped, and she heard a low groan: this time it was a much deeper voice. Every sense in her body was on high alert, she knew that voice, she knew that groan. As she rounded the corner she took in the sight in front of her. Jason was leaning against the wall his head pressed back against it, eyes closed, and that slut Sally was on her knees, her head in his crotch. Erica felt another rush of vomit fill her throat and she lurched to one side. She wanted to run at her and rip her hair out of her dirty head. Slap Jason and tell him he was finished and a cheating bastard. Instead she cupped her hand across her mouth and turned, stumbling towards the car park. She wanted to get out of here.

Pushing her fingers in her pocket she grabbed the keys for her little Peugeot 305, her eighteenth birthday present off her parents. The shame and anger were making her hands tremble. As she got into the driver's seat a voice told her not to do it, to get out and walk home, but that little voice was drowned out by the drunken voice that was shouting louder. That voice was telling her to go, drive home and get away from here as fast as she could: she could show them all that she wasn't going to be treated like this. She had only been driving three weeks, and she loved the freedom it gave to her. So, she started the engine, forgetting to put her seat belt on, forgetting to turn the headlights on. She reversed out of the space, banging into the bumper of the car parked next to her and giggling, then she sped out of the car park.

She was so angry with Jason. Her cheeks were burning, and she couldn't get the image out of her head. The more she thought about it the faster she began driving, putting all the windows down so she could feel the cool evening air whipping her hair around her face. It was dark and Erica hasn't switched her lights on. She didn't see the stop sign or the markings on the junction that she was speeding towards. She didn't see the couple ahead of her at the junction on their bicycles, arms out signalling they were turning right. She didn't see any of it until it was too late, and she ploughed into them at speed. The horrific crunch of mangled metal filled the air as her car drove right through them. She didn't know what she'd hit but knew it was bad. Her brain foggy, for the life of her she couldn't figure out how to stop the car and ploughed straight into the wall of the bridge opposite with a huge bang and a trail of carnage behind her. Mangled bodies, push bikes and pooling blood spreading all over the road. She flew forwards with such force that she smashed through the windscreen, landing in a crumpled heap on the bonnet.

ONE

Sally Lawson always worked late on a Thursday. She always had, partly because it was the busiest day of the week in the salon and partly because she knew that this way she wouldn't have to start making the tea. David was a terrible cook, his meals were like some form of torture, but working late meant she could stop off at the drive-thru and grab herself a burger, eating it slowly, in peace. Then it didn't matter what dross he served up. On rare occasions he gave in and ordered pizza, much to their son Tim's delight. She didn't even feel guilty about avoiding them for an evening because lately Tim was being a complete teenage arsehole with his silent moods, and David was being, well, he was being very David, which was a nice way of saying boring. The queue for the drive-thru was the longest she'd ever seen – she could have parked up and gone inside, but that defeated the object of coming here in the first place. She listened to her audiobook in the car and was enthralled with Lisa Regan's latest instalment in the Josie Quinn series. Everyone seemed to have far more exciting lives than she did, and thank God she had her books and book club to keep her sane. By the time she'd been handed her Quarter Pounder with mushrooms, onions, tomatoes and Swiss cheese it was twenty past seven. Any minute now David would text her to see if she was on her way home.

Parking at the far end of the car park next to the overgrown bushes, she sat in darkness enjoying her burger. She checked her phone and was pleasantly surprised to see there were no messages or missed calls from either David or Tim. She sat back and enjoyed every bite of her burger, chewing slowly, there was no need to shove it down the back of her throat tonight. Normally she only ate a couple of the fries but not tonight; tonight she was a free woman, and she could enjoy them and the white chocolate milkshake. She checked her phone, it was 19.31 and still nothing from either her husband or son, this was a world record. Wiping her hands on the serviette, she got out of the car and walked the short distance to the rubbish bin, which had a large seagull sitting on top of it. She pushed the empty bag inside and shrugged at the gull. It watched her walk all the way back to the car, where she turned the engine on and put the windows down to get rid of the smell of the takeaway. It would take her another five or six minutes to get home; and by the morning the smell would be gone, and Tim would be none the wiser when she dropped him off at school.

Hest Bank Road was in one of the nicer areas of Rydal Falls. Here the houses were detached, with large gardens and drives big enough to fit three cars. Sally knew she was lucky, David had a great job at the University of Cumbria, her salon was thriving, and they didn't have to worry about anything except David's cooking. She had done a lot better than her friends, than her own parents even, and she was acutely aware of this. Sometimes she had to pinch herself as she drove down the street, past the beautiful homes, to reach hers, the biggest and most beautiful of them all. She frowned to see her house in darkness apart from the glow of the kitchen lights reflecting through the stained glass on the double front doors. This was strange, usually every light in the house was left on, signalling Tim and David were home. Neither of them seemed to care about the electricity bill. Sally smiled, maybe the latest one had arrived and now David had seen how much the rising costs were he'd gone around and turned the lights off. Her smile faded though. There was this fluttery feeling down in the depths of her stomach that was foreign to her, something didn't feel quite right about that scenario.

Parking her Mercedes Roadster behind David's brand-new Jaguar SUV she got out and stood on the drive. Not only was the house in darkness, but the drive lights were out too. She had to walk out onto the street to see the nearest house, which was some distance away. Maybe there was a power cut. She could see lights on there, though, and their drive was lit up. That sinking feeling deep down inside the pit of her stomach was telling her something was wrong. What did they call it, gut instinct? Taking out her phone she found she had no missed calls or messages. Grabbing her handbag off the front seat she locked the car and walked towards her front door. The handle twisted and she pushed it open, stepping inside. The bitter tang of copper tainted the air and she tried to place where she knew that smell from. Her entrance hall should smell of fresh apples from the plug-in air freshener, not this.

'David.'

She called again, 'David.' Then much louder, 'Tim, where are you guys?'

Sally was finding it hard to breathe because her heart had begun to race and every nerve ending in her body was telling her to run, get out of there. What if they'd had a terrible accident and she just left them there, injured? Scared to death of what she was going to find, her phone clutched in one hand, she dropped her bag on the floor and walked towards the only light source in the entire house. There was a breeze behind her, and she felt every hair on the back of her neck prickle at the slight change in temperature because of it. Turning her head slightly, she saw a figure stepping out of the shadowy hall closet behind her. They moved fast and before she could do anything, a thick plastic bag was pulled down over her head and she was struggling to breathe. Her long nails reached up trying to scratch at the hands that were holding the bag tight but, panicking, she felt herself being dragged towards the kitchen. Sally knew she didn't want to go in there, she didn't want to see what was waiting for her in her favourite room in the house. She was hot, so unbearably hot, and the bag was steaming up on the inside. Her lungs were on fire, and it was so hard to take in air. She felt her legs going weak as whoever this was dragged her towards the dining table. Dimly, she could see David and Tim. It must be some sick joke, whoever it was would take the bag off her head soon. She felt her body getting weaker, the heat so intense it was too hard to breathe. Then she was thrust down onto one of the chairs. Her eyes watering she blinked and looked towards David. Why wasn't he helping her? And then she saw that both her husband and son were slumped forwards, plastic bags on their own heads. As her eyes travelled down she saw the source of the metallic smell that had hit her as soon as she'd walked into her house. They were both missing their right hands, bloodied stumps where they should be, and so much blood was pooled on the table in front of them. It hit her then, they were dead. Her family was dead. She could barely breathe. If she'd come straight home instead of going for a sneaky burger, she might have been able to stop this. She felt whoever was suffocating her grab her arm, something was tightened around her neck, holding the bag in place. She lifted one hand trying to claw at it to get it off, but the other was in a vice-like grip.

'Do you know what this is, Sally?' The voice in her ear was muffled through the plastic but she could hear it.

'This is the hand of God.'

A glint of silver reflected in the light, and the last thing she saw before she took her last breath was the bloodstained blade of a huge meat cleaver swinging down towards her wrist.

TWO

Detective Constable Morgan Brookes hobbled through the front door of Ben's house and sighed. She loved this house and the man who owned it more than anything. She was tired and her badly sprained ankle had been throbbing all day, making her pop painkillers like Tic Tacs, come to think of it that was probably why she was tired. Will Ashworth, her current sergeant, had dropped her off on his way home. It wasn't really on his way home, in fact it was the complete opposite, but he was far too polite to mention it. He knew she needed to be here in Rydal Falls and, even though she wasn't working on Ben's team at the moment, she was praying she would be sent back any day now. Barrow was all well and good, but she missed her small team, which had become even smaller with Des's murder. Which was why she was here; it was his funeral tomorrow and she wouldn't miss it for the world. The house was silent, and she wondered if Ben wasn't home. A loud miaow came from the direction of the kitchen, and she smiled to herself, setting the alarm on the security system then making her way there. Des's cat, Kevin, had made himself quite at home in a corner of Ben's large warm kitchen. He had a super soft, squishy cat bed that

Ben had brought home from the garden centre the day after he'd been to collect Kevin from Des's empty house, and an endless supply of cat biscuits from the automatic cat feeder he'd also bought. She laughed. This was the man who had firmly said 'absolutely not' to looking after the cat, because he hated them; this was also the man who had let Kevin sleep on their bed on the nights she worked late and couldn't get a lift back from Barrow because of the stupid boot on her foot which stopped her from driving.

A shrill ring filled the air making her jump; no one except for work rang the house phone, and the rare cold caller. Making her way to the phone she picked up the handset. 'Hello.'

'*Detective Matthews there?*'

'I don't think he is, it's DC Morgan Brookes, can I help?'

'*Oh, yes you can. Brilliant, can you get hold of him? He's not answering his mobile. Tell him he's needed at a house fire on Hest Bank Road. Fire said there are a couple of fatalities inside. If you can't get hold of him then can you attend in the first instance?*'

'I'll see what I can do.' She didn't tell them that she wasn't working this area and was on the Barrow list.

'*Cheers.*'

Whoever it was at Control hadn't introduced themselves or even given her the number of the house, although it should be pretty obvious if it was on fire. She sighed; it was never simple this life. Sometimes she wondered if she had been born to do this job – or had the job chosen her? Either way it didn't matter, what was important was that some poor souls had perished in a house fire and that was just tragic. She rang Ben's phone and heard it vibrating upstairs, maybe he was home after all. Kevin was pushing himself against the back of her calves and purring. Reaching the bottom of the stairs she called up, 'Ben.'

'Yeah,' came the groggy reply from their bedroom, and she began to limp up the stairs.

Reaching the bedroom, she saw him curled up on top of the duvet fully dressed, his eyes still unfocused, and she realised he'd been asleep. 'Hey, what you are doing, are you okay?'

'What are you doing? I thought you were staying over tonight?'

She shook her head. 'What and miss this warm welcome, absolutely not, Matthews.'

He chuckled, pushing himself up. 'Well, I'm glad you're here, have you seen—' Before he could say his name, the cat slipped through Morgan's legs and jumped onto the bed next to Ben.

'"I hate cats, I don't want one in my house, it's not sleeping inside."' She rolled her eyes at him with a big smirk on her face.

Ben lifted his finger to his lips. 'Shh, you'll upset him, he has feelings you know.'

Morgan grinned. 'Well, you better say goodbye to Kevin for the time being, Control just rang your house phone. Fire have requested you attend Hest Bank Road for a house fire with fatalities.'

Ben sat up. 'Crap, I never even heard it; I was so tired after he kept waking me up at the most ridiculous hours last night.' He pointed to Kevin who was sitting on the edge of the bed cleaning himself.

'Do you need me? I can help out, there's not much on in Barrow.'

He stood up and was pushing his feet into the shoes he'd kicked off at the end of the bed. 'There's a lot to be said for falling asleep fully clothed you know; it saves so much time.'

She looked longingly at the soft, super king-size bed and sighed.

'Yes, I do need you. Amy isn't back in work yet and I'm not supposed to be working anything too stressful, so if you can spare the time, I would really appreciate your assistance.'

'I always have the time for you.'

He nodded, crossed the room with Kevin behind him and disappeared into the en suite.

Morgan wasn't tired any more, she was ready to visit the house and find out what she could do to help the poor souls who had died.

THREE

Hest Bank Road was lit up like an airfield. It was so bright Morgan had to squint her eyes against the glare from the flood-lights. The noise from the fire engines and generators running the lights and pumps was deafening, not the kind of excitement that neighbours were used to at all. Almost every house was alive with movement and lit up like a beacon. The ones that weren't Morgan had no doubt housed the more discreet curtain twitchers, lights off watching the drama from the safety of the shadows. The fire crew was damping down the smouldering house, which didn't look too badly damaged. Morgan had been expecting to see charred ruins, but the house was still standing. The front windows were broken and cracked, the woodwork and sill were all charred black, but the house was still recognis-ably a house. She turned to find Ben. He was talking to the crew manager. Joining them she couldn't help it and asked, 'How are there fatalities? Could they not escape?'

She was thinking of the fire she'd recently been in that had taken hold of the old farmhouse in a matter of minutes. She'd had to jump out of a first-floor window to save her life, hence the injured ankle.

'They could have, no doubt about that, if they weren't already dead. Paul Wallace.' The crew manager held out his gloved hand to Ben, then Morgan, who both shook it.

'Smoke inhalation?' Ben asked.

'No, it's really weird, you need to see it for yourselves. They're all sitting at the dining table with plastic bags on their heads.'

Ben turned to look at Morgan, asking Paul, 'How many of them, was it suicide?'

'If they cut off their own hands then it was. You can go in as soon as I get the all clear. I'm afraid the front of the house is a bit of a mess with smoke damage, but the kitchen is pretty intact. Luckily the neighbours were going out to pick their daughter up and saw the flames, phoned us and ran to knock on the door. Poor guy ran around the back to raise the alarm and hammered on the kitchen window but knew something was wrong. He said he was going to drag them out but realised they were already dead and thought he better not touch anything.'

'What do you mean, cut off their own hands?'

'Exactly that, they are all missing a hand.'

Morgan had to stop her mouth from hanging open at the thought of it.

'That's shocking to say the least; and I guess he was a wise guy, must have been a hell of a shock for him.'

Paul nodded. 'Very wise, nice too, though he's more than a bit shook up. His wife went to collect their daughter, as he's gone home.'

He pointed to the nearest house, not quite as grand as this one had been, but still beautiful. It was the kind of street you lived in when money was not something you worried about. Morgan would bet that none of the residents ever worried about the rising costs of Lurpak when they did their weekly shop, unlike the rest of them.

'Should we go and speak to him whilst we're waiting, Ben?'

Ben was staring at the cars on the drive, a brand-new 4x4 Jag and a sleek Mercedes sports car. He looked at Morgan and nodded. 'Yes.'

They crossed the treelined street together. It had been cordoned off by officers to prevent the press or anyone getting in that didn't belong there.

'I know that car, it's an old college friend's, Sally. I was only chatting with her the other day in Booths car park.'

Morgan glanced at Ben. His face had paled considerably in a few short minutes.

'Are you okay?'

He nodded. 'I'm fine, thank you. I just can't believe it might be her. We were both talking about holiday destinations.'

'We don't know if it's her yet, Ben, she might not have been home.'

They reached the front door, which was ajar, and Morgan knocked.

'Come in.'

She pushed the door open, and Ben followed her inside. There was a man standing at the doorway to the room that looked out onto the street, his face a mask of misery.

'Hi, Detectives Morgan Brookes and Ben Matthews.'

'Luke Rigg, this is just terrible.'

He turned, walking back inside the room where he sat down on a leather recliner, pointing at the sofa. Morgan sat opposite him, Ben did the same, all three of them, despite the long front garden and drive, could see the drama that was happening further down the road.

'Front row seats, it's dreadful. I mean we all love a good argument and a bit of excitement when it's happening right outside on the street, don't we? But not something of this magnitude. This is horrific. Ava is friends with Tim, they go to school together. What on earth do I tell her when she gets home?'

'How old is Ava?'

He looked at Morgan. 'Fourteen, that delightful age where she thinks she's an adult. I imagine you know it well.'

She smiled. 'It's a tough age, I would say that you tell her the truth, Luke, there's nothing else you can do.'

'But Tim's her friend and he's dead. She'll never get over it.'

Morgan sighed. 'No, she won't, and it will be very painful for her, but she will cope and in time she'll learn to accept it.'

He stared at her, a little too intensely. 'You sound as if you know.'

'I do, I lost a very good friend when I was a teenager and I miss him dearly, but I survived for his sake.'

Luke nodded.

'Can you tell us what you saw, how you knew that Tim was dead?'

'We were getting into the car when I noticed an orange glow coming from David's house. I looked up and had the fright of my life. I wasn't expecting to see flames licking at the front windows. I told Heather to ring 999 and I ran over there, both of the cars are on the drive, so I assumed they were all home.'

He paused and his silence filled the room. Morgan realised he was gathering himself, choosing his words before speaking them out loud, and she wondered if he was regretting his decision to leave them there.

'Then what happened?'

'I couldn't get through the front because the flames and smoke were too intense, so I ran around the back to the kitchen and saw them all sitting around the kitchen table. They looked as if they were about to eat their tea, never mind that the front of the house was burning down around them. I couldn't understand what I was seeing. I hammered on the windows, but they were like statues, they didn't move, and then I realised why they weren't moving. It happened in slow motion; I pulled the handle down on the bifold door and opened it, and found they weren't moving because all three of them had plastic bags over their heads. They were slumped forwards and...' He stopped, a loud noise that was part sob and part gasp of horror escaped his mouth which he quickly covered with his hand.

'It's okay, Luke, you're doing really well. I know this must be hard for you, but we need as much detail as you can give so we can figure out what happened.'

He nodded, closed his eyes and inhaled. 'None of them had their right hands.'

Ben looked at Morgan, then back at Luke. 'Were they on the table still, did you see them anywhere?'

He shook his head.

'They had bloody stumps where their hands should be. I didn't know what I was seeing or what to do, but I knew enough that this wasn't because of the fire and that they were clearly dead. I couldn't see their hands anywhere, but I didn't really look. I couldn't believe what I was seeing. I backed out and waited on the street for Fire to arrive. I took...' He broke off again and lowered his head, his cheeks turning a deep shade of red.

'You took?' Morgan was smiling at him.

'I took a couple of photos, to show you. I'm sorry, I know it sounds like I was being a right weirdo, but I wanted the police to see them in case the fire took hold of them. I should have dragged them out, I know that, but I was a bit scared in case I got caught up in the fire and, well, there wasn't anything I could do to save them. They were already dead.'

Morgan wanted to high five the guy for using his initiative but knew that it would look totally inappropriate. 'There was nothing you could do, but taking the photos is really helpful. Could we see them, please?'

He stood up and, pulling a shiny new iPhone out of his pocket, he passed it to them.

Ben took it from him, while Morgan looked at the screen and felt a stab of fear squeeze her heart. She leaned over, pinching two fingers on the screen to zoom in, and looked in horror at the people sitting around the table, their faces distorted by the plastic bags. She was sitting so close to Ben that she felt his body stiffen as she moved the picture along the screen to see an auburn-haired woman, who he clearly knew, her face contorted in fear or pain, more than likely both. She swiped to get to the next picture, a close-up of the table, which was covered in blood, and noticed that they were all missing their right hands.

'Where are their hands?'

Ben passed her the phone, and she looked up at Luke. 'Did you take any more, and can you confirm who these people are?'

He shook his head. 'No, the smoke was beginning to seep under the door, and I've got to admit I was panicking a lot. I've never felt so scared and helpless in my life. As you can see their faces are distorted and not very clear underneath the plastic bags, but I've been friends with David for years. That is definitely David Lawson, his wife, Sally, and their son, Tim.'

Morgan would have been panicking too. Ben had turned his face away from them and was staring out of the window across at the house.

'Luke, I'm so sorry, I'm going to have to seize your phone because it has evidence on it, and we're going to have to get it downloaded so we don't compromise it.'

She expected him to put up an argument, say absolutely not, they couldn't have it. Phones were the thing people were the most protective of. He nodded his head docilely though.

'Of course, I understand. I only got this yesterday so I still have my old one I can use. I'm afraid it's not very exciting, it's just full of family pics, food, nights out, you know the stuff.'

She smiled at him. 'We only need to download the eviden-tial photos, nothing else. You can have it back when we're done. We really appreciate it, don't we, Ben?' Morgan had no idea if this was true or if they would have to keep hold of it indefinitely, but she couldn't tell Luke that.

Ben turned to look at her. 'Ah, yes, of course we do. Appre-ciate your assistance.'

'What if the person who did this comes back? What if they start picking off families one by one? This is a nice street and, oh God, I don't want to sound as if I think I'm better than anyone. But we all paid a lot of money for these houses because it's a nice street, because we don't have neighbours who are partying and dealing drugs from the front garden, if you get my drift. We have street parties, summer barbeques, Christmas drinks, fundraising events. These are good people; I don't know why someone would want to do this. To come into David's home and kill his family then try to burn it to the ground; obviously they're mentally ill, deranged. What if they decide to come after my family next? How do I keep them safe?'

Luke wasn't shouting but his voice had risen significantly. Morgan understood completely, this was scary stuff. Someone had come into their nice middle-class community and ripped the heart out of it whilst they were all at home eating their evening meals. Luke's questions snapped Ben out of his thoughts.

'These are all valid questions, and we will do our best to answer them, but right now, at this moment, I can't give you the answers you need because we know very little about the circum-stances of what's happened tonight. There will be officers on scene guard for the next few days, there will also be plain-clothes officers on surveillance, and uniformed patrols paying close attention to the whole area. If you so much as see anyone loitering around who you think doesn't belong, then you ring 999.'

'So, you think they might come back?'

Ben shrugged. Morgan knew that arsonists liked to watch buildings burn and if the person who had done this was one, they could well have hung around or even come back once fire-fighters arrived. They didn't know if their suspect was an arsonist though, or whether they had set the fire to cover their tracks. Either way whoever had done this had put a lot of thought into the crime, because it wasn't easy to kill an entire family and chop off their hands.

FOUR

'Luke, have you found out what's happened?'

The woman's voice called out from the front door.

A teenage girl burst into the room. 'Dad, what's happening to Tim's house? Where's Tim, is he okay?'

Luke looked at Morgan and she felt the weight of the world behind his expression. She stood up and nodded her head gently.

'We'll leave you to it, thank you for your help tonight, and we'll be in touch as soon as we know anything more.'

The teenager was staring at the boot on Morgan's foot, her ripped jeans and black bubble coat. Her eyes moved to Ben who looked a lot more like a detective than she ever would, with his smart suit and tie.

'Who are you?'

'Detectives, we've just been talking to your dad about the fire.'

Her attention was drawn away from Morgan and she turned back to her dad. 'What's going on, is Tim okay? Who burned down his house, Sally is going to be furious!'

Luke looked like a rabbit caught in bright headlights his eyes were so wide.

'I'll tell you in a minute, let me see the officers out.'

He walked away from his wife and daughter towards the front door, holding it open for them, and as Morgan passed him, he whispered, 'I can't do it; I can't tell them.'

'You can, but please don't mention the hands, okay? This is something we need to keep very quiet about.'

He nodded. 'I wouldn't, I couldn't. Thank you.'

Ben shook the man's hand again. 'We'll be in touch; we're going to need a statement.'

Morgan turned around. 'Have you noticed anyone strange hanging around? Or someone in the area who you wouldn't normally expect to be here?'

He closed his eyes, massaging the bridge of his nose with two fingers.

'I couldn't say, I work at the university with David so I'm not always home through the day. My wife works too, but you could ask Mrs Wilkes at number twelve. She's retired, walks her dog a lot, knows everything that's going on.'

He rolled his eyes, giving Morgan the impression that Mrs Wilkes was the resident font of all knowledge and maybe a little irritating to her neighbours, which made her the perfect person to speak to.

They walked towards the fire trucks, where Paul was on his phone. He waved them over, ending his call.

'Good news, our fire investigation unit is on its way and because the fire started at the front of the house that is where they'll be focusing. You can take a look at the bodies at the back of the house.'

Ben smiled. 'I'm not sure it's good news but thank you. We can at least get a start on the investigation. Is our CSI allowed in to photograph the crime scene and get it documented for our end?'

'I don't see why not; obviously we will be investigating the cause of the fire and you the cause of death. There isn't much structural damage to the house, it's pretty solid. We're waiting for a fire investigator to arrive because we don't have a level two trained one on our team.' He rolled his eyes, and Morgan knew then that she liked him, he was one of them. Helpful, unobstructive and willing to work as a team. She knew that some partner agencies were an absolute nightmare about sharing crime scenes, how lucky they were that it was Paul's crew who were on shift. It could have been a different matter altogether with another. He walked away, leaving Morgan and Ben facing each other.

'Do we wait for Wendy? Or are we going in for a look first?'

Ben paused. 'Wendy will kill us if we go in, but I don't see that we have a choice. We're only looking anyway; Fire will be handling the majority of the investigation and it's already a complete forensics mess.'

'Fine by me.'

They suited and booted. Most people carried coats, blankets, carrier bags in the boot of their cars; Ben always kept a fully stocked cardboard box of crime scene protective overalls, nitrile gloves, shoe covers, face masks and an assortment of evidence bags just in case something needed to be retrieved before CSI arrived.

There was no need to worry about preserving the entrance along the driveway to the front of the house because that had been well and truly contaminated by the footfall from the fire officers and water from the hoses. They went through the tall wooden gate at the side of the house, where Morgan found that the garden at the back was a lot bigger than she'd expected and perfectly maintained. There was a row of the most delicate pink roses that she'd ever seen, and their sweet fragrance filled the air as she walked past. There was decking outside of the wall-to-wall bifold doors which opened out onto the garden. The decking outside had a dark grey rattan corner suite, and its own built-in kitchen area with the biggest barbeque ever. Morgan nodded in appreciation. This was a beautiful home, how amazing would it be to sit out here on a warm summer's evening, cooking your tea and eating it in luxury? She temporarily forgot the reason they were there and could have been mistaken for thinking this was a house viewing and not a crime scene. She turned to tell Ben they needed an outdoor kitchen and was met with such a scene of total horror and destruction that the words died on her lips. Ben had stepped inside the large airy kitchen and was staring at the industrial-style dining table. Morgan followed, her jaw dropping at the sight of the bodies. All of them were slumped at an angle, leaning forwards onto the table. Luke must have been in complete panic mode earlier to not have realised at first glance that they were dead. The air was filled with the sweet, smoky smell of burning mixed with the sharp, coppery tang of blood. It made her stomach churn as it assaulted her senses. It had been terrible seeing this in a photograph, but to witness it first-hand was next level horrific. Her eyes fixed on Sally, the expression on her face burning itself deep into Morgan's mind where she knew it was going to stay forever. Had that poor woman watched whoever did this to her family knowing it was her turn next? It was incomprehensible to her that someone could do this. She moved her eyes to the smaller figure of the two, Tim. He wasn't a big lad, in fact, Sally looked taller, unless it was the way he was slumped forward, but she didn't think so. He was skinny, the kind of skinny teenage boys can be until they suddenly decide to start working out or they naturally fill out and gain weight. His white-blond hair was stuck to his forehead inside the plastic bag. His eyes were bulging out of their sockets, and she felt a deep sorrow that Tim had been made to endure such a brutal death at such a young age. Finally, she looked at David. His face a deep shade of red, the others were red but his was darker, more like puce. Next she looked around the room. The door had been closed, and had stopped the fire from taking hold inside. The edges were blackened with fingers of soot spreading around the wall. It looked like something from the Upside Down – Morgan had just binge-watched all of *Stranger Things* and it was still on her mind.

Ben, she realised, was fixated on Sally; he looked distraught, and she felt bad for him.

'I can handle this if you need to step outside.'

Her voice had snapped him out of his thoughts, and he turned to her. 'Sorry, I can't get my head around it. She is such a lovely person; I don't get why someone would do this to her and her family. This is some really messed up shit, Morgan, it's pure evil.'

'It is and if you ask me, judging by the expression on her face she was the last one to die; whoever did this wanted her to see her family dead before they killed her.'

Ben turned to look at the other bodies. 'Her son was fourteen last week, she was telling me how much he loves Manchester and wanted to go shopping for the day, but she hadn't been able to arrange it until this weekend. He's never going to go there ever again.' Ben's voice broke. He turned and went back into the garden leaving Morgan standing there.

The perils of living in a small town, almost everyone knew everyone, there was always some connection. First Des and now this. Ben had been doing so well getting on with his life despite living with the loss of his wife, Cindy, and she was worried this would bring that dreadful night to the forefront of his mind, and with his recently diagnosed heart condition... She stopped that train of thought in its tracks: he had put up with all of *her* near brushes with death the last few years, he was made of tough stuff. Turning back to the bodies she focused on Sally.

I don't know what happened for you and your family to end up like this, but I promise you I'll find out who did this and why. Her heart aching for all three of them she turned and followed Ben outside.

FIVE

Ben was sitting on the corner sofa staring into the garden, and Morgan sat down next to him.

'Penny for your thoughts.'

This was the question that Ben usually asked her. He turned to her, a sad smile on his face.

'It's just too...'

She knew exactly what he was thinking. 'It's too much, too sick, too evil, too unnecessary, too sad, too shocking.'

He nodded. 'All of that, plus more.'

She reached out, entwining her fingers in his and squeezing them gently.

'We owe it to Sally to find whoever did this and fast, we owe it to Tim and to David. I get it if it's too hard for you, Ben, you could ask Will to take over.'

He held up his hand. 'No, not again. I'm not getting pushed off my own investigation again. I like Will, he's a good bloke and a bloody good detective, but this is my town, my case and I'm going to solve it.' He paused, squeezing her fingers tight. 'We're going to solve it.'

'And we will because we're also bloody good detectives.'

'We are.'

The gate opened and a white-clad figure stepped through.

'Well look what we have here, if it isn't my favourite crime scene trespassers in the world.'

Morgan smiled. 'Evening, Wendy, we didn't touch anything.'

'Oh, thank you. I'm so grateful to you both for being so considerate. I'm not going to lie it's a nightmare anyway with the mess at the front of the house.'

Another figure followed her through, and she pointed to him. 'This is Nigel Adams, he's the fire investigator.'

Nigel gave them a thumbs up, and then the pair of them walked towards the doors. Morgan didn't give Wendy her usual warning about how bad it was, but she watched her step inside and heard her exclaim, 'Dear Lord, where are their hands?'

Morgan and Ben exchanged glances; they knew exactly what she was thinking. Standing up they watched as the pair of them began to document the scene.

'Should we go and speak to Mrs Wilkes?'

'Would you? I want to see if Wendy finds anything.'

She nodded, leaving Ben staring at the bodies and hoping he was going to be okay.

Mrs Wilkes opened the door before Morgan had even had the chance to knock.

'You must be the police, come on in.'

Morgan followed her into the modern bungalow. These really were exceptionally well built, beautiful houses. It occurred to Morgan how, despite everything that was happening outside, this woman had opened her door to her and invited her into her home, because she'd assumed she was a police officer, without asking for any ID. Morgan glanced at her reflection in the large hall mirror, she didn't look like a conventional copper, is that how the killer had gained access to the Lawsons' home? Had they knocked on the door and said they were from the police? People were always so shocked to have a copper knocking on their door, and it didn't matter if they were in uniform or not, they always assumed they were the good guys, but Morgan knew better: it wasn't always the case. She was taken into a lounge where there was a pot of tea on the coffee table next to a stack of *Good Housekeeping* magazines.

'Please take a seat, I don't know what's going on but it looks just terrible. Poor Sally is going to be devastated, please tell her they are welcome to come here. I suppose they'll have gone to a hotel or to Luke and Heather's house, they're very good friends. Where are they? I saw Sally arrive home, but I haven't seen her, David or Tim since. I've been looking out for them, to offer them a warm place to keep safe. They must be in a complete state of shock. I can't imagine how upset they'll be.'

Morgan knew that the woman opposite her was lovely and full of good intentions, but she was also as bright as a button and didn't miss a trick, which probably irritated her neighbours and would explain Luke's eye roll when he mentioned her.

'I'm Morgan Brookes by the way, a detective with Rydal Falls.'

'I know who you are, dear, everyone knows that. It's a pleasure to have you sitting on my sofa.'

Morgan's cheeks began to burn, of course this woman knew her, the amount of times Morgan's detective work had made it to the papers recently, she probably knew more about her life than she did herself.

'Now, where are Sally, David and Tim? I'm worried about them.' Her tone was forceful this time, demanding, and Morgan realised that there was no point not telling her the awful truth, because in a few hours the Lawsons would be wheeled out of there in body bags and put into waiting private ambulances with blacked out windows, and she had no doubt that Mrs Wilkes would be there watching from her front window seat.

'I have some bad news for you, Mrs Wilkes, I'm afraid they all died.'

The woman gasped so loud that it hurt her eardrums. Her hand flew to her mouth, and she looked genuinely shocked. 'No, I don't understand.' Tears filled her pale blue eyes. Morgan noticed they were crinkled around the edges with laughter lines, or maybe they were worry lines the furrows were that deep.

'I'm afraid that I can't tell you any more than that because we don't know ourselves what has happened. I'm so sorry.'

'Was it smoke inhalation? I've seen it on the television, it can kill you before you get the chance to evacuate.'

'It's hard to say right now.' An image of Sally with a plastic bag over her head and her right hand chopped off filled her mind, and she had to blink to clear it.

Mrs Wilkes leaned forward. 'No, it wasn't that judging by the pained look on your face. Did David go mad and kill them all? You read about it all the time, don't you? Middle-aged man under too much stress goes crazy and kills their entire family.'

Morgan was shocked that the woman sitting across from her could read her so well and she made a determined effort not to show any further emotion.

'Like I said, Mrs Wilkes, we really have nothing we can share at the moment. I'm trying to piece together the last few hours and would really appreciate it if you could talk me through your evening.'

'Maggie, please, I always think Mrs Wilkes is such a mouthful. The neighbours all call me that and I'm not daft, I know what they think, that I curtain twitch all day and walk my dog just so I can be nosy. I'm not, well, I do like to keep an eye on the area, but these are expensive houses, and the neighbours are out at work all day, sometimes away working for days on end. I do my best to make sure everything is tickety-boo, a bit like a one-woman neighbourhood watch.'

'That's very kind of you, Maggie.'

She shrugged. 'Truth is, since my husband, Ronnie, died two years ago, I'm a bit isolated, so to see these gorgeous people and their families going about their business makes my day a little less lonely.'

Morgan felt her heart tear in two for the woman, her opinion of her changing substantially.

'Have you told your neighbours this? I bet they would love to have you over for coffee and a chat.'

Maggie laughed. 'They're far too busy and I would never impose, although Sally, God bless her, would ask me for a coffee when she had a rare moment to herself. I can't believe she's dead. My heart is broken for her and her lovely boy, he was never cheeky or rude like most teenage boys. David was a little more standoffish but that's men in general, don't you think?'

'I suppose so. Maggie, do you know who on the street has CCTV systems, camera doorbells, dashcams?'

'Now, that I can help you with, dear, because we all do. I can't tell you if they actually work or not, but almost everyone has cameras outside of their houses. We are very security conscious.'

Morgan had to stop herself from jumping up and high fiving Maggie. Just this once they might actually have caught their killer on camera. She felt a flicker of hope that they would find whoever slaughtered Sally, David and Tim Lawson, and lock them away for the rest of their lives.

Maggie picked up the remote control and turned on the television. The screen filled up with small squares showing her front, back and side gardens; there was also a view of the front garden and street.

'Can you make that one bigger?' Morgan was standing next to the TV pointing to the view of the street. One click and the fire engines and police cars outside the Lawsons' house came into view. They were some distance away from Maggie's, but it was still good enough. 'That's amazing, can you rewind it too? Hang on, I just need to check what time the call came in. Excuse me a moment, I'll be right back.'

Morgan left the house to go and find Ben, as she didn't have a radio with her, it was in Barrow. Then she realised she could do one better than that. She hurried down the street to find Paul. He was standing talking to Wendy and another guy dressed in protective clothing.

'Hey, what time did the call come in to you guys about the fire?'

'At 19.57 and we arrived on scene at 20.07.'

'Thanks, that's great. Have you seen Ben?' She was asking Wendy, who pointed to the rear of the house.

'He's still there, Morgan.'

'Thanks.'

She left them to it, discussing the best way to work the crime scene.

Ben hadn't moved, he was still sitting on the outdoor sofa.

'Hey, are you okay?'

He turned his head to look at her, the sadness on his face making her want to grab hold of him and never let go, but she didn't.

'We have CCTV, multiple cameras along the entire street.'

He stood up. 'There is?'

She grinned at him. 'There really is, probably dashcams too.' She walked closer and held up her hand, Ben raised his and high fived her.

'Praise the Lord.'

'Had to happen sooner or later, come and meet Maggie, she's the one with the CCTV but she says everyone else has it too.'

'Good job, Brookes.'

She smiled. 'We can figure this out, Ben, find the monster that did this and lock them up so no one else gets hurt.'

He followed her to Maggie's bungalow where Maggie was waiting for them.

'Maggie, this is my boss, Ben Matthews. Ben, this is Maggie.'

Ben reached out his hand and shook Maggie's hand. She gripped his back, shaking it hard.

'Maggie is friends with Sally.'

'I'm sorry for your loss, Maggie. Sally is, was, a lovely woman. She was an old friend of mine.'

'Then we're both grieving her loss, let's do the right thing and find out who did this.'

She pointed to the television screen. 'I'll show you how to work it, take your time, do what you need, and I'll make a fresh pot of tea.'

'Fire was called by Luke at 19.57, they arrived on scene at 20.07. Maggie, do you know what time Sally got home?'

'It was after half past seven. I had just come back from walking Roley, my pug, and was going in the front door when her car drove down the street.' At the mention of the dog's name a loud thump from a room down the hall was followed by the sound of paws tip tapping on the tiled floor, and a loud snorting sound met them before the dog appeared and began to bark at Morgan and Ben.

'Shush, Roley, they've been here ages.'

The dog padded across the floor towards Maggie, and she laughed. 'As you can see, he's not the greatest guard dog, but he is very good company.'

Morgan bent down and scratched his ears. 'Better late than never, Roley, eh?'

Maggie walked out of the room and the dog followed, and Morgan turned back to the television screen and began rewinding the recording.

'Let's see if our suspect leaves the street after setting the fire.'

Ben smiled at her. 'You're good at this, I miss working with you.'

She shrugged. 'I've had a good teacher.'

She pressed play and they watched as Maggie began to walk up her drive with the dog, and a couple of seconds later a white Mercedes sports car drove past as Maggie went inside; the camera captured a good view of the Lawsons' house, and they watched in real time as Sally got out of the car, leaned over to grab her bag and shut the door. The house was in darkness, apart from a single light. She walked to the end of the drive and looked around, then headed towards her house. When Sally opened her front door and went inside, Morgan paused it.

'She must have been ambushed as soon as she stepped inside, because the time stamp on the screen is 19.37 and we know that Luke rang Fire twenty minutes later.'

She lowered her voice so Maggie couldn't hear, but there was the sound of the kettle boiling in the background and Maggie was talking to her dog. 'Could you kill someone and start a fire in that length of time?'

'The evidence is saying yes.'

'Not three people though, David and Tim must have already been dead.'

Ben pressed play and both of them held their breath waiting for someone to come out of the Lawsons' house and walk away. Nobody emerged, and the sinking feeling that they weren't going to catch a break made their shoulders sag. Eventually they saw flames and smoke billowing out of the front window and door, Luke and his wife coming out of their house at the same time. Luke began running towards the burning building whilst on the phone.

'They must have left the back way, where does the garden lead to?'

Maggie walked in with a tray of tea and biscuits.

'Where does Sally's garden lead to?'

'It leads onto the playing fields of the school, very handy for Tim and his friends when they used to be out playing football. Sally would chase them over the back hedge, so they didn't ruin her roses. I don't know what the school thought of them being in there, but as far as I know they only used to run riot on the playing field and not cause any damage.'

'Would it be possible to get a copy of this, Maggie? And I would say the last seven days' footage as well?'

'Of course but it might take me some time. If you come back tomorrow it should be ready for you or I could give you a ring when it is.'

'Maggie, you are amazing. Thank you for all your help and this tea, it's just what we needed.'

Morgan smiled at her and there was no mistaking the tears that pooled in the corner of Maggie's eyes. She nodded, picked up the plate of chocolate covered Hobnobs and offered the biscuits around. Neither Morgan nor Ben had much of an appetite but they both took one.

'Do you think I should go and see if the firemen need a drink?'

'That's up to you, do you have enough mugs?'

Maggie stood up. 'I have a cupboard full of unused ones, I'd feel better making myself busy. The minute I stop and think...' She gulped in a sob that had almost escaped then turned and headed out of her front door, leaving them sipping tea.

'What a lovely lady.'

Morgan nodded. 'She really is, I hope she's okay, she lost her husband two years ago.'

Ben's face creased in pain and sympathy. 'It's not easy, especially if they'd been together for a long time.'

They finished their drinks and stood up. Ben reached down and scooped up another biscuit.

'I'd forgot how good these taste,' he said through a mouthful of biscuit crumbs. He'd been slowly improving his diet, and trying to eat healthier.

She smiled at him, brushing biscuit crumbs off the front of her jacket. As they made to leave Maggie's house, the sound of loud snoring from the kitchen made Morgan turn around, then she saw the dog lying on its bed.

'That dog snores louder than you.'

Ben poked her in the arm. 'How dare you, I'm not being outdone by that, my snores are far superior.'

They walked outside back to reality, and she realised how much she missed working with him, the easy way they could read each other's minds, the way they could make each other laugh to relieve the pressure that otherwise could drag your mind down a dark rabbit hole from where there was no escape.

SIX

Morgan followed Ben into the station wondering if she was going to get sent back to Barrow or if she'd be allowed to stay and help out. She didn't have to worry about it for very long as Marc dashed past them on his way out.

'Oh hey, Morgan, you're here. That's good, I've spoken to Will, he said he doesn't need you and you're good to work this case.'

'Thanks.'

He held up his hand. 'No need, I should be thanking you. I'll see you in my office later for a chat. Got to dash, I'll be back in time for the briefing.'

Their strange, unreadable DI ran out of the double doors leading into the station, leaving Morgan staring after him.

'Finally.' Ben was giving her a thumbs up from the top of the staircase.

She made her way to the lift; there was no way she was trying to navigate those stairs with this stupid boot on, it was a disaster waiting to happen. As the lift doors closed, she lay her head against the cool steel wall and sighed, this was going to be a difficult, complicated case but she was confident they could do it. They could find whoever did this, Ben would leave no stone unturned. They would hold a joint briefing with Fire and Rescue this morning and then in the afternoon they would all get changed into their dress uniforms that they wore to their passing out parade – when they'd finished their two years of training to become fully fledged police officers – and pay their respects to Des. This was going to be a sad day, but they had to keep busy, had to keep working, it was all they could do, and now the terrible murders last night.

The doors opened and she smiled to see Ben waiting for her.

'Hop along, we have a lot to do today.'

'I was just thinking about that, we certainly do. There is a lot to be taking on especially today. Poor Des, what would he say about last night?'

'He'd no doubt blame you, Morgan, he always thought you were the angel of death.'

'Cheers, Ben, make me feel better why don't you.'

He shrugged. 'That was only his opinion, no one else does.'

'Well, that's great to know.'

Cain appeared at the top of the stairs. 'Only whose opinion?'

'Ben was just reminding me of what Des thought of me.'

Cain looked at Ben. 'Des was just a bit superstitious and a little bit afraid of hard work, God rest his soul.'

Morgan smiled at Cain. 'How come you're so diplomatic and he's not?'

'Some of us are natural charmers, some of us aren't. Need to work on those skills, Benno lad, do you want some lessons? I won't charge.'

Ben stared at Cain. 'Did you want something?'

'Yes, actually. Mads is flapping downstairs about the funeral and wanted to speak to you about the guard of honour.'

Ben turned and began to walk back downstairs to speak to Mads, leaving Cain and Morgan.

'Come on, I'll escort you to your desk and make you a coffee. How come you're here anyway? Thought you were still stuck down in Barrow.'

'Right place at the wrong time I suppose. I'd just been dropped off at Ben's when he got called out and I offered to help. Will doesn't need me in Barrow and to be honest I don't think he ever did.'

'Well thank God for that, this place has been boring without you, Brookes. I'm glad you're back.'

She grinned at him. 'You might not be saying that in a few hours.'

'Probably not but it sounds good.' Cain pushed open the door to the empty CID office, and her eyes fell onto Des's empty desk.

'I still can't believe it.'

'No, me neither, I hope those bastards rot in hell for what they did.'

Neither of them mentioned that it could have been Morgan who had been killed. The bedroom wall full of photographs of her meant that one of the killers who got Des had been worryingly obsessed with her.

'You know I'm bloody starving, I've been off the carbs for two weeks now so my tunic will fasten up later. No disrespect, Des, but as soon as this is over, I'm eating the biggest chicken mayo baguette I can find.'

Morgan laughed. 'I thought you looked a little thinner. Why didn't you just get a new tunic?'

Cain looked aghast. 'Never, I'm not admitting defeat and telling stores I'm a fat bastard who can't stop eating.'

'You are not fat, you're just right.'

'And you are very sweet. I needed to drop a few pounds anyway though, I've got my fitness test next month.'

She grimaced. 'I hate them.'

'Me too, you're okay though for now with that ankle. They can't make you do a bleep test with that, can they?'

'That is probably the one and only advantage of wearing this boot.'

Morgan sat down at her desk, while Cain disappeared to go and brew up. The office was too quiet without Amy and Des's continual bickering. As if she'd summoned her the door opened and in walked Amy.

'Hey, how are you doing?'

'Hey, good to see you, Morgan. Better after today; I think once this is over it might be easier you know. Not that I want to forget all about it, but it's like all I can think about. I heard about last night, thought I'd better come in and see if Ben needed a hand. Are you back for good?'

She shrugged. 'Who knows, depends what mood the boss is in. I'm back *for now* anyway.'

Amy lowered her voice. 'That man has more moods than a menopausal woman and I should know my mother was a nightmare.'

Morgan laughed. 'He's certainly something, I'm sure Ben will appreciate you coming back. I don't know what use I'm going to be with this boot on.'

'Role reversal, you can do the Intel checks and CCTV viewings; I'll go out and do the legwork. I might even get a gold star, you never know.'

Ben walked in and his face lit up with a huge smile to see Amy sitting on the corner of Des's desk.

'Before you say anything, yes, I'm back, I want to help out.'

'Thank God for that, it's been far too quiet around here on my own.'

'Yeah, well next time you complain about my attitude remember what you just said, you missed me.'

He laughed. 'I actually did, and I'll try not to forget it. Are you all set for this afternoon?'

'As ready as I can be. I said I'd go with Des's mum in the funeral car, I didn't want her to be alone.'

'Thank you, that's kind of you. It's also going to be hard for you.'

'Yeah, I know, but I couldn't be bothered not eating all week either to fit into my tunic. Why are they so tight? I mean did we not eat when we joined up and were in training or something?'

Ben shrugged. 'We were younger, a lot fitter.'

'We were definitely something, imagine if this was one of us instead of Des, he'd be laughing his socks off because his tunic still fits him perfect with his weird dietary choices. He's getting buried in it. I'm telling you now if I die on the job for the love of God bury me in my pyjamas. I want to be comfortable for all of eternity. I'm not haunting you lot in a tunic that's so tight I can't wave my arms around in it to scare the shit out of you all.'

Their laughter filled the room and suddenly it felt a little lighter in there despite the gravity of the Lawsons' horrific murders and the fact that they had to attend Des's funeral this afternoon.

Cain walked in with a tray of mugs, and they all picked one up and followed Ben down to the briefing room.

SEVEN

The briefing room wasn't as full as it usually was for a murder investigation. Ben had the policy book tucked under his arm and the mug of coffee in his hand. Marc came in behind them, taking a seat at the head of the table. Wendy came in next, and behind her was Nigel from the fire service. Ben, Morgan and Amy took seats as the sound of heavy footfall on the stairs signalled the arrival of task force. Al was in the lead, his team following behind. Once everyone had shuffled into place, they waited for the room to be silent before Ben began to talk.

'Today is not the best day to be starting a triple murder investigation, so I appreciate everyone turning up and I know that the majority of us will be attending Des's funeral this after-noon, but right now, we need to focus. Sally Lawson, her husband, David and fourteen-year-old son, Tim, were brutally murdered last night, and their house set on fire. We need to find out who did this and why this happened, we need to figure out who the victims were, if they had any problems with friends, family, neighbours. A few of you may already know Sally if you go to The Hair Bar on the high street. Morgan, maybe you could fix up speaking with the staff at the salon for me.'

There were a few murmurs and nods, the expression on Al's face one of pure shock.

'You're joking. Sally? Who always gives a discount for blue light workers and is always smiling?'

Ben nodded. 'I'm afraid so. What we know up to now is that Sally arrived home at 19.37 and a neighbour called Fire twenty minutes later. When Fire arrived at 20.07 the front of the house was burning, but the back of the house was mainly smoke damage. The crew discovered the bodies of Sally, David and Tim at the kitchen table. I think it's easier to show you.'

He opened the photos that Wendy had sent him, and the Lawsons' kitchen filled the Smart TV. He clicked on the next one, a close-up of the family all slumped forwards, with thick, clear plastic bags on their heads. Morgan knew what was coming next. Ben clicked, and the camera zoomed out enough to show the bloodied stumps of their right hands.

'Jesus, where are their hands?' Al was staring at the screen his eyes wide, his lips parted.

'We haven't located them yet.'

Morgan noticed the big US-style fridge freezer in the corner of the kitchen. 'Did we check the freezer?'

Wendy shook her head. 'I photographed and documented the scene, focusing on the bodies before they were moved. Nigel and I are going back this morning to do a thorough search once we have the go-ahead from Fire that it's safe to do so.'

Nigel smiled. 'I'm Nigel Adams, Fire Investigator with the North Cumbria Fire Service. I'm usually based in Carlisle but cover the entire county when needed.'

Ben nodded. 'Pleased to have you on board, Nigel. Anything you need see either myself, Morgan or Amy, although I'm sure Wendy is looking after you.'

'She certainly is, thank you. I have to say I've never seen anything quite like this. I've attended multiple fatalities over the years and a couple of suspicious deaths, but this is...'

'Next level?'

He looked at Morgan. 'Yes, it is. I mean the missing hands, the bags over their heads, it has to mean something to whoever did this but to me, I'm at a loss.'

'I know what you mean, I think this is personal, very personal. It also bears similarities to some of the murders committed by Richard Cottingham the Times Square Torso Killer. He killed prostitutes and would butcher them in hotel rooms, cutting off their hands, breasts and heads then set them on fire.'

Ben's mouth fell open, she heard Cain whisper, 'Jesus, Morgan.'

She stopped and looked around the room, everyone was staring at her. But she couldn't help it, her fascination with true crime and cold cases would creep into investigations, and it hadn't done them any harm up to now, in fact if anything it helped them catch the killers. She continued, 'I'm not saying that this is the case here, I'm just stating the similarities, but it's quite obvious this isn't something a killer would walk in off the street and do. For a start they would know that they needed three bags, three lengths of rope. They would have had to have watched the family for some time, so they knew when the best time was to kill them. One of the neighbours said that Sally always worked late on a Thursday, that gave them time to take out David and Tim before Sally got home; and I noticed Sally was wearing a silver crucifix necklace and a ring on her left hand, so it wasn't a burglary gone wrong.'

Ben was scratching the side of his face. 'A crucifix? That's odd, she wasn't religious. Even made some comments when we were catching up. Let's make sure Wendy bags that up. So why do you think Sally was killed last?'

Amy pulled a small gold crucifix on a delicate chain out of her shirt. 'You don't actually have to be religious to wear one. I love my little necklace, it was a present from my gran. Sally's might have been a gift from someone.'

Morgan hesitated; she didn't know if this was right, but it felt right to her. They might laugh and poke fun at her because she enjoyed reading true crime books and listening to podcasts about it, but at least she had an open mind when it came to the motives of killers.

'I think whoever did this had an issue with Sally, they wanted to kill her last so she could see that her entire family was already dead before she died. Torture her in the worst possible way, just before they killed her.'

Al was now staring at Morgan along with the rest of the room, making her squirm a little in her seat but she stood her ground. 'At least that's my theory.'

'Sally was the target, David and Tim were in the way?'

'Basically, yes. The killer waited for her to come home. If they only wanted David or Tim, they could have left before Sally arrived.'

Nigel was nodding his head. 'Looking at their house, life-style, I would put their victim risk factor as low. I can't see that the life they led put them in the high or medium risk category and caused them to be the victims of crime, well not unless you find out something that contradicts this. I agree that this appears to be something very personal.'

'We need a timeline of events, let's watch Maggie's camera footage and see who came home first, what time it was and if anyone was loitering around in the street or if they had already gained access to the house. The killer didn't leave out the front door, so they must have run across the school fields at the back of the house. Maybe they also gained entry to the property that way.'

'Amy, can you go to the school and ask to view their CCTV footage? Find out where the cameras are, and see if you can gain access to the playing fields without crossing the school playground. Then I want you to have a walk around the field and see if there are any gaps in the bushes that the killer could have used to get in or out.'

She looked down at her watch. 'Okay, but then I'm going to need to be back here at dinner to get ready and get to Mrs Black's house for the funeral.'

Morgan realised that Ben had forgot all about Des's funeral in a few hours, so tied up with trying to solve this case and bringing Sally's killer to justice.

'Of course, we're all going to need to do that. You do what you can, Amy, and then get yourself off. Morgan, you're going to have to stay here and be my video monitor, you can't go hobbling around on that ankle all day. Is that okay?'

He was wearing an expression of worry and she knew he was waiting for her to object.

'Of course, that's fine.'

'It is?'

She nodded, watching as he breathed out a small sigh of relief, wondering if she was usually too hard on him and deciding that she wasn't. She liked to be in the middle of things, but she'd clean the office, stack the papers and sort out the filing cabinets if Ben asked her to, because at least it meant she was here, back where she belonged, instead of feeling like a fish out of water down in Barrow.

'I'll get the PCSOs to carry out extensive house-to-house and CCTV enquiries focusing on Hest Bank Road to begin with. Once we have the relevant footage secured, we can start watching it. The good news is there is no shortage of houses with cameras and Ring doorbells; the bad news is we are drastically short of officers to sit and view it. I'll figure something out though.'

Marc stood up. 'This afternoon is going to be a hard one for anyone attending Des's funeral; if you're taking part in the guard of honour then please make sure you're back in time to get yourself ready and get to the cemetery.'

Morgan felt sad that Des's funeral was only at the crematorium and not at the church, but it was hardly fitting to hold his funeral in the very place they had found his body. Too painful, without putting his poor mum and everyone else through that. Besides she didn't get the impression Des was a very religious man; at least this way it wouldn't be a long, drawn-out affair. Then she scolded herself for even thinking like that, the least they could do was to give him a good send-off. He deserved it, he had died on the job even though he did his best to avoid working. She thought about his cat, Kevin, and hoped he was okay whilst they were out at work. Did cats know when their owners had died or were they as ruthless as they seemed, only caring about whoever it was with a fresh pouch of food and someone to rub behind their ears?

'Morgan, are you good to print out some questionnaires for the PCSOs?'

She nodded; of course she could, anything to keep her mind off Des until she really had no choice but to face him for the final time.

EIGHT

They all went their separate ways: Amy left to go to the school, Al and his team following, ready to head in the direction of the Lawsons' house and begin a painstaking fingertip search of the back garden and school playing field for any discarded evidence. Wendy escorted Nigel back down to her office, no doubt to come up with a detailed plan of how they were going to approach the scene. Marc left too and Morgan wondered what on earth he got up to and where he went every time he dashed out of the station. He either had his own stash of case files he followed up on, more meetings than anyone should, or he was having an affair with someone, which was the usual reason colleagues disappeared mid shift without a valid excuse. She didn't care as long as he left her alone.

Ben turned to her. 'I've spoken to Will, who kindly offered to attend David and Sally's post-mortems today. I don't want to put them off because of Des. I still can't reconcile the lively, bubbly woman with the corpse we discovered. Would you be able to attend Tim's with me though? Kids are hard to watch.'

'Of course, do you want me to go with Will today?'

Morgan hated funerals. For someone who was only twenty-four she'd been to more than she cared to think about, and then she realised she was being utterly selfish; she couldn't leave Ben to go on his own. He'd had his fair share too over the years.

'Sorry, forget that suggestion I wasn't thinking straight.'

'Actually, I would like you to attend, but I kind of think we owe it to Des.'

'We do, and Will has probably asked Adele to go with him anyway, she's his right-hand woman.'

'Just like you're mine.' He winked at her. 'I couldn't live without you, Brookes, you saved my life in more ways than you could ever know.' He reached forward, pulling her close for the briefest of hugs then stepped away.

'Do you want to go and grab the footage from Maggie?'

Morgan laughed. 'I would, I still can't drive though.'

He looked down at the boot on her foot. 'Damn it, sorry, I forgot all about that. You're probably the only copper in this entire county who would still come to work with a badly sprained ankle and not moan about it.'

'I could get Cain to drive me, he's around.'

'You're resourceful too.' He winked at her then turned to leave the too small, stuffy room.

'Ben.' He turned back to her. 'Are you okay, like deep down okay with this? I'm worried about you, your heart.'

'My ticker is just fine, the tablets they gave me seem to have done the trick. I'm saddened beyond belief but I'm good and I think I'll feel even better once we get today over with; it's going to be a long one.'

He disappeared up the three little steps out into the corridor, and she let out a sigh, yes today was definitely going to be a long one.

Hobbling to the lift she went to the ground floor in search of Cain, who was leaning against the door of the patrol sergeant's office, arms crossed, laughing at whatever joke Mads had just finished telling.

'Cain, are you busy?'

Mads was shaking his head. 'Don't answer that one, she'll have you chasing around after killers and making you work for a living.'

'Not at the moment, Morgan, what do you need?'

Mads groaned. 'Sucker, you'll regret it.'

Morgan glared at him. 'I need to grab some CCTV footage from Hest Bank Road. If you could give me a lift, I'd really appreciate it.'

She walked away, and Cain followed. 'Hey, wait up he's only joking, Morgan.'

Stopping in her tracks she turned to him. 'I know, I'm not in the mood that's all. I'm fed up wearing this boot, my ankle is hurting, and I don't want to go to Des's funeral.'

Cain's mouth opened wide. 'You having a bad day, kid? You never complain, come on let's grab a coffee and go get that CCTV.'

'Thank you.'

He shrugged. 'That's what I'm here for, always happy to help.'

Cain parked outside The Coffee Pot. 'I'll go grab a couple of lattes; do you want anything to eat?'

'No thanks, I feel sick to the bottom of my feet, I don't think I could eat anything.'

'That is probably why you should eat something then, empty stomach, too much stress, it's not a good combination.'

'I'm fine, thanks.'

Shrugging he strolled into the café, his hands in his pockets; he looked the epitome of cool, calm and collected. Morgan flipped down the sun visor to look at herself in the tiny mirror, and sighed. She looked pale, there were dark circles under her eyes, and she was tired beyond belief. Tired of all the death that seemed to edge the fringes of her life, tired of losing people she cared about, tired of just about everything. She pushed the visor back and lay her head against the seat, closing her eyes. The door opened and the strong aroma of fresh coffee wafted into the car. She took the drinks from Cain.

'I love the smell of fresh coffee, it's like an instant hit of joy to my brain.'

'I know what you mean, I also love the smell of bacon and the sweet aroma of freshly baked cake, which is why I bought you a white chocolate and raspberry cupcake. You look as if a sugar hit might perk you up. No arguments, and besides I wanted one but couldn't stuff my face in front of you when I'm supposed to be eating healthy.'

Her laughter filled the car, and she took the paper bag from him, peeking inside.

'You did the right thing, these look amazing.'

It wasn't lost on her that the last time she'd seen Des alive he'd wandered away from her with a similar paper bag containing freshly made scones. Did he ever eat them, she wondered, before he died? She hoped he had, that he'd eaten all of them and enjoyed every single morsel.

'Hey, why are you on a healthy eating kick? Is it really for the fitness test?'

'Bella has just lost a stone doing keto, and I thought I'd give it a go.'

She turned to really look at him. 'Bella?'

His cheeks burned pinker than the raspberry sauce drizzled over the buttercream icing on the cupcakes. 'Isabelle, Dr Burrows.'

It was Morgan's turn to grin. 'Are you two seeing each other?'

'Kind of, we're taking it slow for now, actually we have no choice with her living eight hours away at the far end of Wales.

But we talk on the phone all the time, message each other, and she's coming here for a couple of weeks' holiday.'

'Cain, that's brilliant, I'm so happy for you, she seems lovely.'

'She is, I really like her. Obviously not as much as I like you, but you're already spoken for so it's out of the question, and I can't spend the rest of my life pining for something I'll never have.'

Her mouth dropped open, and he nudged her gently in the side. 'I'm only kidding, well maybe there's a little bit of truth in there, but I want you to be happy and as much as my poor heart is broken, Benno makes you happy so it's fine, I can live with that.'

She turned away from him frantically blinking away the tears pooling in the corners of her eyes. 'You say the sweetest things, I want you to be happy too and I think Bella is perfect for you.'

He shrugged. 'Yeah, thanks, kid. There's just this problem of the mammoth drive to take her out for coffee.'

She laughed. 'You'll sort it, you could always put in for a transfer to work for the police near her, or she could move to Lancaster University.'

'What and leave this glamorous life behind with all the excitement of a Netflix series? I don't think I could do it; I don't speak Welsh either.'

'Love will find a way so that you can both make it work.'

'You think so?'

She nodded. 'I know so and, by the way, Cain, I bet Bella loves you just the way you are so don't go depriving yourself of your favourite foods.'

'Haha, it really is actually more for the fitness test but thanks, Morgan.'

He sipped his coffee, took a large bite of the cake and then began driving towards Hest Bank Road. Morgan's frozen insides began to thaw a little as she sipped her latte, nibbled her cake and realised that she was ridiculously happy that Cain was seeing Bella. He deserved so much happiness and if Bella could give that to him, then Morgan liked her even more than she already did.

Driving down the road she could see the PCSOs on scene guard outside the Lawsons' house and the others knocking on doors in the street. Maggie's front door was ajar, and she took that to mean she had invited inside whoever had knocked on her door. Bless her, she was lovely but naïve beyond belief.

Cain parked the car. 'Do you need me?'

'No, thanks I'm just grabbing the CCTV. Are you okay to wait for me though?'

He gave her a thumbs up.

She walked down the driveway, knocking on the open door.

'Come in.'

Maggie's voice filtered down the hallway to her. Pushing the door, she hoped to God that the woman wasn't this trusting to everyone who wasn't in a uniform. Inside, Cathy was sitting at the kitchen table nursing a mug of tea, a plate of biscuits on the table in front of her. She stood up and Morgan shook her head.

'Sorry.'

'Don't apologise to me, I did the same last night. Maggie makes a wonderful cup of tea.'

'Hello again, dear, how are you, any news? I asked your colleague here, but she said there wasn't anything she could tell me.'

'I'm afraid Cathy is right; we have nothing yet. Did you manage to download the CCTV for me?'

Maggie beamed at her. Standing up she picked up a pen

drive from a shelf and handed it over. 'I did, I also checked it actually worked and it did.'

Morgan wanted to kiss the woman's cheek; instead she reached forward, patting her arm.

'Thank you, this is wonderful.'

'I didn't sleep a wink last night, as exciting as all of this is my heart is aching for that poor family. No one deserves this, I don't care if you're the most miserable, meanest person in the world they still wouldn't deserve to be murdered. Not that I'm saying Sally or David were, in fact they were the opposite, but you know that it's hard to think of a reason they could have upset somebody enough to...' Her voice broke, the tears began to flow, and Cathy stood up, tearing off a piece of kitchen roll and passing it to Maggie.

'Thank you, dear.'

This time Morgan couldn't stop herself; she took a step forward and hugged the sobbing woman, holding her tight in her arms, and Maggie clutched onto her hard. Morgan rocked her, the way Sylvia used to do when she was a child and upset. Cathy was watching them, a look of discomfort across her face. Eventually Morgan gave Maggie a squeeze and released her, and she dabbed her eyes with a corner of the paper towel.

'I'm sorry, it's been a long time since I've had a hug, thank you.'

Morgan smiled. 'Sometimes a hug is all you need.' She thought of Cain; his famous bear hugs when she'd been feeling low had cheered her up no end despite the fact that she wasn't really a people person or a hugger.

'Maggie, do you still have my phone number?'

She nodded.

'Well, if you ever need someone to come for a tea and a chat or a hug then you ring me, okay. I'll probably be back and forth for the next few days anyway, and the PCSOs are here too if you need anything.'

'Thank you.'

The words were little more than a whisper. Morgan smiled at Cathy who was watching both women with a quizzical look on her face.

Clutching the pen drive she walked out of the house, and on reaching the front door she turned and called out, 'Maggie, promise me you'll lock this door when Cathy leaves and don't open it for anyone unless they show you official identification. No leaving it ajar, not until we know what's happened, okay.'

'I promise.'

Morgan walked out, closing the door behind her to the sound of the dog's loud snores coming from the sofa. He was the worst guard dog she'd ever come across, and she hoped that the woman would take her safety seriously.

NINE

The mood in the station was sombre to say the least when Morgan and Cain returned. Officers were milling around in their dress uniforms ready to go to the crem for Des's funeral. Even though it wasn't her fault, Morgan couldn't shake the feeling deep down inside that it was; once again a killer's obsession with her had brought them to this dreadful outcome. When was it going to stop and why was she such a good target for anyone who wasn't remotely like the rest of the population?

'Brookes.'

Mads's voice snapped her out of the worries that were creasing her forehead and her mind. She turned to look at him. 'Yes, Sarge?'

He beckoned her over to his office where he was standing, leaning against the door frame. He turned and went inside, and she followed him. 'I forgot to ask you, did you want to be a pallbearer?'

She did not, could not think of anything worse but thought it was sweet of him to ask.

'No, thank you. I'd be afraid to trip with my sore ankle and drop the coffin.'

Mads laughed. 'Erm, there is that, just thought I'd better check. I also wanted to ask how Benno was, he's a bit quiet.'

She looked at him. 'I never realised you had a compassionate side to you. I always thought you were all jokes and sarcasm.'

'Hey, even I have feelings now and again. He's upset over Des, it's hard to explain but when you're in charge of a shift, or in his case a team, you kind of feel responsible for them, it won't be easy to live with, and now the family last night, word has it he knew the mother.'

She nodded, he did.

'Terrible situation that, well if either of you need anything, you know where I am.'

'Thank you, that's really sweet of you.'

'Yeah, don't go around telling everyone about it though, it doesn't happen very often.'

Smiling, she walked away. Her uniform was hanging up in the ladies' loo upstairs where she'd cleared a space on the coat hooks for it earlier, ready for her to change into, and there was no avoiding it any longer. She called the lift and stepped into it, glad to be away from everyone even if only for the briefest of moments. When she arrived on the upstairs landing, Amy walked out of the office in a smart two-piece suit, looking uncomfortable.

'Hey, you look great.'

She laughed. 'Liar, but I'll take it. I haven't eaten much all week to make sure the bloody buttons fastened. I bet your tunic fits like a dream, have you even changed size since you were measured up for it?'

'Yeah, living with Ben has seen a definite change in my trousers fastening. I don't survive off dried cereal any more, he's a good cook.'

A shadow crossed Amy's face then was gone in the blink of an eye. 'You really fell on your feet you know with Ben. He's a nice guy and he cooks too. Jack can't cook an egg and thank God he doesn't even try.'

Morgan wanted to say maybe it was mutual and maybe Ben had fallen on his feet with her, but she couldn't because there was that doubt deep down inside her that she was like a cursed talisman which emitted some invisible frequency that drew in bad luck. Maybe she should go see her aunt Ettie for some kind of crystal. Morgan wasn't sure how much she believed in her aunt's charms, but the teas she mixed up for her had always helped, and it wasn't like she had anything to lose.

Before she could reply, Amy frowned and said, 'Sorry, I didn't mean that how it sounded, did I upset you?'

She shook her head. 'No, you didn't and it's fine. Are you going to be okay? It's going to be tough being with Des's mum, has she got any other family to support her?'

'Aunts, cousins, I'm not looking forward to it but I'm doing it as one last favour for Desmondo because there's nothing else I can do for him. I need to get going, see you at the crem.'

Amy walked away, and Morgan went into the office where Ben was staring out of the window down onto the car park. His shoulders were hunched and she wondered if he was crying. Despite being in work she crossed the room and wrapped her arms around him. He breathed out a loud sigh and pushed back against her.

'How are you doing?'

'Rubbish, you?' Turning around he looked at her.

'I feel as if this is all my fault.'

'Hey, it's not and you know it. The only person whose fault this is, is behind bars. This is not your burden to bear, Morgan. How did you get on with the CCTV? Amy managed to get the footage from the school grounds, but I'm not holding much luck seeing as how the camera only really covers the perimeter of the school building. But we need to check, we might get something.'

'Well, I'll do my best with it. I got the CCTV from Maggie. When are we coming back?'

'I think we'll have to come straight back. I don't even know if there's a wake, and I can't really afford to take the time to spend a couple of hours in a pub when there's Sally's post-mortem going on this afternoon. This is about as shit as life can get. I never thought I'd say this but I'm kind of fed up dealing with this much death.'

'I'm with you on that one. You look really good in your tunic though.'

This made Ben let out a loud laugh, breaking the feeling of impending doom that had seconds ago filled the air.

'You're too good to me, I look awful.'

She shook her head. 'You don't, I guess I should get changed too. As soon as I get back later, I'll start watching the CCTV footage and hope we catch sight of our guy sneaking around. I could go speak to Sally's colleagues at the salon too.'

'That would be great, see if she was having any trouble with anyone, that kind of thing. I'll speak to Declan and Will, see if they've found anything we can work with. Come on, you better get changed so we can get to the crematorium for the guard of honour. Mads will have a duck fit if we're late.'

Morgan gave him a quick salute, then turned and headed down to the ladies to get changed.

TEN

Morgan sat in the front of Ben's car holding her breath as he drove down the quiet road that led to the black cast-iron gates of Lancaster and Morecambe Crematorium. Rydall Falls wasn't big enough to have its own crematorium, so it had to be either Barrow or here and Des's mum lived closer to Lancaster. There was already a long line of police vehicles parked along the route, officers were milling around with sombre faces, none of them wanting to be here because they all knew that this could be any one of them. Being killed in the line of duty was a scarily real possibility that all officers had to face at some point. The sea of black and white as officers lined up along the private road outside made Morgan's stomach churn. Ben was a pallbearer, along with Cain, Mads and a few officers whom Des had done his training with that she didn't recognise. She took her place in the line, while Ben waited at the front with the others for the hearse to arrive.

The sound of cars in the distance travelling slowly along the road brought a hush to every person standing there. Heads bowed they stood tall, white gloved hands behind their backs as the undertaker leading the procession walked into view with the hearse carrying Des's coffin behind him, and next to him was Father Theo Edwards who smiled at her on his way past, and behind came a solitary funeral car. Des's mum sat inside, staring out at everyone, Amy next to her. Des's solid oak coffin went past and a cold shiver wracked Morgan's entire body, tears pooling in the corners of her eyes. She closed them and whispered, *I'm so sorry, Des.* Amy's face was ashen and as her eyes met Morgan's, she gave her a half smile; Des's mum was talking to her, but she knew Amy was struggling and she felt dreadful for her.

As the coffin, draped in a Cumbria Constabulary flag, with Des's old police helmet on top, was carried inside the building, Morgan hung back, and she watched as Amy held Des's mum's arm, guiding her in behind the coffin. A few civilians followed her inside and she guessed they were his cousins and aunts. Then the officers filed in behind them, and she still didn't want to go inside but someone grabbed her elbow and pushed her forwards. She turned to see Cathy, Sam and Tina all wearing their PCSO finest ushering her inside. She was touched by their kindness; they were looking out for her, and she loved them so much for it. Cathy guided her to a bench, where they all crammed in behind the family, and she wanted the ground to open up and swallow her whole. Cathy leaned into her and whispered, 'My arse is killing me; I can't stand up for an hour. I fell off my niece's scooter last night and I think I broke something inside my buttock.'

Morgan had to suppress a giggle. Cathy always had a way of making her laugh. She ended up letting out a strangled cough so loud that the whole row in front of her turned around to stare, making her feel even worse than she already did. She spied Ben watching her, the look of pain etched across his face snapping her out of it. Morgan lowered her head, but nudged Cathy in the side all the same. Theo began to talk about Des, and she found herself drawn to his voice, it was so soothing, he certainly had a gift. She found herself watching him, smiling as he delivered an amazing eulogy that did Des proud. His eyes fixed on her, and she felt as if he was talking directly to her when he began to talk about seeking forgiveness. In fact he kept his gaze on her until she began to feel a little uncomfortable, wondering if he was as nervous as she was, and using her because he knew her better than everyone else in the room. The alternative was that he was trying to make her feel even worse than she did. She had to break his gaze first, looking down at the order of service that had been placed on her chair. Morgan didn't know which was worse: Theo's intense gaze or Des's eyes that had once been full of life staring up at her from the photograph on the order of service in her hands. Morgan closed her eyes, lowered her head and tried to think of anything other than what she was doing here, to stop the tears.

When the curtains closed on the coffin she finally looked up, it was over for now. The guilt she carried deep inside her wasn't going to be pushed away so easily but at least this part was done. Everyone stood up and began filing out to Bette Midler singing 'Wind Beneath My Wings'. She didn't imagine this would have been Des's choice of song, it must have been his mum's. It had all got too much for Des's mum, who was being led towards the funeral car by a woman who looked just like her, probably a sister. Amy was outside leaning against the brick wall, looking relieved.

Morgan made her way to stand with her.

'Are you okay?'

She nodded. 'I am now. Christ, that was weird, she never stopped chatting all the way here, bless her. I don't think it had sunk in until just before the end when she couldn't take her eyes away from the coffin and began to sob.'

'God love her, you did great.'

'Yeah, if he was here, I'd make him buy the first round of drinks for putting us through this shit.'

Morgan smiled. 'You'd be lucky, he wasn't always forthcoming with his rounds.'

'Tight as a crab's arse was our Des, no doubt about it. Can I grab a lift back with you and Ben? My car's at Felicity's house but I don't want to go back with her to get it.'

'Of course, you can.'

As if speaking of him had instantly transported him to where they were, Ben walked towards them. He reached out and hugged Amy, who squirmed but hugged him back.

'How are you?'

She pulled away from him. 'Better than poor Felicity that's for sure.'

He nodded. 'At least that's over with.'

They turned to walk back to Ben's car when a voice boomed, 'Morgan.'

She stopped in her tracks, turning around to face Theo who was striding towards them.

'How are you all? Thanks for coming.'

Amy bristled, she nodded at him but carried on walking with Ben, leaving Morgan to talk to Theo alone and she was furious that they'd just dumped her.

'That was a lovely service. It was as if you knew him.'

'Thank you, I spent quite some time with his mum and aunt, although not at the same time, apparently they don't get on, but I'm happy to see they seemed to have buried the hatchet for today.'

'I guess death has a way of making you realise how short life actually is.'

'True, I was wondering, do you think I should come into the station and have a chat with some of your colleagues? Grief can hit us when we least expect it. I'd like to offer my services of a listening ear if anyone needs it.'

Morgan looked deep into his eyes, there was a genuine warmth there which she hadn't expected.

'I'd have to ask the boss and let you know, if that's okay, it's not up to me to say really, Theo.'

'I understand, I wanted to ask how you were specifically, Morgan. You had a terrible time, and I think we got off on the wrong foot. The same applies to you, if you need to have a chat, you're welcome to come to the vicarage for a coffee anytime.'

'Thank you, that's good to know.'

She smiled at him then turned and hurried after Ben, who was leaning on the car waiting for her. They got inside, none of them speaking until the engine was on and he was turning away from Theo's gaze.

'What did he want?'

'Said he was here if anyone needed to chat, might do you some good, Amy.'

'Absolutely bloody not, I'd rather go stark raving mad than sit and talk to him about how I'm feeling, it's not happening.'

Ben laughed. 'He's kind of hard to figure out, don't you think? I can't decide if he means well or is just meddling.'

Morgan glanced in the wing mirror to see him shaking the chief constable's hand.

'I think he might mean well, maybe we're being too harsh on him.'

They drove the rest of the way back to Rydal Falls in silence.

ELEVEN

Any moment now she would come out of the quirky coffee shop where she went for lunch every day at the same time. Natalie White. She always ate the same thing, a tuna mayo jacket potato with salad, large cappuccino and a slice of tray bake for dessert. Each day she went in with a different friend. Monday it was yoga day and she went in with a dark-haired woman, both of them wearing flowy yoga pants, tight vests and with a rolled-up mat underneath their arms. Tuesday it was fell-walking day and she usually arrived with two other women, all wearing walking boots, North Face trousers and gilets. Wednesday, she met her husband who was a good twenty years older than her; he was always late, she was always early, waiting for him with her coffee whilst reading this week's copy of one of those awful celebrity magazines. Thursday her daughter would arrive, sometimes with a friend in tow, wearing her school uniform, a backpack slung over one arm and a look of either misery or anger etched across her moody face. Friday was by far the most interesting day, because on Fridays her lunch date was a younger man. The person watching wasn't sure who he was, but they knew that Natalie always dressed up on Fridays, more than any other day. Which led them to question if he was a friend, or maybe a lover, they weren't too sure because they never managed to get a table close enough to her on a Friday. It was always too busy, and the staff reserved Natalie's table every day because she must spend a small fortune in there. Natalie and the man never left together, always going their separate ways with a quick peck on the cheek, which really piqued their interest.

Today was a long, leisurely lunch with several coffees involved. The watcher had seen it all from the shop across the road where they worked. They sighed happily; Natalie was still blissfully unaware that her clock was ticking, and her time was running out. Sometimes they wondered whether, if she knew that her glorious, privileged life was drawing to an end, she would live dangerously and try a roast chicken sandwich for a change. They smiled; it was a weird thing, knowing how much power they held after all those years of having none. They'd known since they were a small child that they were different, but hadn't realised how much so until they'd finally put their plan into action. Some people didn't deserve to live, it really was as simple as that. Beauty could be bought, but it was only ever skin deep. Look at Natalie, who had a fresh blow dry every week, roots retouched every four weeks and three-monthly Botox injections to keep those wrinkles at bay. She was exquisitely beautiful on the outside, yet when you peeled back all those layers you could see quite plainly that she was like a wizened, bitter and twisted witch from a Grimm's fairy tale. It was a shame that people were so taken in with the glamorous woman who supported charitable causes with her husband's wealth. The watcher saw through her though. They got a little kick out of the fact that her teenage daughter seemed to hate her almost as much as they did. Perhaps, when the time came, they would spare the daughter. Perhaps the open contempt she so publicly threw her mother's way would save her life, they weren't sure yet. It all depended upon how the plan went, they were open-minded, adaptable to small amendments. The Lawsons' deaths had gone splendidly, much better than they'd anticipated. And it had inspired them to make the Whites' deaths even more spectacular.

TWELVE

It was almost teatime when the car arrived back at the station. Ben and Morgan rushed to get changed out of their stuffy, heavy black cotton tunics into something more breathable and cooler, not to mention less restrictive. Her ankle was feeling much better. She'd noticed when she stood up and down for the hymns at the service that it wasn't hurting her as much and she could bear weight on it much better. As she stripped off her uniform in the ladies, she sat on the toilet lid and tried to wiggle her foot, making small circles with it. It niggled a little but nothing she couldn't cope with. Standing up she tried walking on it without the boot the hospital had given her and realised, much to her relief, that she could as long as she didn't put too much weight on it, which meant that she'd also hopefully be able to drive. Pressing the palms of her hands together she closed her eyes and whispered *Thank you, God, the universe, whoever is watching.* Morgan hadn't realised how much she'd loved the freedom of being able to drive wherever she wanted until it had been taken away from her. Sitting back down she tugged on her one highly polished Doc Marten boot and put her uniform in a bag to take to the dry cleaners, hoping that she wouldn't need it again for a very long time.

She walked to the lift with one boot on, the other waiting downstairs for her in the locker where she'd left it in the hope that soon enough she'd be able to wear it again. She still wasn't going to attempt the stairs, better not push it too much, but it also meant she wouldn't have to be stuck in the station. She wanted to be out there talking to the Lawsons' friends and colleagues, and trying to figure out who had hated them enough to kill them all in such a barbaric way.

Ben was back in his office, wearing a shirt and trousers but no suit jacket or tie. Amy had gone for a quick drink at The Black Dog with the officers who hadn't been on shift, to raise a glass for Des and let her hair down for a bit. Morgan knocked on Ben's door and he waved her inside.

'I know you wanted me to view the CCTV, but I need to get out of here for a bit and I can drive now. I could go and speak to Sally's colleagues and see if they know anything about her home life, if she'd ever mentioned any problems.' Her fingers were crossed behind her back, desperate for him to say yes and give her some freedom back.

'What do you mean you can drive now?'

She lifted her Doc Marten clad foot in the air, waving it in his direction. 'Look, I can bear weight okay without the supportive boot. We can't afford to waste any time, we could be losing precious leads.'

Ben sighed. 'Okay, I'm glad your ankle is much better, that's great. If you want to chase up some of Sally's colleagues, friends that would be great. I'll see if any of the PCSOs can view the CCTV for us. I'm waiting for Will or Declan to update me about the post-mortems.'

'Cool, I'll go to the salon and see if anyone is around.'

She left him to it, knowing that he had a lot on his mind and that a bit of time alone might be what he needed.

. . .

The Hair Bar was on the high street. Morgan squeezed the plain car into a space and crossed the road. There was a woman hovering around outside by the door, by a handwritten note taped to the glass window of the door, 'Closed Due to Unforeseen Circumstances'. That was one way of putting it.

'Is anyone in, do you know?'

She shook her head, eyes full of unshed tears, looking sad, and Morgan felt sorry for her.

'I just came down to check everything was okay. We didn't think it was appropriate to open up today.'

Morgan looked at the woman standing in front of her. She was early forties, with shoulder-length bobbed platinum hair and a pair of huge hoops dangling from her ears.

'Can I help you? I'm Jackie Thorpe, I help to run the place when Sally isn't here.'

'I'm sorry for your loss, it must have been a terrible shock for you all. Is it okay to have a chat about Sally? I'm Detective Morgan Brookes, I'm on the investigating team.'

Jackie nodded. 'I'm sorry I didn't bring my key, my head's all over the place.'

Morgan smiled. 'I bet it is, what a terrible shock for you. Should we sit in my car?' Morgan pointed across the street, and the woman nodded, though she looked a bit unsure.

They crossed the street and got back into her car. Jackie wore a strong perfume that filled the air, making Morgan feel a bit sick. She put the window down slightly not wanting to offend the woman who looked devastated.

'Before we begin can I get your details? Your full name, date of birth and current address, please, for my records.'

'Jacqueline Thorpe, the twelfth of April 1982, I live above the shop. I can't believe it; she was fine yesterday. We were working late last night. I left around five to seven, and Sally was going to lock up and now she's dead. We don't even know how or what happened. I've been trying to get hold of David all day, but his phone's turned off, understandably.'

A chill settled across Morgan's shoulders as she realised that Jackie had no idea about David and Tim.

'I'm sorry to be the one to tell you this but both David and Tim are dead too.'

The woman sitting opposite her laughed, it was a high-pitched sound, then her hand flew to her mouth, and she whispered, 'You're kidding me, right? This is some kind of sick joke, why would you do that, are you even a copper?'

Morgan pulled her lanyard out from underneath her T-shirt, holding it up for Jackie to read. 'This is no joke, I'm serious.'

'What's going on, I don't understand?'

'How did you know Sally was dead?'

'Facebook, well Messenger. The salon girls have a group chat and one of them saw a picture of Sally's house on Facebook with the fire engine outside, and one of the neighbours said she died in the fire. No one has been able to get hold of her and that's not like Sally. She's a right gossip, she'd have been the first to let us know her bloody house burned down. Such a gorgeous house too. Poor David and Tim, God love them, did they all die in the fire?'

'We're looking into that. Did Sally ever say she was having trouble with anyone, an angry customer? Did she fall out with any family members, friends?'

Jackie shook her head. 'No arguments with anyone but she said she felt spooked a couple of times.'

Morgan sat forward, every sense in her body on high alert. 'How was she spooked?'

Jackie sighed. 'She said she thought she was seeing things, a dark shadow out of the corner of her eye, the feeling she wasn't alone, that someone was watching her, but she could never see an actual person.'

'Did she tell the police or David?'

'Not that I know of. She said she felt stupid because she thought it was a ghost.'

Morgan's mouth dropped open; she had not been expecting that.

'A ghost?'

Jackie laughed. 'Yeah, a ghost. It's not unheard of you know, they do exist. My old house used to be haunted when I was a kid. I told her she should go to that shop in Bowness, the one that sells all witchy books and tarot cards, with a little coffee shop on one side. Apparently the woman who owns it is psychic and can see things, and there's a woman there who is also good and reads cards. A few of us have been for readings and she knows stuff there is no way that she should. Sally went there last week; I think she had a reading, but nothing came of it, and then she bought some tarot cards. We had a laugh about it because neither of us know what the hell to do with them, but she said the woman who owned it was so lovely she didn't want to leave without buying something.'

'Did she speak to her about her experiences?'

'She must have done I suppose. Poor Sally, I guess it wasn't a ghost after all. My mum always said it's the living that can harm you not the dead and she was right, God rest her soul.'

Morgan was stunned by this revelation. 'What's the shop called?'

'Practical Magic, it sells these really cool coffees and stuff.'

'Thank you. Is there anyone else Sally was close to here that I could speak to?'

Jackie shrugged. 'She got on well with everyone. She only told me about being haunted though, she didn't want everyone to think she was crazy. I had to swear to secrecy, and I did, it's not my business. I can't believe she's really gone, that she's not going to walk in tomorrow, it's so weird. What's going to happen to this place now?'

'I have no idea, I'm sorry, I can't help you with that side of things. I'm here purely on investigations to find out how she died.'

'What, wait, are you saying that she didn't die in the fire?'

Morgan wanted to kick herself. 'We can't assume anything until the post-mortem has been conducted. I can't tell you anything else. Thank you for your help and again I'm sorry for your loss.'

Morgan stared at the car door, suddenly feeling hot and needing to be outside in the cool air. It was hard to breathe inside the stuffy car, with the overpowering smell of Jackie's intense perfume. Jackie opened her door and got out of the car. She turned back to smile at Morgan who smiled back, relieved to have the car back to herself.

She watched Jackie as she crossed the road, tried the door handle of the shop to make sure it was locked then turned and walked away, but not before waving at Morgan. She waved back as she put down all the windows in the car, to try and get rid of the lingering smell of fragrance that felt as if it had seeped into every piece of fabric.

THIRTEEN

Morgan drove towards Bowness and the shop, hoping that it might still be open although she wasn't holding out much hope. Her mind was a blur with everything Jackie had told her. She didn't believe that Sally was being haunted, but there was a very real possibility that Sally was being stalked by someone so good at it they were as stealthy as a ghost. Or had they tried to make her believe that she was seeing things that didn't exist? Abandoning the car on the opposite side of the road to the shop, Morgan turned the hazard lights on and hoped for the best. She looked up at the sign above the shop; *Practical Magic* was one of her favourite movies, one she'd watch on her own curled up on the sofa with a mug of hot chocolate on a rainy day off, when she'd lived alone. It never failed to cheer her up. Her own aunt Ettie reminded her a little of Aunt Jet, and once again she wondered how her life would have turned out had she been allowed to live with her aunt instead of being put into care to then be adopted by Sylvia and Stan. Lost in her own thoughts she heard the sound of a door being slammed shut and saw a dark-haired woman about to lock the shop up. Dashing across the road she called out, 'Excuse me.'

The woman turned to look at her and an overwhelming feeling of déjà vu washed over Morgan. She felt as if she knew her but that wasn't possible, was it?

'Can I help you?'

'I hope so, I'm Detective Morgan Brookes, I wondered if I could ask you a few questions? If you have the time, it's important.'

The woman turned the key and pushed the door open. 'Of course, come inside.'

Morgan followed her in, the smell of ground coffee lingered in the air. She looked around at the coffee shop, which was full of lush green plants, an assortment of statement piece crystal towers and prints of the actual house from the movie it was named after. 'Wow, why have I never been here before? This place is amazing.'

'Well, I'm a firm believer in things happening at the right time, so this is your time to discover my little shop and café, welcome to Practical Magic, I'm Annie.'

Morgan turned to stare at her. 'Annie Graham?' Will had told her about this place and his wife's brushes with all sorts.

'Yes, technically, although I'm Annie Ashworth now.' Annie arched an eyebrow at her. 'I don't believe I know you though, although I know your name and I've heard a lot about you, Morgan.'

Morgan's cheeks burned red. 'Will?'

Annie laughed. 'Yes, Will, he's a bit of a gossip, in the nicest way possible.'

'He's a nice guy, a good boss, I worked for him for a few weeks.'

'I think he's pretty good too. Why don't you take a seat. Would you like a coffee? And then you can tell me how I can help you, Morgan.'

'I would love a latte, if it's not too much trouble, it's been one heck of a long day.'

'A latte it is, would you like some peppermint slice? I find it the perfect pick me up when I'm lagging and need an energy boost, it's also great for clearing headaches.'

'Oh God, yes please, that sounds perfect. Do you mind if I look around the shop?'

'Help yourself.'

Morgan began browsing the shelves. There were so many books on witchcraft, the moon, spirituality, then there were pretty hardback versions of some of her favourite classics: *Dracula, Frankenstein, Wuthering Heights, The Picture of Dorian Grey*. She turned around and spied a shelf full of jars of familiar herbal teas. Picking one up she smiled. 'You know my aunt Ettie.'

Annie put the tray of coffee and cake down on a table and walked to where Morgan was standing. 'Is she your aunt? It's a small world. She's a gorgeous woman and her teas are the best thing ever. They really work. I had to beg her to let me stock them as she was quite opposed to it at first, but then she said yes; and I believe there's another shop in Kendal that sells them now. I love her to bits, she's so kind.'

Morgan nodded. 'She is a lovely lady, and this is such a wonderful shop. I'll be back tomorrow to buy one of everything.'

Annie laughed. 'They must be paying you better than they paid me when I worked for the police then.'

'Haha, definitely not, but I can't resist those books.'

They sat down and Annie pointed to the peppermint slice. 'Have some of that and then we'll talk.'

Morgan had never felt so comfortable in another woman's presence. She felt as if she'd known Annie forever. Through a mouthful of cake, she told her, 'This is amazing, do you make it yourself?'

'No, I'm afraid as much as I love baking it doesn't love me. My mother-in-law is an amazing baker, and she makes all the cakes.'

'Pure heaven, do you need anyone else to help out?'

'Something tells me that you love your job too much to leave it, the thrill of the chase, the hunting down the bad guys and helping out the people who need it most. But if you ever do decide enough is enough then I would happily find space for you, Morgan. There's something about you that is so familiar, yet I can't figure out what.'

She laughed. 'You're right, at the moment I love it too much even though I've been in some terrible scrapes, but I do like the thrill of the chase and hunting down the bad guys as you put it.'

'So, what's brought you to me today?'

Morgan paused for a second, wondering how much she could tell Annie and decided that she could trust her. She'd been one of them and her husband was a DS just like Ben, so she would be acutely aware of the need for discretion.

'This hasn't been released yet, but we're investigating the murders of the Lawson family last night. Well, the press and public know about the house fire, but not that they were killed before it started. I know I can trust you with this information.'

Annie looked sad. 'You can, that's just horrific but I don't think I know them.'

'Sally Lawson came to visit the shop last week, when she thought she was being haunted. I think she bought some tarot cards.'

'Oh no, not that lovely lady who owns the beauty salon in Rydal Falls? She never told me her surname, but I remember now she introduced herself as Sally. Bless her that's awful.'

'It is, I spoke to her colleague at the salon before I came here, and she told me that Sally was concerned she was being watched. Could you tell me anything she said to you about it?'

'I can't believe it; her entire family are all dead. Let me tell you what happened. She rang up and asked if she could come in for a card reading, usually Magda does those, I prefer the hands-on kind of readings, but she was away, so Sally asked to do a session with me instead. So, Sally turned up, I spoke to her, and she told me she thought she was being haunted. I sat with her for fifteen minutes, but I really couldn't see or feel there was anyone who had passed on lingering around trying to get her attention. I told her that I didn't think it was a haunting and that maybe there was another reason for how she'd been feeling, perhaps she had a stalker. She laughed at that and asked who on earth would want to stalk her, said she lived a boring life and survived off the gossip from the salon. I advised her to be careful and speak to the police, but she didn't think there was any need. Sally still wanted to buy some cards, said she might try it at home or in the salon, in case the ghost was attached to one of those locations. Bless her, I feel awful thinking about it now because once upon a time I would have been able to go into police-mode, but I really never saw it coming.'

'That's not your fault, how were you to know any of this was going to happen?'

Annie sipped her latte. She looked sad, and Morgan felt bad that she'd upset her.

'Sally thought you were lovely, she told Jackie that.'

'I can't believe she's dead, it's so senseless, and her family too. I'm sorry I haven't been much help, Morgan. The only thing I can tell you for sure is that she wasn't being haunted, at least not by the dead.'

Morgan popped the last piece of cake in her mouth and finished her latte. She nodded. 'Thank you for staying behind to speak to me and for this, it's truly the best coffee and cake I've ever eaten.'

She stood up and felt an overwhelming urge to hug Annie, but she didn't. What was happening to her lately? She wasn't usually a hugger.

'If you need anything, let me know, the only days I'm not here are Sundays and Mondays.'

Morgan nodded; she had a feeling as she walked away that

this wouldn't be the last time she visited the shop.

FOURTEEN

Ben was waiting for a phone call from either Declan or Will, maybe both, but hopefully not at the same time. When the pair of them walked into the office he thought he was seeing double, and managed to dribble the mouthful of coffee he'd just swigged all down the front of his white shirt. He stood up and grabbed some paper, blotting the stain with it.

'Would you look at you, can't take you anywhere, Matthews. Do you need a bib?' Declan grinned at him.

He smiled for what felt like the first time in hours. 'Good afternoon, Declan, Will, what brings you here?'

Declan crossed the room to where Ben was standing and before he could speak wrapped his arms around him, hugging him tight for the briefest of moments before letting go and stepping back. 'I've been longing to do that for years. How are you holding up? It's been a tough day for you, and Will here told me that you knew Sally Lawson?'

'It's been crap, in every way you can imagine.'

'I'm sorry I couldn't make the funeral. I thought I'd help you in the only way I could by not delaying Sally's and David's postmortems. Look, the reason we're here is to drag you to the pub for a pint and to discuss my findings with you in some quiet corner, what do you say?'

'That sounds bloody great, yes, thank you.'

'Good, it's not often you listen to your uncle Declan, but I'm glad to see you're learning. Where is that feisty fire pot, Morgan?'

Will was smiling and Ben joined in.

'Gone out on enquiries. I think she needed to escape for a bit. She blames herself for Des.'

'What, why? You two are a pain in the foot. Well reel her in and tell her I'll buy her a pint too.'

'I will, but maybe she'd be better doing her own thing, she's driving again, and I think she'll be enjoying her freedom.'

Declan shrugged. 'Whatever you think, come on let's go, it's been a hell of a day for us all, and I only have an hour before the love of my life finishes work and arrives to pick me back up. Your good man Will drove me here to come check you were okay. You have some good friends, Benjamin.'

Ben smiled at Will; he was fortunate that he did have friends because they were all in this together.

The Black Dog was relatively quiet considering it had been Des's unofficial wake a couple of hours earlier. Ben had thought there would be a few stragglers hanging around, and he was relieved there weren't. He ordered two pints of lager and a half for Will who had to drive back to Hawkshead, where he lived. He'd texted Morgan, to see if she wanted to join them, but she'd replied she was busy. That made him smile and worry at the same time, but he was glad she was out doing what she was so good at. They took their pints to the billiard room and Declan began to set up the balls, at least no one would bother them in here. There were only a couple of blokes sitting at the bar, nursing their drinks and watching the news on the television.

Declan picked up a pool cue, handing it to Ben, then grabbed one for himself.

'So, the cause of death for both of them was suffocation and clearly the manner of death is homicide. Thankfully, David Lawson was killed before he had his hand cut off with a razor-sharp instrument. You're looking for something along the lines of a professional meat cleaver, the kind that a chef or butcher would use, you know. I entered the information onto the data-base, and it should come up with a complete match of make and style, but that might take a little time.'

'I suppose that's something, that the injuries were post-mortem.'

'Ah, I haven't got to Sally yet. I'm awfully sorry to tell you this but her injury was perimortem and sustained whilst she was still alive.'

Ben leaned over and took his shot, smashing the white ball so hard that the rest of the balls flew violently across the table. He stood up inhaling deeply and downed half of his pint in one mouthful.

'How could you tell? Is there a chance you could be mistaken?'

'Ben, I'm going to pretend you didn't just insult both my intelligence and professionalism with that tasteless remark. I could tell because in perimortem injuries the haemorrhaging after losing a large amount of blood is associated with clotting. When you are breathing and hurt yourself enough to bleed the clots are laminated, firm and variegated. Wounds after death can cause a slight haemorrhage of the venous vessels, in which case clots are not present or if they are, they will be soft and non-laminated with a yellowish appearance. David had no clots in or around his injury, but Sally did and, to further back this up, her wound edges were gaped and swollen, while David's had no swelling around them.'

Will was shaking his head. 'It's terrible, they killed David before his wife.'

Ben took another shot whilst he processed the information Declan had relayed to him.

'What about the boy, Tim?'

'I haven't looked at him, I'm hoping for his sake that his were the same as David's. I'll be able to tell you more tomorrow, Ben.'

'So, whoever did this, it's likely that David and Tim were killed first, because Sally was the last one to arrive home. Then not long after the neighbour saw smoke coming from the front of the house. This is personal, whoever did this wanted Sally to see her family dead with their hands chopped off.'

'Yes, it looks that way. Obviously I can't give you a definite on Tim's injuries until tomorrow, but I'm hoping to God that whoever this sick bastard is didn't make a fourteen-year-old boy suffer any more than he had to. This is the kind of thing that gives me nightmares.'

Ben hadn't thought today could get any worse, how wrong he'd been. Now Declan had confirmed Morgan's theory and his own worst fears. He couldn't comprehend the terror Sally must have felt walking into her home, the place she should be the safest, and seeing her husband and son dead. Then to have someone put a thick plastic bag over her head and chop off her hand whilst she was dying was just incomprehensible. Declan wasn't the only one going to have nightmares tonight. He wasn't sure if he'd be able to close his eyes without seeing those three bodies slumped at the table, bloodied stumps in front of them and their eyes bulging from their sockets as they gasped to try and take in oxygen that wasn't there.

FIFTEEN

The ride into work was quiet. Morgan was worried about Ben. He'd been tossing and turning so that neither had slept much last night. She'd managed to grab a few hours at one point, but she'd then woken to find the bed empty and heard him downstairs in the kitchen. The next time he got in bed she got a faint whiff of whisky fumes that tainted his breath.

Amy was already in the atrium when they arrived, chatting to Mads. She looked a lot better than she had yesterday, funerals were hard. The dread and sadness leading up to them was magnified a hundred times, not that the grief ever left you. Morgan knew this all too well; she'd spent years battling with Stan, her dad, only to finally start to get along with him in the weeks before he'd been cruelly murdered. The grief ebbed and flowed in waves, she'd be okay and not even thinking about him and then out of nowhere something would remind her of him, and she'd want to curl up into a ball and cry buckets. She guessed guilt was what was eating away at Amy, but she had nothing to be guilty about. It was her, Morgan, who shouldered that particular guilt over Des: as she was the last person to be with him, she should have stopped it happening. Instead, she'd been relieved when he'd left her at that spring fete because he'd been getting on her nerves. The thing that upset Morgan over it all was that she'd never get to apologise to Des about what had happened. He had worn a protective shield whenever he had to work with her because he was scared she'd get him killed, and look what happened, she'd done just that.

Ben went up the stairs, but Morgan veered off to the downstairs toilets because she was afraid she was suddenly going to cry right here in the middle of the station. She never used to be this way, she used to be tough, feisty. But, she reflected, she also used to be lonely with no real friends since leaving school. She realised this was the price you paid for having people you cared about in your life: the more you liked someone, the bigger the impact from anything happening to them. Blotting her eyes with a piece of toilet paper so as not to smudge her eyeliner wings, Morgan asked herself would she rather be lonely so there was none of this and she realised the answer was no, she didn't want to go back to the lonely girl she'd been before she joined this team.

When she came out of the toilet everyone had disappeared. Amy was now in the office along with Ben and Marc, who looked at her and smiled.

'How are you all doing? It's been a rough few days for everyone.'

Amy shrugged, Ben nodded, and Marc's eyes fell on her.

'Okay I guess,' she answered him.

'I wanted you to know that I'm going to be putting a post up on the intranet, asking for offers of interest to fill Des's position.' He held up his hand. 'Before you rip my head off, Amy, I'm not trying to replace him, I wouldn't want to. But what I see is a hard-working team who are overworked, underpaid and a team member down. Regardless of what you think of me, I can't let you go on without an extra pair of hands. Even if we get someone in temporarily, that's a big help.'

He was grimacing and Morgan found herself feeling a bit sorry for him, despite her past run-in with him.

Amy shrugged. 'We need the help.'

Ben nodded. 'We do need a hand, there's a lot of investigating to do. Thanks, boss, that's very much appreciated.'

'Obviously I'll run the likely candidates past you all, I'm not going to throw someone in who won't get along with the rest of the team. That would be counterproductive, I want it to be someone you all think you can work with. Morgan, could I have a word with you in my office?'

Amy raised her eyebrows at Morgan, who nodded and followed him down to his office wondering what he was up to.

'Come in, take a seat, this won't take long.'

Reluctantly she did as he asked, noticing the picture frame of the family he'd had on his desk was gone.

'I'm going to be honest with you because there is literally no point in not being; you seem to have a good handle on people, which is an excellent trait by the way.'

'Honest about what?' She had her hands tucked under her knees, hoping that he wasn't going to say she was being moved again because she didn't know if she'd be able to control herself.

Marc sighed heavily. 'I have been a nightmare; I came in here guns blazing wanting to make the best impression, but I realise now that I have done nothing but mess things up and in a spectacular fashion too.'

She nodded, not sure if she was supposed to agree with him or not.

'I'm sorry for causing you a lot of unnecessary stress. I shouldn't have moved you to Barrow like that. I was angry, not with you but with myself. I thought that I was going to be working things out with my family and it didn't happen. In Ben's words I have been a complete arsehole and I want you to know that I'm going to really make this move work. Now that the investigation I was under in Manchester has been closed, and my name cleared, I can relax a little and see things for what they are, and I've realised that I needed to sort myself out.'

'That's good, I'm glad to hear it.'

He nodded. 'My wife filed for divorce, but the girls still want to come visit so at least that's something. I was in a bad place for some time, but I promise you that I'm over that now and I want you to feel that you can come to me if you need anything work or personal wise. I've already spoken to Ben and apologised, and when Amy is up to it, I'll be speaking to her too. You are now officially back in the Rydal Falls CID team, no more moving departments.'

'Is this the real Marc talking or are you going to change your mind next time someone puts you in a bad mood?'

He looked at her then laughed. 'I deserve that, in fact that's a lot kinder than the reaction I was expecting. This is me; I'm not saying I won't annoy you ever again because there's probably a very good chance I will. What I'm hoping is we can put the last couple of months behind us and move forward.'

'I guess we can.'

She stood up to leave.

'I also wanted to ask your opinion about someone I think would be a great asset to our team, but I didn't want to ask in front of the others in case it was a bit awkward.'

'Who do you have in mind?'

'Cain, I've seen how well he works. How you all seem to get on with him. He's going to have to sit his exams before he's a detective, like you did, but I think he'd be okay with them. What do you think, would he be interested and would you all like to have him on board if so?'

'He would be amazing, he's practically one of us anyway. Have you asked him?'

'Not yet, I wanted to run it past you.'

'Why me and not Ben?'

'Because you and Cain get on well, and I didn't know if it would interfere with you and Ben. You know how complicated office dynamics can get; it can turn into a nightmare. I don't want to upset things any more than I already have.'

He looked genuinely remorseful, and she found herself warming to this improved version of her boss, hoping this time he was being honest.

'There would be no problem, Cain and I are friends, and there is nothing between us and never has been. In fact, he is seeing someone at the moment and is really happy. I think he'd be very interested in joining us.'

'Thank you, Morgan, that's great. I'll go and find him, see what he says.'

She opened the door. 'Actually, it's not Ben you need to worry about, Mads will be furious if you steal Cain away from him.'

'I can handle Mads, I need to put my team first, and anyway Cain might not be interested. But I wanted to give him first refusal. Maybe don't mention it until I've spoken to Cain; if he says yes, I'll check with the others if they're happy to have him on board too.'

She walked out of his office with a huge grin on her face, thinking Cain would be fantastic, someone she could work with easily and even Amy liked him. There would be no friction or the feeling that he was replacing Des because Cain was Cain. She just hoped that he hadn't decided to transfer to Wales to be with Bella just yet.

SIXTEEN

The shop was always busy on Saturdays. They passed the day splendidly and they actually focused on their work because Natalie didn't visit the café across the road on weekends. For the last ten minutes for example, they'd been busy mopping the floor after a customer had managed to drop an entire bottle of shampoo everywhere. It had exploded into a hundred pieces of plastic, green, gloopy slime and it was taking forever to wash away the bubbles that kept forming every time they added water. They were proud that they hadn't told the customer to get out. It had been on the tip of their tongue, but they couldn't. For a start it wasn't their shop, they'd upset the supervisor if they did that, and they couldn't afford to put her in a worse mood than she was already in. Taking the mop bucket outside to pour down the drain they caught sight of a familiar Porsche pulling up outside the coffee shop. Lifting their head they watched as Natalie climbed out of the passenger side, laughing at something her husband had said. This was interesting, a deviation from her usual routine. All thoughts of pure hatred towards the dopey customer were obliterated as they realised they'd have completely missed this opportunity without them.

It was almost lunchtime, they could take a break and go over the road to grab something to eat, see what she was doing there. They had to know. Natalie was their obsession; they were drawn to her for the same reason they'd been drawn to Sally – her husband and kid were an unfortunate part of the game plan. Necessary to make her realise that you don't get away with the things she did, at least not to them.

Going back inside they slipped on the wet floor, almost breaking their neck, and realised they forgot to put the 'wet floor' sign out. Good job the supervisor was busy chattering to a customer, otherwise she'd have gone crazy. They rushed to the cleaning cupboard, grabbed the yellow sign and stood it in front of the wet floor. Then grabbed their jacket and pointed across the road.

'Is it okay if I go grab lunch, I feel a bit faint? Do you want anything bringing back?'

The supervisor didn't, but she nodded with the smallest look of concern showing in her eyes, then her attention was diverted away as she carried on whatever gossip she was in the middle of. She could grab her own lunch, the lazy cow, they were just being polite to her so they could escape for thirty minutes.

The café was busy. Lady Natalie wasn't sitting in her usual seat, which pleased them a lot more than it should have. A family were sitting there, eating toasted sandwiches, and she was at a table next to the breakfast bar that ran along one wall, meaning there was one stool left at the bar, so they threw their jacket across it to snag it before anyone else, then went to order something. This was perfect: they couldn't have planned it any better if they'd tried. Their stomach was jittery and their hands were a little shaky but that was okay: they'd calm down once they were sitting next to her with a slice of cake and a pot of tea. They weren't a tea fan, but they could make a pot of tea last longer than a mug of milky coffee, plus tea was cheaper. Another thing that made them rage at Natalie. They had to scrimp and scrape to pay the bills, and buy food and live, whilst she was splashing the cash around as if she was printing it herself. They were sure she'd never done a solid day's work from the day she married her wealthy husband. Ironic really, they were convinced she'd stalked her rich husband so she could live a trophy wife life, and now they were stalking her so they could finish what she started that day thirty years ago when she made the worst decision of her life.

SEVENTEEN

Morgan let Ben drive to the Royal Lancaster Infirmary to attend Tim Lawson's post-mortem, and neither of them spoke much on the way. Ben had updated her earlier on the findings from Sally's and David's autopsies. Now the thought of watching the PM of a healthy teenager who should not be in one of Declan's freezers weighed heavy on their minds. When they got out of the car Ben reached out for her hand, squeezing it.

'Thank you.'

'For what?'

'This, agreeing to come with me. I could have asked Amy.'

She shrugged. 'I think Amy has enough to deal with at the moment, although she seemed a bit brighter this morning. Of course, I'd come, I'm not going to wimp out on you. I know this is going to be hard for you. Did you know Tim?'

'Only from what Sally would tell me whenever we bumped into each other.'

They talked as they crossed the road, walking towards the mortuary entrance.

'What was she like back then?'

'A little more outspoken, she hung around with a group of

girls who were a bit like the ones in the Lindsay Lohan film, the one with the burn book.'

Morgan turned to look at Ben.

'You've watched *Mean Girls?*'

His cheeks tinged with the slightest pink colour as he laughed. 'I have, I shouldn't have admitted that, should I?'

Morgan was giggling as they walked on. 'There's nothing wrong with that, I just wouldn't have pegged you as a fan of those kinds of movies.'

Ben shrugged. 'I'm not really, Cindy enjoyed them, and I'm going to tell you something I've never told anyone else, ever.'

'I can't wait, I'm holding my breath.'

'I had a thing for Lindsay Lohan.'

Morgan stopped dead in her tracks, folded her arms across her stomach and bent double with laughter.

'What's so funny, she's attractive. Or was, I don't know what she looks like now.'

'Nothing, it's just funny.' She stopped laughing. 'Oh God, tell me you didn't have a crush on me because we both had red hair?'

'Now you're being plain ridiculous. Well okay, maybe I did a little.' He began to laugh and the pair of them stood there for a few seconds holding each other. Morgan lifted a finger to wipe her eyes that were watering.

'I don't know whether to be insulted or not, I can't make up my mind.'

'I fell for you because you're you, not because you reminded me of her. I shouldn't have told you.'

Morgan squeezed his arm. 'Don't be daft, sorry, it really tickled me that's all.'

As they reached the door to the mortuary their mood shifted back to one of sombre dread for what they were about to observe.

She pressed the buzzer on the intercom.

'Hiya.'

'Morning, Susie, it's Morgan and Ben.'

'On my way.'

After a couple of minutes Susie opened the door. Her hair this month was surprisingly blonde. Morgan decided that she preferred her rainbow-coloured hair a million times over, though she had every right to do what she wanted with it. Ben was gawping as per usual, and before she could say anything he spoke.

'Your hair.'

Susie looked at him. 'What about it?'

'It's normal.'

Morgan glared at him.

'Are you going natural, Susie?' she asked.

Susie shrugged. 'Not sure, thought I'd give being blonde a go but I'm not really feeling it you know, it's a bit boring. Be different if I was a natural fiery redhead like you, but this mousy blonde is a bit bland.'

'I think it looks nice.' Ben was still getting over the shock.

Susie laughed. 'Well then if it looks nice, I think I need to go neon pink, Ben, *nice* is not the kind of reaction I'm after. I quite enjoy shocking people. Hey, enough about me, what books have you read since I last saw you?'

'I haven't had time to read any.'

Morgan smiled, she knew that Susie was a major bookworm who loved to tease and put Ben on the spot.

'Ask him what his favourite film is instead.' she asked.

'What's your favourite film?'

Ben glared at Morgan, then shook his head. 'Erm, *Fast and Furious*.'

This set Morgan off into a fit of giggles. 'He's fibbing, it's not.'

'Why is it you three are like a bunch of naughty school kids, while the rest of us are ready and waiting? In your own time please, Brookes and Matthews. Susie, for the love of God, stop corrupting our officers of the law.'

Declan was standing with his arms folded across his chest. Susie scurried off towards the mortuary, and Morgan headed into the ladies' changing room to escape Declan's glare. She loved him to bits, and he was as funny as any comedian, but when it came down to his job he was deadly serious in more ways than one.

As Morgan walked into the mortuary, she realised that the strong, chlorine-like disinfectant smell hadn't bothered her as much as usual, and she took this as a bad sign, that she was getting far too used to being in here. Ben was the last to enter the room, his face much paler than it had been minutes before, and she felt bad for him. It wasn't that long ago that they'd been in here to watch Shea Wilkinson's autopsy. That had been a tough one for them all, God love her.

Susie had already got Tim's body out of the fridge, and he was lying wrapped tight inside the black body bag on the steel table in front of them. Wendy was there with Claire; they were such a good team Morgan wondered why they didn't work together all the time. Declan had Rock FM playing in the background, which was quite a change from usual, but she knew he would have a reason. The music was such a lovely distraction, at least it was for her anyway, she could look down at her boots and forget where they were momentarily when a great song came on.

Declan cut the tag sealing the bag and began to unzip it. There was no awful decomposition smell yet because Tim had been found less than a couple of hours after his murder. She steeled herself as Declan and Susie expertly rolled Tim out of the bag then unwrapped the white sheet from around him. She'd flinched at the plastic bag, still cable tied around his head.

She'd forgot about that part. Her eyes were drawn down to his missing right hand, the red bloodied stump looked so wrong. All of this was wrong. She noticed he was wearing an Iron Maiden T-shirt, and nodded appreciatively at Declan's choice of music. He was such a sweetheart; he must have noted it at the house before the bodies were moved. This single, kind attention to his victim's details made the corner of her eyes pool with tears.

They weighed, measured and X-rayed Tim's body before Declan began his external observations. Susie took fingernail clippings from his left hand, then they began to remove his clothes for Wendy to bag up.

'I think it's pretty clear what Tim's cause of death was, but we still need to go through the motions. Tim, bear with me please, this isn't nice and I'm sorry, but we will look after you in the best way possible, mate. It will be over soon, no one else can hurt you now.'

This time it was Wendy who let out a loud sniff. No one looked her way, they had all been there at some point. Declan was so lovely; his care of his patients as he did this final thing for them was always so poignant and fitting. Morgan hadn't worked with any other pathologists, but she thought that they probably were the luckiest coppers in England to have him working on their team.

He cut the tie sealing the plastic bag and passed it to Wendy to bag up and be tested for any DNA evidence, then he removed the bag. Tim's blond hair was stuck to his forehead, his eyes bulged from the lack of oxygen, his tongue protruded from his mouth.

'What a cruel way to kill someone, watching them struggling to gulp in air that isn't there. Horrid, it really is, I'd like to get my hands on whoever did this. Tim should be watching *Stranger Things* and practising his guitar riffs right now.'

No one disagreed with Declan, they were all thinking the same thing.

Ben finally found his voice. 'What about the hand, can you tell if it was done before or after?'

'Clearly after, same as his dad's, no visible clotting. At least that's some small token of comfort. Unlike his poor mum, who suffered the pain of watching her dead family whilst her hand was chopped off before she suffocated to death. Same cut marks too, so it's the same instrument.'

'Can you tell who died first?'

'Pretty difficult to determine. If I had the knife or whatever that might help to determine, if the blood is on there in layers.'

Morgan tore her eyes away from Tim's body to look at Ben. 'Wouldn't Tim have been home first? School finished no later than four. If the killer was waiting, he might have killed him when he arrived, then David must have come home next, and we know for sure Sally was the last one, killed only minutes after she arrived home. It would be far easier to pick them off one by one than to try and take out both of them at the same time.'

Ben nodded. 'Declan, are there any defence wounds on any of them?'

'None whatsoever, this was a quick, efficient method of disposal, although I'm praying that one of them managed to scratch our man's hand and we get lucky with some DNA under their fingernails that will lead you straight to your killer's front door. We've got scrapings from all of them now anyway, and we'll let you know as soon as we get results from the lab.'

Morgan hoped they had, that Sally had done her best to leave them with something to find the monster who took out her entire family, and lead them to him.

EIGHTEEN

Once they were back at the station, they made their way to the small room where Cathy and another PCSO, Sam, were sitting at two separate monitors viewing the CCTV footage they had seized.

'How's it going?' he asked.

Cathy shrugged. 'Rubbish. Sorry, Ben, but we're almost at the end of the footage from the school and there's nothing.'

Morgan saw his shoulders sag and felt bad for him. He'd been relying on this to give them a much-needed lead. 'Bollocks.'

'Yes, it really is. We still have a little bit left though, so you never know, we could strike it lucky. And before you ask, yes we have been paying attention, our eyes have been glued to these screens and we haven't missed anything.'

'Thank you both. It's very much appreciated, and I didn't doubt you for a moment. Sounds like I shouldn't hold my breath though.'

'Hmm, I bet you didn't. I'll come find you if there's anything.'

He gave her a thumbs up, then walked out of the room. Morgan stayed behind.

'For once, it would be great to have the killer caught on camera, wouldn't it?' Cathy said, clearly not as devoid of hope as Ben was.

'Yep, it would.'

'Hey, is it true that Cain is joining your team?'

'Gossip really spreads fast in this place, does he even know yet?' Morgan laughed, trying not to give anything away, it wasn't really her place after all.

'Not gossip, I heard it straight from the horse's mouth. He was dancing around like one of those Irish Riverdance people at the brew station earlier. I thought Mads was going to have a heart attack, his face was a picture.'

'Phew, he must have said yes then.'

'Whoa, what's this?' Sam, who was viewing Maggie's CCTV, had paused the screen.

Morgan bent over and she pressed play. Two figures came into view, one wearing school uniform, walking side by side down the street and heading for the Lawsons' front door. A tingling sensation at the base of Morgan's spine told her they might be onto something. The teenager wearing the uniform took out a key, then opened the door, and whoever was with him stopped and slowly turned to look up and down the street.

'Why's he bothered who's watching them?' asked Sam.

'He's checking to see if anyone has noticed him going inside. Sam, this is a gem, thank you!'

They continued watching as he eventually turned, stepped inside the house and closed the door.

'Be back in a min.'

Morgan walked as fast as she could to their office. Pushing open the door she grinned to see Cain sitting there opposite Amy. 'Where's Ben?'

'Didn't come in here.'

She turned to catch him coming out of the gents. 'Follow me, you need to see this.'

She led the way back to the room, Ben almost bursting with excitement.

'Show me what you have.'

As Sam rewound the CCTV, they all crowded around her, the small, windowless room getting hotter by the second with their combined body heat. Morgan noticed that Ben was holding his breath. As they all watched the guy with Tim turn to check out the street, Cathy muttered, 'Well, if that's not creepy.'

'That's our guy, it has to be. Can you zoom in on his face, Sam?'

'I can try, but this is not my area of expertise. I can only really fast forward, pause and rewind. You need to get it to the video imaging unit to get stills printed off.'

She did manage to zoom in, but the face was blurry. One thing was clear though: whoever this was looked older than the teenager he was with, and wasn't wearing a uniform.

'Who do you think he is?' Cathy asked.

'I think he's the guy we're looking for, that's who I think he is. What did you do, Tim? You led a monster in through your front door, why?' whispered Morgan.

'Monster indeed. We need to go back and search Tim's room. Does he have an iPad, computer, phone that might give us some idea who this is?'

'His phone was seized by the search team, I think a laptop too, but I'm not sure about anything else. All this time we were focusing on Sally but what if it's Tim who is the link? He brought the killer home with him, we need to find out why, what their connection is to each other. Come on, Morgan, we're going back to the house. And so we don't miss any more angles,

Amy and Cain can go and speak to David's colleagues at the university, see what he was like, if he had any problems with students or staff. But the most important question right now is who is this mystery guy?'

NINETEEN

They drove down Hest Bank Road, both feeling more positive now that they had a lead. Even if it turned out that the guy with Tim wasn't involved, at this moment he was the last person to see him alive, he'd surely know something.

'If we get stills, we could go to Tim's school and ask his friends if they know who he is, and we need to go there anyway, so this could be a huge help in identifying the man.'

'This is why I love working with you, Brookes. I've been so focused on Sally because she was killed last. Why do you think he saved her until the last though?'

Morgan shrugged; she was driving. She glanced at him then looked back at the road as the car crawled towards the Lawsons' house, which was still taped off with blue and white police tape. A lone PCSO was sitting in a car parked in front of the drive. Despite all the excitement about the man with Tim, she still had a feeling that there was something significant about Sally's death having been last, only she had no idea what it could be.

She said her thoughts out loud. 'Could he have been a school friend of Tim's? He looked older in the video, but it wasn't very clear. What if he had some strange crush on Sally, or maybe she didn't like him and told Tim he wasn't to hang around with him? It seems extreme, but this killer is clearly extreme. Something upset them to the degree that he felt that murdering her family was acceptable. She must have really pissed him off. Or maybe it was simply because she came home last; he might have killed them in the order they arrived home. He could have fallen out with Tim, killed him then realised he had to kill his parents if he wanted to get away with it. But, then the hands, why the hands? There has to be some meaning to it somewhere, buried deep, we need to uncover it.'

'Deep, that's deep but I think you're right. If he'd had a falling out with Tim, wouldn't he have killed him and then got the hell out of there? I mean what kind of person kills an entire family to right one wrong, if there even was any wrongdoing?'

They got out of the car and headed over to the PCSO on guard. Tina dangled one hand out of the car window, a keyring containing a bunch of keys attached to it.

'Afternoon.'

'How's it going? Have you seen anyone loitering around?'

Morgan noticed the empty mug on the passenger seat. Tina shook her head.

'Nothing, there's been a bit of traffic with residents coming and going. That old lady who lives in the bungalow is a feeder. She's brought me cakes, biscuits and two mugs of coffee. In fact before you go, can I use the toilet?'

Morgan smiled at her. 'Nip off now, Maggie will let you in to use her loo.'

Tina got out of the car and stretched. 'Thank God, I'd have wet myself if I had to hold it in much longer.' She strolled towards Maggie's house, with the empty mug in one hand and her hat in the other.

'You know, we should ask Maggie if she saw the guy with Tim, if she recognises him. He might be a regular at their house.'

'We will, let's go inside first though and see what we can find. Then you can go speak to her. I'm too scared of that angry pug.'

'You're such a wimp at times, boss.' She laughed and shook her head.

'I know, I'm not hardcore like you.'

They walked around to the back of the house, which wasn't fire damaged, and once again, in the muted afternoon light, Morgan was struck by how perfect the garden was. It must be nice to have the time to appreciate what you had by spending balmy summer evenings cooking and eating outside.

'You like this garden an awful lot, don't you?' Ben said.

She nodded. 'It's nice, great for entertaining your family and friends, don't you think?'

He laughed. 'Definitely nice, if you have family and friends to entertain. We have each other and are married to the job, but if you'd like something like this, I'd get someone in to build it.'

She looked at Ben, then shook her head. 'Maybe when we're older, retired, maybe have some family and friends. I don't suppose we'd get to use it much now, but it's just nice to look, you know, and imagine what your life could be like.'

He was unlocking the bifold door but turned back. 'Would you like a family one day?'

She shrugged. 'I don't know, not something I've ever given much thought to. I mean it's not all it's cracked up to be, is it? Sally and David had the perfect family life, or at least they did from the outside, and now they're all dead. How cold and cruel is that? Maybe we should stick with each other for the time being.'

He laughed. 'You're right, I wasn't offering to get you up the duff, Morgan, it was just a thought.'

'Up the duff? You have such a way with words.'

He pulled open the door, stepping inside, and he didn't answer, though she didn't expect one. They were here, once again, at the awful scene of the crime, looking for clues that only they could find.

'Do you want to take Tim's bedroom? You're closer to his age, you might have a clue what to look for. And I'll check Sally and David's?'

'Fine by me, although I'm hardly a teenager I'll just have a look downstairs first.'

Ben didn't answer, he was already making his way up the stairs.

Morgan looked at the heavily bloodstained table. That thing needed burning, no matter how much it was scrubbed they would never get all the blood out of the grains of wood. She wondered where the hell the Lawsons' bloodied hands were. Had the killer taken them with him, or had he left them here? She crossed to the American-style fridge freezer and opened the door. Wendy had looked in here, but had she been through every drawer? She knew that she would have, she was thorough and a complete professional, but still she had been delayed getting here and it wouldn't hurt her to take a quick peek.

Pulling out each drawer Morgan sifted through the contents with her gloved hands. Lots of joints of meat, one drawer full of fish, shellfish, every kind of fish. There was a drawer filled with pizzas, burgers, Hamwiches, God she remembered those when she was a teenager. Stan used to buy all their weekly food shop from Iceland, and he always threw in a pack of them even though she didn't really like them. She stared at the bag, wondering if they had made them bigger, because it looked bulkier than she remembered. She looked closer, surely not, everything these days was significantly smaller not bigger. Then why was this bag so lumpy? A sickening feeling of dread filled her stomach. Grasping the bag by the corner she picked it up. It was too heavy, there was no way it was full of those funny, triangular cheesy bits of ham. There was an ordinary pink household peg holding the bag closed. Morgan lifted it fully out of the drawer and stared at it, a queasy feeling in her stomach.

Was that a drop of blood on it?

'What are you doing?'

Morgan shrieked, jumped away from the freezer and dropped the bag with a heavy thump on the kitchen floor. The peg sprang open and flew across the tiles as the contents of the bag spilled out onto them.

'Jesus Christ, that's a hand,' Ben yelled from behind Morgan.

Lying on the floor, looking out of place on the marble tiles, was a bloodied, frozen hand. Morgan nodded. It was indeed a hand, one she hoped wasn't going to come to life and skitter across the floor on its fingertips like Thing in *The Addams Family*.

Ben pushed past her and bent down to look at it, prodding it with his pen.

'It's solid, no wedding ring either. Sally wore one, not sure about David but I'd assume he did.'

A wave of sadness washed over Morgan. 'Tim's?'

She looked at the empty bag where it had been hidden inside. It had been placed in the drawer full of junk food that a typical teenager would eat. Giving the hand a wide berth, she went back to the freezer drawers.

'Did Sally ever tell you what kind of food she loved to eat?'

She was already thinking that the other missing hands could be in different drawers hidden inside the plastic packaging.

'I think she ate a lot of seafood; she was always trying some fad diet; we talked a lot about diets.'

Morgan was already looking through the drawer, noticing nothing in there as bulky as in the other one, but Sally was quite petite, she wasn't going to have a huge hand.

'Hang on, we better get CSI here to document this and let Wendy or whoever is on call go through the rest of the drawers.'

Morgan knew this, of course she did, but she was eager to see if her hunch was right. Nodding she pushed the drawer shut, closing the freezer door. She turned around to see Ben still kneeling, staring at the hand.

'I don't get it, why the hands? I mean what does it mean? Is it some kind of clue, a symbol, or is he just a sick bastard?'

Morgan was wracking her mind, what was that saying Sylvia used to say, something about the hand of God? It was that long ago she couldn't remember exactly – being judged by the hand of God maybe?

'My mum used to say they'd been dealt the hand of God when she was talking about people sometimes, but I have no idea what she meant. Have you heard of that saying?'

Ben shrugged. Standing upright his knees creaked loudly in the silence of the kitchen.

'What, like a religious thing?'

She looked down at her own hand, slender fingers with painted black nails as Goth-like as she could get whilst on duty, along with her neat eyeliner wings.

'Maybe, we could ask Father Theo, he might know.'

'I thought you disliked him more than my beef stew?'

'He's not that bad, and your stew would be okay if you made it in a slow cooker instead of the oven. My teeth aren't tough enough to chew through it on a good day.'

Ben smiled at her. 'Father Theo, I suppose he might know something. Do you want to go and pay him a visit whilst I check out Tim's bedroom and wait for CSI to arrive?'

'What, as in you're going to stay here and stare at that hand until there's a free unit? You're not going to delegate it to me to sit and wait?'

'I feel as if I owe it to Sally to see this thing through. Are you okay with visiting the good vicar?'

'Might as well.' She turned to walk out of the open bifold doors and paused, looking back at Ben.

'Hey, tell Wendy or whoever comes that that peg that spun across the floor looked as if it had a tiny drop of blood on it.' She pointed to the corner of the table where it was lying as out of place on the white marble tiles as the decapitated hand.

Outside in the fresh air she waved at Tina who was on her phone but waved back. She walked down to Maggie's house, annoyed to see the front door ajar. Knocking, she walked inside.

'Maggie, hello it's me, Morgan.'

The pug began to bark from somewhere, not bothering to come and see who she was.

'Hello, dear, I'm in the kitchen.'

Morgan walked down to where the woman was rolling out pastry. Maggie turned to look at her with a dusting of flour on the tip of her nose.

'How lovely to see you, your friend has just been in to use the loo.'

'Maggie, did you forget what I said about keeping your door locked?'

'Of course not, but nothing's going to happen when there are police officers guarding the street.'

Morgan tried not to roll her eyes or let out a loud sigh. She couldn't tell her that Tina's priority was guarding the Lawsons' house and not everyone else's.

'When Tim came home from school that day, did you see him?'

She shook her head. 'I don't think I did, no I definitely didn't.'

Morgan did sigh this time, it escaped without her even realising.

'Is it important, should I have seen him?'

'It is important, but no it's not your responsibility. He came home with someone else, and I just wanted to know if it was someone you may have recognised.'

'Have you got a picture?'

'Not yet, but we'll get one to you as soon as we can. Did Tim often bring friends home with him?'

She shook her head. 'Not that I know of, he was a quiet boy. He sometimes walked home with Ava from over the road, but not as much lately. Have you spoken with her? She may be able to tell you more.'

'Not yet, thank you, Maggie. As always, you've been a great help, but please, for my sake so I don't have to go home and worry about you, keep your door locked.'

Maggie laughed. 'Okay, I will. Would you like a cup of tea, some cake? I'm making a caramel apple pie. It will be ready in around an hour, if you fancy a slice when it's warm with some double cream.'

Morgan did fancy a slice, lately she had a terrible sweet tooth, but she shook her head.

'Maggie, I'll never be able to fasten my jeans if you keep on feeding me cakes and biscuits.'

'Get away with you, if there was anyone that needed feeding up a little it's you. There's nothing to you. I know it's none of my business, dear, but do you eat enough?'

Morgan laughed. 'I certainly do, I guess the only good thing I got from my parents was the ability to eat like a horse and not gain too much weight.'

'Lucky you, I've spent my whole life on one diet or another. After my husband died, I decided that I wasn't doing it any longer and to eat what the hell I wanted, accept myself for who I am. What's that song that gorgeous woman sings? I follow her on Instagram and she's just wonderful, I wish I could have been more like her, she's such an amazing role model.'

Maggie screwed up her face in concentration then burst

into song. She even did a little wiggle, waving her finger at her which made Morgan grin.

'"About Damn Time" by Lizzo, yes, she's brilliant. I love that song; I love all her songs.'

Maggie nodded. 'Me too, she's like a breath of fresh air and I think we should all be more Lizzo.'

'I do too. Well fine, in that case maybe you could save me a slice of that pie and I'll pop around tomorrow.'

Maggie's face lit up; she was positively beaming. 'Of course, I'd like that, and it will taste just as good tomorrow.'

'Amazing, now if you lock up behind me, I'll be even happier.'

Maggie followed her to the front door. 'All of this sadness, yet deep down I feel a little bit lighter than I have since Ronnie died and I think it's because you've been so kind to me, Morgan. You're a lovely young woman, I hope you have someone who makes you as happy as Ronnie made me.'

She nodded. 'I do, I'm very lucky, I met my best friend and soulmate a couple of years ago. Good evening, Maggie.'

The sound of the key turning in the lock once the door was closed made Morgan put her hands together in prayer and look up to the sky. 'Thank you.'

The Riggs' house was in darkness, no lights on, there were no cars on the drive either. She would have to come back to speak to Ava Rigg, but for now she'd go and visit Father Theo Edwards, to see if he could help her to figure things out.

TWENTY

Morgan parked the car outside of Saint Martha's church and felt a crushing sadness inside of her chest, wondering if she would ever be able to disconnect this beautiful place of worship from Des's battered, bleeding body. Probably not, that image wasn't going to fade anytime soon and a part of her wished that she hadn't ever gone inside to see him that way. She would have much preferred to remember him sloping off to his car with that bag of freshly baked scones.

Walking up to the gate, she could hear voices filtering out through the church door, which had been left ajar. The voices began to sing, and she smiled; choir practice. At that moment, the man she was looking for came out of the church, closing the door softly behind him.

'Father, could I have a word?'

He looked across to the gate where she was leaning, and a look of concern crossed his face before he broke into a huge smile and beamed at her.

'Detective, how nice to see you, of course you can.'

He walked across the gravel path, the tiny stones crunching

underneath the Doc Marten boots that were peeping out from under his cassock.

'I'd offer to take you inside the church but even in the vestry I wouldn't be able to hear a word you said through that racket.'

He laughed, which set Morgan off.

'Aren't they your celestial angels singing?'

Theo leaned towards her and lowered his voice. 'They're definitely something, but celestial is not the word I would use. Come on, let's go next door to the vicarage and grab a coffee; you look as if you could do with one.'

She hated how he seemed to read her; he was either a bit psychic or had a very good sense of people.

'Coffee would be nice, thanks.'

They reached the red front door of the vicarage, he pushed it open, stepping inside, and Morgan followed him.

'You don't lock the door?'

'Should I?'

'I'd like to say no need, this is a lovely quiet place, but truthfully, I wouldn't leave it open. Too much bad stuff happens around here for anyone to be able to live a simple, crime-free life. I'm afraid the freedom of living without locking up is long gone.'

He nodded. 'I guess you're right, I'd never have left it open in Birmingham. The place would have been burgled and ransacked before I'd finished the Lord's Prayer. I will endeavour to remember to keep my windows and doors secure, Detective, whenever I pop across to the church.' He saluted her, and her cheeks began to burn.

'You're being sarcastic?'

'Maybe a little, tea or coffee?'

'Coffee, please.'

The kitchen was still decorated in the awful sixties wallpaper from when she'd last been here. Theo had a new coffee machine and set about making her a much-needed cappuccino.

'You haven't heard how long you're staying here then?'

'My, you are astute; you don't miss a trick. No, I haven't been given any official timescale, which is why I'm reluctant to strip these monstrous walls bare.'

Morgan smiled. 'Maybe you'll come to love it in time or if not, you could open it up as a sixties museum.'

Theo boiled the kettle, pouring the hot water onto the teabag in his large mug, then he finished frothing the milk and pouring her drink. He passed it to her.

'Chocolate on top?'

She nodded, watching him as he picked up a small canister and sprinkled drinking chocolate on top of her coffee.

'Thank you.'

He beamed at her. 'You're more than welcome as long as you haven't come here to accuse me of murdering someone. We really need to get over this thing we have going on. I'm no killer, so if you could take my name off the top of the list you have it written down on, I'd very much appreciate that.'

'I haven't come to accuse you of anything, I also don't have your name on any list, at least, not at the moment, but should I? You tell me.'

He nodded. 'Glad to hear it and no you should not have my name on any list, except the one that is there as a reference for anyone seeking solace or comfort. So how can I help you then?'

'Have you heard of the saying "the hand of God"?'

'Yes, I'm a vicar, it's my thing, why?'

Morgan let out a small laugh. 'Sorry, of course it's your thing. What does it mean then? My mum used to say it all the time, that someone had been dealt the hand of God.'

'It's an interesting phrase, one which is quite old and outdated now. There are several ways I've heard it used. For instance, my nan used to say that too, but she meant it as if the person she was talking about had been judged and their fate was in God's hands, or that's what I took it she meant.'

Morgan sipped the coffee whilst she processed this.

'I think that's what my mum meant by it too. What else could it mean?'

'In technical terms from my standpoint? The hand of God is mentioned multiple times in the Bible and there are references to God's right hand in Mormonism and Judaism.'

'The victim had a silver crucifix necklace, does that help?'

'Yes, in that case the one that sticks out for me is, and this isn't a direct quote but similar, "The hand of the Lord is mighty, it's also dangerous and deadly against his enemies." The first time we come across it in the Bible it speaks of the "hand of the Lord" and it's in connection with the judgement God was going to pour out onto the Egyptians.'

Morgan thought about this, was the killer judging the Lawsons? Had he taken the hands as punishment? If he thought they had been dealt the hand of God then it seemed to mean he had decided they had done something that deserved retribution. What though, what could a beauty salon owner do that was so bad it meant her entire family was killed because of it? Morgan needed to look closely into Sally's life, her background, had she done something that had caused whoever had killed her to punish her entire family in revenge?

'Is that any use to you? I could give you actual Bible readings if you like but I don't think you'd enjoy that much.'

'Yes, thank you, it's very useful.'

'Good, this is nice, Morgan, I like you and spending time in your company is quite enjoyable when you're not wanting to handcuff me and march me into the station. Although I'm quite partial to a bit of handcuffing now and again.'

He laughed, and she felt her skin crawl. She did not want any more insight into Theo's preferences – she had enough on her mind without picturing him handcuffed to something. Although, the first time they met Theo had referenced a notorious serial killer, so she hoped that was all he was talking about.

'Sorry, that was a bit out of order, wasn't it?'

'I, erm, I wasn't really listening to the last part.'

'You look as if I've just scared you to death. Don't worry, you're quite safe with me, I'm not after handcuffing you to my bedpost or the other way around. Even though I think you're a lovely girl who has excellent taste in footwear, it wouldn't matter how lovely you were. I'm not into girls, women, ladies. Are you getting my drift, Morgan?'

She wasn't, not one little bit; instead, she was wondering how she could get out of here and quick.

Theo let out a sigh. 'I think you need to know who I am so you can relax around me, it might make you feel a little more comfortable if you knew.'

'Knew what?'

'I'm gay, Morgan, and have been since I was old enough to realise that girls, teenage girls at the time, did nothing for me in the slightest.'

She sat back down. 'Oh, I didn't know.'

'Why would you? I try to keep it under my collar, at least until I've fully settled into a place. I like it here; I think I'd like to make a go of it in Rydal Falls but I don't want to alienate my congregation, at least not yet.'

'You won't alienate anyone, there's no problem with you being gay and it's no one's business but yours. Have you come across anything that's made you uncomfortable, Theo? We don't stand for that here. You could use a third-party reporting system if you didn't want to speak to officers about anything.'

He held up his hand. 'Morgan, thank you that's very kind of you but I'm okay, and you're right, everyone seems to be very kind and nice.'

She smiled. 'That's because most of the women fancy you though, they're going to be devastated that you're not available.'

He laughed loudly. 'Oh, I'm available, but not to them.'

'Have you got any friends around here?'

He looked at her. 'I was hoping that once we got over this thing where you think I'm responsible for all the crimes around here that we might be friends.'

'What thing? I haven't had you arrested for a couple of weeks, we're well over that.'

Theo laughed.

'Good, I'd like it if we could be. You know, I don't always talk about God, I do have other levels of conversation.'

'Brill, next time we go to The Black Dog I'll let you know. It would be nice if you could join us, our quiz team sucks really bad. We always come last, so you might improve our chances.'

'Thank you, it would.'

They both smiled, and finished their drinks in companionable silence. As Morgan was getting ready to leave, Theo spoke again. 'Look, this hand of God thing, you have to ask yourself is your guy seeking revenge for something that has wronged him in the past, is he passing judgement? It's worth thinking about especially if your victim was wearing a crucifix around her neck.'

Morgan stood up for a second time. 'Thanks, Theo, it's definitely worth considering and thank you for the coffee. I need to get back to work now, there's a lot going on.'

He nodded. 'There certainly is, is it always so busy here? Stay safe.'

Smiling at him she shrugged then walked towards the front door.

Once outside she had to stop herself from running to the car. She hadn't told Theo why she was interested in finding out the reasoning behind that saying. Yet he'd said 'your guy seeking revenge'. She never told him Sally was wearing the crucifix either? How the hell had he known that was what she was thinking? Was she really that easy to read, or did Theo Edwards know a lot more than he was letting on?

TWENTY-ONE

Natalie White knew that she was walking a fine line between coping and, well, basically screwing things up. All these years she had done her best to keep to the promise she'd made to herself. As she arrived home the house was in darkness, again. Lexie much preferred being at her friend's house, and Jasper would be at the golf club until closing time. She pressed her thumb against the pad on the front door and it clicked open. The lights automatically turned on as she stepped inside the airy entrance hall, where the old period features of the property blended with the modern innovations Jasper had had installed. The hallway was so big she could have invited her regular Monday yoga class to hold it inside of it should they ever need a new venue. Not that she would, because Jasper wouldn't be able to stop himself from gawping at the flexible women in skintight clothing; he seemed to be getting worse as each year passed despite the fact that he was almost seventy. Now that Natalie wasn't the pretty young thing he'd met when she was twenty-three, his eyes seemed to rove all over the place. Not that she was bad-looking for her age, forty-nine; she kept up with every beauty treatment available, to keep her looking young. Her breasts were the perkiest they'd ever been, but she knew he still couldn't stop looking. She wondered if it would be so bad if he did leave her for a younger woman, deciding she'd keep the house because of Lexie; and maybe that would fix their relationship. Though if it didn't, she could always palm her off on Jasper, and spend weeks by herself, now that would be fun. She was tired of playing this game; she would quite like to just be herself, not that she really remembered who that even was. In the kitchen Natalie opened the fridge and stared at the open bottle of Chardonnay. It had been so long since she'd let a drop of alcohol pass her lips she wondered if she'd even enjoy it now. This house, which was as big as any boutique hotel, wasn't the kind of place you could ever feel at home in. She had begged Jasper to buy a quaint country cottage with a rose garden, but he had laughed at her and without even consulting her had bought this mausoleum. He was hardly here, and Natalie kept herself busy through the day, so she didn't have to wander around lonely, wishing she'd chosen a different life for herself. She hadn't though, this was the life she'd so wanted when she was younger, and she'd been determined to have it. Now it was empty. Her life, her heart, even the bloody house was empty. The only things that kept her going were her weekday meetings with her friends, especially her Fridays when Harry would put her first before his other commitments, unlike her husband. She'd heard the terrible news about Sally Lawson today and she'd felt sad ever since. Sally had caused her so much heartache as a teenager, but she'd managed to forgive her. They'd been stupid girls, who had both done things they weren't proud of; and poor Tim had been a friend of Lexie's. It was all such a mess.

As she began to take out the ingredients from the fridge to make a spicy chicken pasta bake, she heard a sound upstairs, the slightest of creaks from the master bedroom above her. Natalie tilted her head, maybe Jasper was home and had put his car in the garage. He was never home at this time though, what if he wasn't well? A part of her thought that she wasn't that lucky, the other wondered if she should go and check. Picking up her phone from the white Italian marble worktop she checked to see if she had any missed calls from him, she didn't. There were no more noises, so Natalie dismissed the noise and went back to cooking. She placed the pan of water on the range cooker and turned on the gas, then began to chop the peppers. Suddenly the hairs on the back of her neck prickled and she got the uneasy feeling that she was being watched. Natalie stopped chopping. What was going on? At least she had a sharp knife in her hand, but it was ridiculous to think she'd need it. Who could be watching her? She always felt like this alone in this bloody house. She'd begged him not to buy it, had actually said it was probably haunted. It was that old God knows how many people had died in here. She wasn't psychic, didn't have a sixth sense, but she did believe in ghosts – she'd heard too many stories about them. That's why she loved the café she went to for lunch every day, it was full of women talking about weird and wonderful experiences. The owner was gifted, maybe she could invite her here for lunch and repay the favour? She could have a wander around and tell her if her house was super creepy because it was haunted or if she was just imagining the odd sounds she'd hear, the cold draughts, the feeling of being watched. She had mentioned it to Jasper once and he'd laughed so hard that he'd had tears rolling down his face, telling her she was ridiculous. Lexie was different, super moody, hated her with a passion, but she hadn't laughed when she'd asked her if she ever felt uncomfortable when she was here alone. She hated that her daughter would rather listen to podcasts or Spotify to avoid having a conversation with her, but she hoped one day she might grow out of it and realise that her mother was a human being in need of love and laughter. A tear leaked from the corner of her eye, and she brushed it away with her sleeve telling herself it was the onion – only she hadn't even peeled the onions yet. She froze as another creak from upstairs broke the silence. The thought that someone was in the house came back. She gripped the handle of the knife and held it behind her back in case someone had broken in, but she knew she better check to make sure Jasper or Lexie weren't home first. The house had a top-notch security system, enough to put off any intruder and it had been locked up when she got home.

The stairs were best described as sweeping. The oak banister was intricately carved with vines and leaves. As much as she hated the house, she had to admit it was a thing of beauty, and she couldn't wait for Lexie to have her prom photos taken on this staircase. Natalie wished she'd had a prom, but they were only coming into fashion when she'd left school. Standing at the foot of the stairs she listened for any movement. She wasn't afraid of burglars but the thought of something she couldn't see gliding around her house unseen scared her to death.

'Jasper, Lexie, are you home?'

She called, her voice falling flat as it echoed up to the first floor. The house had two upper floors; they rarely used the second floor. No one answered, so she carried on. Reaching the landing she looked around, then flicked the light switch on. Downstairs was as modern and hi-tech as you could find, but up here they hadn't started to fully renovate it yet, so it was still quite old-fashioned.

'Jasper, Lexie.'

Still no answer. A part of Natalie wanted to go back downstairs to where the LED lighting left no dark corners, but another part of her would feel forever guilty if Jasper had taken ill and she'd been too afraid of the dark corners up here to go and check on him. Marching down to their bedroom she flung open the door, reached her hand inside and turned on the light.

'Oh,' she whispered, it was empty. She had expected to see

Jasper, but the bed cover was crumpled, as if someone had been sitting on it. Had she left it that way earlier? She couldn't remember. Closing the door, she went to check Lexie's room at the opposite end, but it was empty too. She would be at her friend Ava's house; she was always there. That left two more bedrooms up here and the bathroom. She opened each door in turn: nothing. The rooms were empty, granted she didn't check under any beds or in wardrobes, but she reassured herself that she didn't need to. If anyone had got inside who didn't have the security code, the alarm system would have been blaring when she'd arrived home. She looked at the end of the hall where the stairs to the second floor were, should she check it? Her phone began to ring down in the kitchen, making up her mind for her, and she turned, leaving all the lights on, and jogged back downstairs to answer it, forgetting all about the ruffled bed cover.

TWENTY-TWO

Morgan drove back to Hest Bank Road, and this time the Riggs' house was lit up. The CSI van was parked behind the plain car Tina was still sitting in. That hadn't taken them too long. Things were moving, not as fast as the whole team would like but they were getting there. She got out of the car, her stomach growling as she glanced over at Maggie's house. The thought of warm, gooey caramel apple pie and fresh cream was almost too much to bear. *Focus, Morgan, you can feed your stomach later, this is important.* She curled her fist and hammered five times on the door, her official-police-business knock loud and clear. Footsteps in the hall came towards the door, and she smiled through the crack at the teenage girl peering out at her.

'Ava?'

'Who's asking?'

'Detective Constable Morgan Brookes, can I have a word with you? Are your parents home?'

'Let me see your badge.'

Morgan tugged it out from underneath her jacket, holding it up for Ava to read. She was impressed, obviously the security over here was much better than at Maggie's.

'Hang on. Dad, there's a copper here, should I let her in?'

Heavy footsteps came towards the door.

'What have I told you, Ava? You're not to answer the door to anyone we don't know.'

'I looked on the Ring app, she doesn't look like a homicidal maniac.' Ava turned and walked away.

The door opened wide, and Luke Rigg shrugged at her. 'Oh, it's you. Sorry, we're a little on edge about what happened.'

'That's good, I think it's far better to be vigilant, Ava's a bright girl.'

'She is when she wants to be, come on in, it's Morgan, isn't it?'

She smiled at him. 'It is. I wanted to have a chat with Ava, if that's okay. Did the PCSOs check your doorbell camera coverage?'

'I did myself, I'm sorry to say that before the fire I only had it covering the start of our drive; I'd turned it off ages ago from covering the street. I couldn't keep up with the notifications every time Maggie walked that dog past. I've reset it now and changed the parameters, so it does cover anyone walking past, just in case.'

'Thank you, that's probably wise.'

'You haven't caught the bastard yet then?'

She shook her head. 'Unfortunately not, but we're getting close.' She didn't want to tell him they had no idea who it was, he looked so on edge.

'Come in, I'll get Ava to come back down, she's with her friend.'

He led her into the same lounge that she'd been in the night of the fire. She sat on the chair leaving the sofa free for Ava and her dad to sit on. He disappeared, moments later returning with the teenager, who had a look of annoyance on her face.

'Hello again, Ava, can we have a little chat?'

She rolled her eyes in Morgan's direction but nodded.

'Your dad told me you and Tim were good friends, I'm sorry for your loss, this must have come as a terrible shock for you.'

'We *were*, yes. I feel sick every time I look out of my bedroom window at his house. I can't believe he's dead, I mean who would do that?'

Suddenly Ava didn't look quite as grown up as she had when she'd answered the door. Luke reached out his hand and patted her back, but she shrugged him off.

'I know, it's horrible to think someone would hurt him, which is why I need your help. I need to find this person and lock him up where he can't hurt anyone else.'

Ava's eyes opened wide. 'You think he's going to do it again?'

Morgan could have kicked herself; she didn't want to be frightening the girl. 'No, at least I hope not, but we'd rather have him in prison to make sure that he can't.'

The girl nodded.

'You said you and Tim were good friends, what happened, did you fall out?'

'Not exactly, we used to always walk to school and back, hang around together at lunchtime, break time that kind of thing. Stick up for each other when we needed it.'

Morgan thought back to her school days, they were tough, but she'd had Brad, he had always been a good friend to her when she needed it.

'And then you weren't?'

'He started playing this stupid computer game online, it was all he talked about, then he would be late in a morning, and I didn't want to get in trouble, so I'd leave without him. When he was late in, he'd get a detention, and I wasn't hanging around for him after school. So I guess we just started seeing less of each other. He was different, too.'

'I don't blame you; I wouldn't have waited either. What was the computer game called?'

She shrugged. 'I don't know, it was top secret, but he began to get friendly with another guy who played it too. He was always talking about him; it was a bit weird to be honest, it was like he really looked up to him. But how can you look up to someone you only know online? I told him that he might be grooming him, and Tim laughed. He told me not to be so stupid; he knew what that was, and they were just mates.'

Every nerve in Morgan's body was sparking little jolts of static electricity.

'Did he ever tell you his friend's name?'

'It was weird, really old-fashioned. Isaiah, I think? No idea about his surname.'

Morgan hadn't ever come across anyone called Isaiah. 'That's a strange name, did you ever meet him?'

'God no, he was Tim's big secret, he only told me because I kept giving him grief about being so late for school all the time. He said he wasn't telling anyone because they wouldn't get their friendship. I left him to it, left him to his game playing and keeping secrets. David would have gone ape shit when our reports come out next week. Tim was moved out of the top sets for everything and put in different classes.'

'Didn't the school contact his parents?'

She glanced at her dad, then lowered her eyes.

Luke looked at Morgan who nodded at him.

'It's okay, Ava, I'm not going to shout at you, you're not in any trouble.'

'Tim stole his mum's phone one morning, along with the letter they sent home about him that he'd opened before his parents did. I phoned the school and pretended to be Sally. I couldn't speak to Mr Mackintosh, his form teacher, straight away, so he phoned back, and I had to go hide in the toilets to have a conversation with him about Tim.'

'What did you tell Mr Mackintosh?'

'That we were going through a rough time at home,

that... that David had been having an affair and that Tim was very upset by it all. I'm sorry, I know I shouldn't have done that, but he begged me, and he gave me fifty quid. I never thought anything really bad would happen.'

'Ava, I can't believe you did that.' Luke seemed stunned.

She lowered her head further. 'I'm sorry.'

Morgan reached across and patted her arm. 'You weren't to know this was going to happen, Ava, try not to beat yourself up about it. Thank you for being so honest with me, that takes courage. On the day Tim died, he is on camera walking down the street with someone else, did you see them?'

'No, I was late home that night. I went to my friend's and then Mum picked me up and told me Tim's house was on fire. I can't believe I'll never see him again.'

'Thank you, that's it for now. When I get a still of the person with Tim is it okay if I bring it round to show you, in case you recognise them?'

Luke and Ava both nodded their heads at the same time.

Morgan left them to it. They were so near yet so far, every corner they turned something else popped up throwing them another line of enquiry. One thing was perfectly clear though, Tim had been dragged into this and they needed to get the tech department to fast track his laptop. Morgan wanted to know what game he'd been playing and who the hell Isaiah was.

TWENTY-THREE

By the time Morgan left the Riggs' house Ben was back outside of the Lawsons' fire damaged home. She wondered briefly who would buy this once beautiful house now. She wouldn't want to live in a place where a whole family had been brutally murdered. Although she'd heard someone had bought the Potters' house after it had lain empty for a couple of years. If the price was right, she guessed you might be able to push the horrible history to one side. A picture of *The Amityville Horror* house flashed across her mind, and she shivered; she wouldn't live in that one if they gave it to her. Ben was leaning against the side of the CSI van talking to Wendy. She headed towards them both.

'Did you find anything else?'

Wendy nodded. 'What I'd thought was a joint of pork turns out to be a rather large hand. I'm so mad that I missed them, thank God you took another look, Morgan. Imagine whoever had the job of clearing that freezer out finding them.'

Ben reached out patting Wendy's arm. 'They were pretty well hidden.'

'It doesn't matter, I should have found them. I've also

collected all the laptops in the house. I'll send them over to the tech department.'

Morgan understood, she would be feeling the same if it had been her job to search. Both of them cared deeply about doing the best job possible for the victims they tried to help.

Morgan leaned closer. 'I have some news; do you want it now or at the station?'

'You're not keeping me in suspense, spill,' Ben said.

She looked around, then leaned towards them both, lowering her voice. 'Ava Rigg' – she pointed towards the Riggs' house – 'was very good friends with Tim until he got involved in some online game he wouldn't tell her about. His grades dropped, along with his punctuality. He became friends with someone called Isaiah, but he wouldn't share any other information about him.'

Ben nodded. 'That's a great lead. We need to fast track his laptop, iPad, phone.'

'Yes, we do.'

'Bloody hell, I thought it was Sally this was about, but now it's back to Tim again. I wish I could make sense of it. Let's check our records for anyone with the name Isaiah. If he got involved in some seedy online game, God knows who he was talking to.'

Wendy spoke. 'And what he brought into his life. Isn't Isaiah a biblical name? I've heard of Isaac but never really heard of anyone called Isaiah.'

'I think you're right, Wendy, let's get back to the station.'

'Not me, I need to get these hands delivered to the mortuary before they defrost all over the back of the van.'

Wendy climbed into the driver's seat, gave them a wave and drove off.

'That was perfect timing, Brookes, come on let's go back to the office and you can make me a coffee whilst we start to try and piece this jigsaw together.' He grinned at her outraged face. 'I'm kidding, I'll make you one.'

Amy and Cain were in the office when they arrived back, Cain perfectly at home sitting behind the desk. Gone was his fluorescent yellow body armour and he looked happy sitting there in a black polo shirt and combat trousers.

'The workers return, we missed you, didn't we, Amy?' Cain smiled happily at them.

Amy rolled her eyes. 'Not really, how did you get on?'

Ben smiled at her. 'We hit the jackpot, or at least Morgan did.'

Amy leaned forward. 'You did? What did you find, the killer hanging around with a bag full of evidence? Please say you found him, so we don't have to work double shifts for the next month.'

'Not exactly, but we're getting close I can feel it.'

Amy turned to Cain. 'This means he *thinks* we're getting close but in reality, we still don't have a clue what's going on.'

Morgan couldn't help it and she began to laugh. 'No, we're getting somewhere, we really are.'

She picked up the whiteboard marker. Underneath Tim's name she wrote a list.

- *Secret Online game? What is this, speak to classmates, teachers see if they have heard anything around the school.*
- *Isaiah – who is he/she? Is he the guy that came home with Tim on the day of the murders?*
- *The hand of God – passing judgement, you have been judged by God and this is your punishment?*
- *Motive – ??*
- *Who was the intended target? David, Tim or Sally?*

Amy asked, 'Whoa, what's this hand of God stuff, Morgan? Did you find a Bible or what at the scene, and what about David, are we ruling him out as bringing this horrific fate to the family?'

'Not a Bible, but there was that crucifix Sally was wearing. What if it wasn't Sally's but the killer left it, like a calling card? Then we're on the right track thinking this is all linked to a religious killer. Where is it now?'

Ben looked at her. 'Wendy will have sent it off for forensics; maybe there's a nice fingerprint or DNA sample on it. Did you manage to speak to any of David's colleagues, Amy?'

'Yeah, he was a nice bloke, bit of a loner, he wasn't having any affairs that anyone knows of. Worked hard, was good to his students, they seemed to like him; he was a decent guy by the sounds of it. Morgan, seriously, what's the hand of God? It's kind of freaking me out, I hate churches at the best of times.'

Morgan thought about Des, then pushed the thought away.

'So I have a theory that maybe the hands symbolise something and the first thing that I thought about was a saying my mum would sometimes use. I went to speak to Theo about it, and he agreed with me that being dealt the hand of God was a saying people would use when someone had been judged, or something happened to them that was a bit like rough justice, or bad karma, I suppose. I think the killer chose the Lawsons, or one of them, for some reason and judged them. The hands are symbolic and probably a huge clue if we can figure out *what* they're being judged on.'

'Theo, as in the vicar we had down as a number one suspect for Shea Wilkinson's murder?'

Morgan nodded.

'Jesus this is getting better by the minute. Oh well, that makes it nice and simple then, Morgan. No problem, I'm sure we'll figure this out in the next hour and be home in time for a mug of cocoa.'

Cain laughed, and Morgan felt her cheeks begin to burn.

It was Ben who answered. 'Then we'll focus on Tim for now. The video game is a solid lead; we all know what sick, twisted predators there are lurking on the internet. Morgan, I want you to get on to the tech department, find out as much as you can about the secret game, and can you go back to speak to Theo about the Isaiah angle and get his opinion? Amy, you and Cain can go back to the school, and get a list of friends from his form teacher, then I want you to find out what they know about Tim and if he told them about any games he played. I'll ask Intel to run some checks on our systems, to see if the name Isaiah comes up as an alias for one of our better-known criminals.'

'Of course.'

'Not now, I think for now we need to go home, eat and try to get some sleep, it's been a long day. Thank you for all your hard work, we're getting closer.'

Amy and Cain stood up at the same time, and grabbing their jackets they said goodnight, leaving Morgan and Ben to follow them out. Morgan's ankle was aching, it had been a long day and perhaps she had pushed herself a bit too far. She wanted a long, hot soak in the bath and wished she could do so without forever thinking about how Ben's wife Cindy had killed herself in Ben's bath. It didn't make for much of a relaxing soak and she often ended up having a shower instead. Well whatever she decided it had to be followed by fresh, hot pizza from Gino's.

TWENTY-FOUR

Amy and Cain, who was dressed in a shirt and navy chinos, arrived at Alfred Barrow Academy before the bell rang to signal lessons were starting. The school had been closed yesterday, Sunday, so they'd progressed what they could from their desks at the station, but now they were here, bright and early, at the start of the week. There was no one to buzz them in to the reception area, so they waited, leaning on the counter for someone to sign them in.

'Blimey, this makes a change, I normally come here in uniform to give school talks about the dangers of drugs or to bollock some pot-smoking kid for doing it on the school grounds.'

She laughed. 'Yeah, I remember those days well, and I've got to admit I don't miss them at all. Mind you I'm not that fond of working murder investigations either.'

'Really? I thought you enjoyed it.'

'It's different since Des, things have changed. I mean I like being a detective, but I don't like the heartache that comes with it sometimes. I honestly don't know how Morgan copes; I mean look at what she's been through. It's enough to send any man or woman to the nearest mental health facility and no one could blame her if she did have a breakdown, but she keeps turning up, day after day, giving it her best.'

He smiled. 'She's a tough cookie is Morgan; I think they broke the mould when they made her.'

'Do you think it's because of her dad, I mean I've been thinking this through a lot since Des.'

'Stan? I don't think so, he was a nice bloke but a bit of a drinker. I get the impression he wasn't given good coping skills, he went to pieces after Morgan's mum died. So the opposite of Morgan's ability to keep on trying.'

'No, not Stan.'

'Oh, you mean Gary Marks, her piece-of-shit biological dad?'

She nodded.

'What are you saying, Amy, I'm not sure I understand?'

'That he was a very determined man, he did what he wanted without a second thought for anyone else. Maybe she gets that determination from him. But if so, she clearly has more of her mother's genes, thankfully.'

Cain blew out his cheeks. 'Possibly, hey you better not let Morgan hear you talk about that; she'd be mortified if she thought she was anything like that scumbag.'

'I wouldn't, I like her, I'm just thinking out loud. There's been days since Des died that I just want to give all of this up and go work in a shop.'

'Nah, you'd have to actually work if you got a job in a shop, they're always rushed off their feet. You are too lazy for that; you're used to a slower pace of life.'

Amy glared at him, but he winked, and the corners of her mouth turned upwards ever so slightly.

'*Can I help you?*'

Both of them jumped at the loud voice that came from the speaker on the wall next to them.

'Police, can we speak to you?'

The door to the left of them clicked, and Cain pushed it open. 'Works every time that magic word, Police.'

They were standing on the other side of the counter, the receptionist was standing there, her arms crossed and an angry look on her face.

'How can we help you, officers?'

Amy answered. 'We need to talk to Timothy Lawson's form teacher and his friends, if possible.'

The name printed on the receptionist's lanyard read, Amanda Hughes; her face thawed at the mention of Timothy. Cain gave her his best smile.

'We'd really appreciate it if you could arrange that, Amanda, it's very important.'

She sighed. 'It's so awful, Tim was a lovely boy, one of those who never gave you cheek or answered back. Always so polite too.'

'Did you know him well?'

She shrugged. 'Only the last few weeks, his attendance began to slip, and he never seemed to make it before the bell. The doors are open for pupils until 8:50. If they arrive later, they have to sign in here.'

'Did he ever speak to you about anything troubling?'

She laughed. 'He was a teenage boy, he didn't speak much at all except to say sorry, thank you, have a nice day.'

'Thank you, if you could take us to his form teacher, we'd really appreciate it.' Amy smiled at her, taking a leaf from Cain's book.

After signing them in and giving them red visitors' lanyards to wear, she led them down a long corridor that went on forever, then down a flight of stairs to the basement area where there were lots of empty rooms. They reached a peeling orange painted door with a sign on it that read 'Staff Room'. Pushing it open they were hit with the smell of freshly brewed coffee, and it smelled divine. There were a couple of teachers on the sofa, mugs in their hands. They looked at them. Amanda pointed to Amy and Cain.

'Detectives, they need to speak to you, Ian, about Timothy.'

Ian, who was the younger of the teachers, stood up.

'Of course, such a terrible tragedy. We'll go to my unofficial office, I'm Ian Mackintosh.'

He held out his hand and shook both of theirs, then he led them a few doors along to a large dark office. Holding the door open for them, he felt along the wall for the switch. When the light decided to stop flickering and come to life, Amy nearly jumped out of her skin. The room was full of life-sized mannequins.

'Sorry, I should have warned you. Technically this used to be the art and sewing class back in the day, and no one has the heart to throw these things out in case we ever need them one day. They'd cost a fortune to buy now.'

'It's creepy, how do you manage to work in here with all those eyes looking at you?'

He laughed. 'I guess I don't even notice them any more. I used to share an office upstairs, but the other teachers were forever sending their unruly pupils to me, and I'd spend most of my free time babysitting. I moved down here because it's out of the way and a lot easier to hide, plus none of the kids like it in here either so they don't bother me. It's a win-win situation.'

He pointed to a couple of chairs. 'Take a seat, I'll help you as much as I can although I don't know an awful lot.'

Cain looked to Amy, she nodded.

'I'm Detective Constable Amy Smith and this is my colleague, Cain Robson. We've had some information that Timothy had got involved with some online game that he was very secretive about. So involved that he was late for school often and his grades were slipping. Have you heard any of the kids talking about it or overheard Tim mentioning a game?'

His eyes opened wide, and his head shook. 'Really? Wow, this is the first I've heard about it. Do you know what it's called?'

'Unfortunately, we don't, that's what we're hoping to find out today.'

'I'm sorry, I don't know.'

'Were Timothy's grades slipping? Could you give us some background on what he was like?'

'Tim was essentially a good kid. Up until the last couple of months he was always punctual, worked hard in class, very quiet, well-mannered. There had been a change in all of that recently though. I wrote a letter home asking for a meeting with his parents because I was worried that maybe he'd got in with the wrong crowd after school. His mum rang me about it and explained what was going on at home, that they were having a tough time, his dad had been having an affair and they were in the middle of splitting up. Tim was taking it badly, she said, he was a sensitive boy, which I suppose he was. Poor kid, it explained the lateness and lack of attention in class, and to be honest I was relieved it was that and not drugs. As hard as it is when your parents split up at least you can still keep your life on track.'

Amy glanced at Cain. 'Ian, I hate to tell you this, but you didn't speak to Tim's mum.'

A look of confusion crossed his face. 'What? I did, I definitely had a conversation with her. What are you saying, that I imagined it?'

'Not at all, but it wasn't Sally, it was one of Tim's classmates.'

'I rang her back on the mobile number we have on record as his next of kin, of course it was her.'

'I'm sorry but you didn't. Tim opened the letter before his parents got home from work, and the next morning he stole his mum's mobile and got a friend to phone the school pretending to be her. His parents had no idea what was going on with him, they also to our knowledge weren't in the middle of splitting up.'

Ian's mouth opened, then closed as he tried to process what he'd just been told. 'They weren't?'

Amy shook her head. 'What we believe happened is that he got involved in this online game and that was taking up all of his time. We really need to know what it was and whether anyone else played it. For all we know his killer could find more victims this way, so we need to find him and stop him before anyone else gets hurt.'

'Sorry, I'm trying to get my head around the level of deviousness Tim displayed. Who pretended to be his mum?'

'I can't disclose that, I don't want to get anyone in trouble when there's a lot going on. The night of the murders, Tim walked home with another older-looking lad. He may have been wearing a uniform but it's hard to tell from the CCTV footage and he was wearing a hooded top. Can you tell us who his friends are, if he hung around with any older boys?'

'I don't know, in school he was good friends with Ava Rigg.' He stopped talking and stared at Amy. 'It was Ava, wasn't it? She phoned up pretending to be his mum, that's the kind of thing she would do.'

'Like I said, I can't disclose that to you. Can you write down a list of his friends, and is it possible to speak to them?'

Mr Mackintosh looked angry; he was annoyed that he'd been played by a couple of teenagers.

'Well, I suppose you've talked with Ava; she lives near to Tim. Then there's Josh, Shane, Carl, aside from them he kind of kept to himself. I don't know about anyone he might have associated with out of school.'

'Have you heard the name Isaiah? Did he ever mention any friends who were called that?'

'As in out of the Bible?'

'Maybe, we were thinking more along the lines of a mate called that.'

'Definitely not. I'll go and round up Josh, Shane and Carl though; you can use this classroom to speak to them.'

'Thank you, we'll need an appropriate adult, can you sit in?'

'I'm afraid I can't, I have class very soon; however, I can ask one of the TAs to sit in.'

He walked out of the door leaving them staring at each other. Cain smiled at Amy.

'I think he's really pissed that Tim got one over on him. Do you think he holds a grudge? If he does that poor Ava is going to have a miserable year at school.'

'Surely not, that wouldn't be very professional of him, and besides I never grassed on her for that reason. She has enough to contend with losing her friend. She doesn't need some angry teacher breathing down her neck.'

While they waited for the Tim's friends to be rounded up, Amy took out her phone and texted Morgan.

The teacher doesn't know anything about Isaiah, but he asked if it was like out of the Bible.

Slipping her phone back in her pocket she looked around at the creepy mannequins, glad that she didn't have to work down here alone.

TWENTY-FIVE

Morgan was alone in the office for a change, Ben had gone to speak to the DI, Amy had taken Cain to Tim's school, and she was catching up on her emails. The desk phone began to ring.

'Morning, CID.'

'Morning, is this Morgan Brookes?'

'It is, how can I help?'

'It's Bev, from the high-tech unit at headquarters. I just wanted to let you know that I've sent you an email with the images downloaded from the phone you sent in, for you to look at. There were only a few recent ones and an older album, so I've sent them all. Not like my phone where I've got almost two thousand that I can't decide what to do with. I've also started working on the laptop that has had a fast-track request. It's early days but I can tell you whoever was using this they were connected to the Dark Web a lot.'

Morgan felt a chill run down her spine at the thought of Tim using the Dark Web. She didn't know a lot about it, but it couldn't be a good thing. It was a hiding place used by child abusers, drug dealers, criminals, to name a few. The sick feeling in her stomach made her put her mug of coffee down.

'How can you tell?'

'It has the Tor browser bundle downloaded on it.'

'Tor?'

'It's short for The Onion Router, when you're connected to it the sites don't end in the usual dot com or dot org, they end in dot onion.'

'Wow, I had no idea.'

'You wouldn't unless it's your thing, trust me you don't need to know this stuff, you'd put me out of a job.' Bev was laughing on the other end and Morgan smiled, she had an infectious laugh.

'Basically, everyone thinks that the Dark Web is this terrifying, complicated, secret place full of encryption and complex codes. Honestly, it's no more complicated than using any of the apps you already have downloaded on your phone. Tor supports multiple Dark Web forums and markets. Literally all you have to do is type in the address and download the browser onto your computer. I wouldn't though, in case you're considering it. You'd have PSD having a shit fit unless you've been given authority. Anyway though, yea, even my mum could get on the Dark Web and she's a pain in the backside when it comes to anything remotely techy.'

'Really? I always thought it would be so secretive and difficult, that's unbelievable.'

'I know, there is no Google on the Dark Web but there are some search engines. Generally though you need to be sent a link to find what you're looking for.'

'So, assuming the game Tim was playing was hosted on one of these sites, you're saying that someone must have sent Tim a link to find it?'

'Yes, like an invitation to an event sort of thing. Like I said it's early days, but I just wanted to give you a heads-up that your user was accessing Tor regularly.'

'Bev, can you search the computer for the name Isaiah? He

might be the one who sent Tim the link in the first place so he could access it.'

'*Absolutely, leave it with me. Have a great day, Morgan.*'

'You too, Bev, thanks for the update it's very much appreciated.'

Bev hung up, and Morgan sat back in her chair, she had not been expecting that. How had Tim got involved with some secret game on the Dark Web, and why had it ended with his whole family dead? This was getting more complex by the minute. She sipped her coffee, hoping to get her brain fired up, and logged in to her email account. There was the email from Bev with attachments of the photos from Luke Rigg's phone. She opened them and waited for them to load. There were a couple of photos of food taken in a restaurant, and then she clicked on the album and watched in shock as image after image of Sally Lawson appeared on the screen. These weren't photos taken at one event, because in them she was wearing different clothes; they were taken in different locations. The last few were of a BBQ, Sally talking to John, Sally on her own sitting on the outdoor sofa, they were creepy, and Morgan wondered if Sally knew Luke was photographing her.

The next picture showed Sally eating a hot dog, where she had tomato ketchup dribbling down her chin, her mouth open. The next image was of the Lawsons, all dead, sitting around the kitchen table.

'What you got there?'

Ben was moving across the room towards her, and she looked up at him.

'Honestly I don't know, boss. I'm thinking that we *might* have got a motive, but it's not necessarily got anything do to with Tim.'

'Really?'

She went back to the first image. 'What do you see?'

'I see the lovely Sally.'

'Look closer.'

Ben leaned across her shoulder, he smelled of his favourite aftershave, Eau Savage. 'What am I looking for?'

Morgan touched the screen. 'Look, apart from the last couple they're all of Sally on her own. Why is he taking photos of his neighbour's wife?'

'Okay, yes they are.'

'Now look at this one.'

She showed him the one of Sally about to eat the hot dog, then the one of them all dead.

'Don't you think this is bizarre? He told us himself that it's a new phone, he only just got it, and the only photos he has on it are of him, Sally and her dead family. But these look as if they were taken over a long period of time. We haven't had any warm enough weather for a BBQ for weeks, so it wasn't taken the day he got his phone. He would have had to physically transfer those from his old phone to his new one, yet he hasn't transferred any of his own family, do you think that's just a bit weird?'

'Well, when you put it like that, yes I do.'

'What if he had a thing for Sally? She might not have been interested in him though. Bev from the tech unit rang whilst you were out to say that Tim had been accessing the Dark Web on a regular basis. Luke teaches at the university right, what if it's computer science? Then he would know all about the Dark Web, or what if he's a computer geek? We need to find out, and I think we need to bring him in for more formal questioning about his relationship with Sally Lawson. I also think we need to speak to his wife, to ask if she knows about the photos because if she did then maybe we need to look closer at her. There is nothing like a woman scorned and don't they say that revenge is a dish best served cold?'

'I think you're right, Morgan, but right now the mystery

man with Tim is still our most solid lead, let's not drop the ball on that.'

'I've been thinking about Isaiah too. What if it isn't a person, what if it's the name of the game Tim was playing? I've asked Bev to search for it anyway, but it's worth keeping an open mind.'

'Have you checked our systems for Isaiah? I'm still waiting on Intel to come back to me.'

She shook her head, then logged into the intelligence system and typed it in. After a few seconds the screen loaded with a message saying there were no matches.

'There's your answer, nothing.'

Morgan knew they were onto something; she could feel it deep down inside that once they figured out what or who Isaiah was, they were going to find who killed the Lawsons.

TWENTY-SIX

Natalie White walked into the café and sat at her usual seat, brushing past Annie who felt a cold shiver run down the entire left side of her body where they had touched. Instantly, Annie knew something was wrong, she hadn't had a reaction to someone like that in ages. She found herself staring at Natalie. She was one of her best customers and came here without fail every weekday unless she was on holiday. Something was wrong though, and she turned away, not wanting Natalie to catch her staring, but Annie knew she had to do something. She went to the little storeroom in the back and perched on a large cardboard box. Ever since Sally died she had been sensing things a lot more than she had for quite some time, though she wasn't sure if it was her gift kicking in or whether she was being more open to reading people because she'd let her guard down and now Sally and her whole family were dead. She hadn't been able to sleep properly the last few nights, worrying whether she could have done something to prevent what had happened. Will had sensed something was wrong and had sat her down at breakfast this morning to ask if she was okay. She felt terrible that she had done something she hadn't had to do since she'd left her job as a police officer: she'd lied to him and told him she was fine, a little bit stressed with work but nothing she couldn't handle. She hated not telling him the truth, but he'd nodded and kissed her before she'd left for work. It was his day off, so he was dropping Alfie at school and picking him up.

Magda came into the room, took one look at Annie and tilted her head.

'What's wrong? You look like you've seen a ghost.'

Annie held up her hand to signal to leave her be for a moment. Was that it? Had she seen a ghost? One that was still breathing, but not for much longer. Oh God, Natalie White, was something awful going to happen to her? She stood up, and looking around for her phone she realised she didn't have Morgan's phone number.

'Magda, have you seen my phone?'

'Not today, did you bring it with you?'

Annie couldn't remember if she had or not. 'It doesn't matter, I'll use the shop phone.' She looked at Magda who was normally quite perceptive and whispered, 'Can you see the woman sitting alone at the table in the window?'

'Natalie, yes, I can see her. She's not a ghost, she's solid flesh and blood.'

'I didn't mean that, can you see anything wrong with her?'

'Like what, she has an extra ear, two heads?'

'No, like her aura, can you see that?'

Magda shook her head. 'I can't see anything today, Annie, I'm hung-over.'

Annie looked at her then smiled. 'Magda, it's a good job you're not doing any readings then.'

Annie needed to speak to Natalie, but how could she do that without appearing weird? She was going to have to just do it. Where was her friend today? She normally came in with her yoga friend on a Monday. In fact, she noticed now that Natalie wasn't wearing her usual fitness leggings and crop top, maybe that's what was different. She was dressed in a pair of jeans, with a baggy T-shirt and her hair was in a scruffy topknot instead of its usual sleek high ponytail. Still, she couldn't ignore it, so she walked over to her and sat down.

'Hey, sorry for intruding but I wondered if you were okay.'

Natalie turned her gaze from staring out of the window to stare directly into Annie's eyes, and she felt that coldness seep down her back again. It was like looking into two black holes with nothing behind them.

'Excuse me?'

Annie sucked in a breath. 'I was just checking you're okay.'

Natalie laughed. 'Of course, I'm okay, why are you asking?'

'I... you looked a little distracted, not like your usual self.'

'I do? I'm tired I suppose. I haven't been sleeping very well, thank you for asking though and for noticing, that's kind of you. Jasper hasn't asked me if I'm okay for at least three years. It's that bloody house. We should never have bought it, and now we're stuck there or at least I am, and I hate it.'

'Have you talked to him about it? Why do you hate it so much?'

She shrugged. 'You'll think I'm crazy if I tell you.'

The waitress brought Natalie's large cappuccino over, placing it on the table, and Natalie thanked her, picked up the spoon and began to stir it.

'I wouldn't, if you knew half of the stuff I've been through, you'd have me certified insane and carted away. I've seen an awful lot of things that can't be explained and even more that can.'

Natalie looked at Annie properly. 'You're psychic, is that why all of this?' She waved her hands in the direction of the shop, the prints on the wall, the crystals and plants.

Annie laughed. 'I am a bit sensitive to things others can't see, but in all honesty I loved *Practical Magic*, the book and the movie, so much I thought it would be a cool idea to open a café based on it.'

Natalie smiled. 'It is cool, that's why I love it in here.'

'So what's wrong with your house?'

Natalie picked up her coffee, taking small sips.

'I don't know for sure and please don't laugh at me, but I think it's haunted.'

If Annie had felt a cold chill earlier, it was nothing compared to the arctic blast that washed over her as every single nerve ending in her body stood on end.

'See, you think I'm mad, your expression says it all.'

'No, I don't, not at all. Please tell me about your house.'

'It's stupid really, I just hear things and it always feels as if there is someone there who I can't see. It feels as if I'm being watched, but in reality, who would want to watch me? It must be a ghost and they must be really bored to be hanging around watching my boring life.'

'It's not stupid, have you checked to make sure no one is in your house watching you?'

'Oh yes, we have a fancy alarm system and there are cameras outside of it. I always check all the rooms but there's never anyone there.'

Annie was struck by the similarities between Natalie and Sally. 'I could come to your house and check it out for you, if you like, see if there's anything there that shouldn't be?' Looking back, she wished she'd offered to do that for Sally when she came to see her.

'You could? That would be amazing, I'd pay you for your time of course.'

Annie shook her head. 'You help keep this café afloat with your valued custom, it's the least I can do.'

Natalie laughed. 'It's not my fault, I'm addicted to that peppermint slice. No one makes it like that and believe me I've tried every café and bakery in a fifty-mile radius.'

Opening her bag, she took out a notebook, scribbled down her address then phone number and tore the page out, handing it to Annie. 'I can't tell you how much it would mean to me. When is the best time for you?'

'Today when I've closed the café? Around five, my husband is off work, so I don't need to worry about childcare.'

'Perfect, thank you, Annie. I feel better already, phew it's helped telling someone who didn't laugh at me.'

Annie stood up. 'I'll see you later. Would it be okay to bring a friend with me?'

'As long as she's not going to tell the whole world Natalie White is stark raving mad.'

'She wouldn't say a word, I promise.'

Leaving her to drink her coffee, Annie walked into the office, and closing the door behind her she sat down at the compact desk and picked up the phone, and dialled 101 to get through to the Cumbria Constabulary. She needed to speak to Morgan before something terrible happened to Natalie White. She was certain that there was something hovering on the horizon that she couldn't see yet, and if they didn't stop it she wouldn't be able to live with herself.

TWENTY-SEVEN

Morgan had tried to phone Theo yesterday, but there was no answer then resorted to Google where she'd been inundated with links to Bible study websites, so Ben had offered to accompany her to the vicarage, then they were going to visit the Riggs' house and speak to Luke and his wife, Heather. She had done a search of the police systems to see if there was any intelligence on either of them, but had come up with nothing, other than a criminal damage report for the family car having its wing mirror smashed off a couple of years ago. On paper they were the perfect family: Facebook was full of happy family photos, holidays, meals out, the usual stuff. Ava Rigg was a lot more tech savvy than her parents, who had their pages set to public so the whole world could see what they were doing. At least Ava was sensible, she didn't want her parents to know what she was doing, assuming she even bothered with it. She was probably into TikTok and Instagram more, but Morgan wasn't interested in Ava, who had a rock-solid alibi that had been confirmed by one of the PCSOs. She was interested in Luke and Heather.

'Should I come with you?'

She smiled and shook her head. 'No need, he might not be in anyway.'

Ben shrugged. 'Your call, Brookes.' His phone began to ring, he answered it, distracted already, and she rolled her eyes. Shutting the door she left him talking to whoever that was.

'Morgan.'

Theo's voice called her from the door of the church, and she stopped, turning to look at him, hoping he wasn't going to make her go inside. He beckoned her over and she muttered *bollocks* under her breath. Turning she made her way to the door of the church and followed him inside.

'We have to stop meeting like this, people are going to talk.' He winked at her, and she laughed.

'We do.'

'What's your boss doing, isn't he coming in?'

'He's on a call, I just wanted a quick word with you.'

He looked her up and down. 'No handcuffs, are we getting a little more trusting?'

'Theo, if you give me a reason to arrest you I will. I honestly don't care that you're a vicar.'

He started laughing; it was so loud it echoed around the empty church.

'I love teasing you. Sorry, that was mean of me. How can I help you?'

He didn't go any further into the church, keeping her inside the entrance, and she was grateful for that, she didn't need an image of Des's mutilated body to distract her.

'Have you heard of Isaiah, is it a biblical reference?'

'Is this some kind of trick question?'

She shook her head.

'Oh, okay you're being serious. Right, well, let me see if I can recall something off the top of my head from it. The book of

Isaiah is in the Old Testament, and it outlines Israel and its nations' coming judgement.'

Morgan shrugged.

'I think it also talks about the coming of the Messiah. Verse 19:16: "God is salvation, on that day the Egyptians will become like women, they will tremble and be in dread because of the waving of the hand of the Lord that he is going to wave over them". Don't quote me on that, it's not perfect but something along those lines.'

'The hand of God, judgement, it all leads back to that.'

'I suppose if you're referring to what you came to ask about on Saturday then yes, it is all linked.'

She leaned back against the cold stone wall and closed her eyes for a moment, trying to process everything.

'Are you okay, do you want to sit down for a moment, Morgan, and take five minutes?'

She looked at him. 'I'm good, thanks. I have this tornado going around in my head. It's driving me mad all this stuff, how it all relates.'

'Look, I'm not stupid as well as not being a serial killer and this is a small place. You're obviously working on the terrible murder of that family. Can I give you my opinion?'

'Of course.'

'For what it's worth if this person knows about the book of Isaiah and is using it to live their life by, I would say they learned it at Sunday school many moons ago, when they taught that kind of stuff. Whoever it is thinks they are either God, or carrying out His work, that's my thought.'

'That's helpful, Theo, thank you.'

She turned to go back to the car. Ben was standing outside leaning against it waiting for her. He got back inside when he saw her hurrying towards him.

Morgan almost threw herself in, putting her seat belt on.

'Isaiah is from the Old Testament and it's all about judging the Egyptians. I think this is all about revenge.'

'Revenge for what?'

'Something that happened a long time ago, maybe. Theo said they used to teach this stuff in Sunday schools, so maybe the killer was forced to go to a Sunday school, or they had a strict religious upbringing where the Bible was rammed down their throats regularly? If Luke Rigg's advances were turned down by Sally was this his revenge? Or if his wife knew about his feelings towards her, did she take her revenge on Sally and her family? One thing I do know we need to ask both of them, and not when they're together, is if they ever went to a Sunday school or if they go to church.'

'What about Tim's online game on the Dark Web?'

She let out a sigh. 'I don't know, this is all way too complicated.'

'You're telling me.'

Ben drove towards Hest Bank Road as Morgan stared out of the window and tried to piece everything together.

TWENTY-EIGHT

Luke Rigg answered the door in his pyjama bottoms and a shirt and tie.

'Oh, I thought you were the delivery guy.'

Morgan smiled at him, by the look of disappointment on his face he'd been expecting something a lot more exciting than them. 'Can we come in, Luke, and have a word?'

He didn't seem as reluctant to let them in as previous times, but nodded and opened the door for them.

'I have a Zoom meeting in fifteen minutes, will this take long?'

Ben took the lead. 'Not at all, just a few loose ends we need to tie up. Is Heather here?'

'No, she's out shopping or meeting her friend for coffee. I don't really know to be honest, she kind of leaves me alone if I have meetings.'

He pointed to the sofa, and they both sat down.

'How can I help?'

'Did you say you worked with David at the university?'

'I did, not in the same department but we shared an office.'

'David was an English lecturer, I believe?'

'He was, a very good one too. The students liked his easy-going manner; he was very enthusiastic, too, when discussing his favourite books.'

'I should imagine his death will be a huge loss.'

Luke nodded.

'What do you teach?'

'Computer Science.'

Morgan had to push her hands under her knees and force herself to sit straight, not looking in Ben's direction. Before Ben could say anything else she smiled at Luke.

'I bet that's really interesting, what kind of things does it cover?'

'It is, it covers all the basics really: programming, security, gaming, networking, web technologies.'

'Oh wow, I'd have liked to have done that if I hadn't joined the police. It would be so cool to be able to write your own programmes and stuff.'

She didn't dare look at Ben, who would be questioning everything he knew about her at this moment in time. It was a tiny lie to keep Luke talking, she wasn't remotely interested.

Luke laughed. 'It's fun, but also very boring at times.'

'What about games, have you ever had a go at writing your own?'

'I have, only a couple of basic ones though, unfortunately I'm not that hot at development. Why do you ask?'

'Oh, I just wondered, those game developers must make a lot of money.'

'Some of them do, it's like everything else though, competitive. If you can come up with an interesting concept that the public will buy then yeah, I suppose you can practically print your own money.'

Ben interjected. 'Does Heather work?'

Luke shook his head. 'She used to, she doesn't any more.'

'What did she do?'

'Worked in the butchers on the high street, but she got fed up with the stench of the meat in the summer and gave it up. She's currently trying to write a novel, but I don't know how she's getting on with it. She doesn't talk about it.'

'That's amazing, what genre? I love reading.'

'I think it's women's fiction. Look I don't mean to sound rude, but my meeting is going to start soon.'

Ben smiled but didn't move. 'Of course, sorry just a couple more, did you go to Sunday school?'

Luke began to laugh. 'Sunday school, what has that got to do with anything? I maybe went a couple of times as a kid because I was in the Scouts and we had to go to church now and again. I can't even remember to be honest it's that long ago.'

'Have you heard of a game called *Isaiah*?'

Luke screwed up his eyes and shook his head at Ben.

'I can't say that I have, but then again it's hard to keep up with all these online crazes these days.'

'Thanks, Luke. One last question, were you having an affair with Sally Lawson?' Ben was watching him closely.

Luke's mouth dropped open, and he looked around as if checking that Heather hadn't just walked through the front door.

'What do you mean by that?'

Morgan smiled at him. 'The pictures on your phone we seized, they were very telling. Does Heather know you had a thing for Sally?'

'I most certainly wasn't having an affair with Sally; I'd never cheat on my wife. How dare you come into my home and insinuate such nonsense. Do you know how much trouble you would cause if Heather had heard this? She is a very jealous woman and she's not been well lately, she's having trouble with her meds and trialling new ones that don't seem to be working too good. You would cause such trouble talking like this.'

Morgan thought that maybe Heather was the one they should be talking to. Could she be their killer?

'I want you to leave now and don't come back talking such utter nonsense unless you have proof of anything more than a couple of photos.'

'They were hardly a couple of photos. Why did you only upload the photos of Sally to your new phone, and then the ones of her dead family?'

Luke's face had paled significantly since he'd let them into his home. He looked around flustered. Then lowered his voice. 'I liked her, okay, there's no crime in that.'

Ben looked him straight in the eyes. 'You liked her, in what way? As a friend, a good neighbour, a lover?'

'I can't believe this, that you would come in here speaking about her like that.'

'We're not speaking out of turn, and I'm sure she would want us to do whatever we had to, to find the person who killed her and her family.'

Luke turned to Morgan. 'This is your doing; you think you're smart, don't you, but you're not and you know nothing about me or my life. Get out of my house and don't bother to call again unless you have enough evidence against me to secure a warrant for my arrest.'

He marched to the front door and stood there holding it wide open.

They walked out but before he could close it Morgan turned back and stared at him.

'We need to speak to Heather, so we will be back, or if you'd rather avoid that, please ask her to come to the station for a chat. It's your choice, but that's how it is. The Lawsons' murder investigation is our top priority not sparing your feelings because you can't admit how you really felt about Sally. Enjoy your meeting.'

With that Morgan walked back to the car, closely followed

by Ben. They heard the door shut firmly behind them, not quite the slam Luke Rigg would have wanted because he'd know Maggie, or her security camera, was probably watching, and he wouldn't want to give her an inch of gossip.

Ben drove away, not speaking until they turned out of the cul-de-sac.

'Well, that could have gone better.'

Morgan began to laugh. 'Sorry, I couldn't help it, the smug arrogant bastard. Did you see how he changed when we asked him about Sally? He went from a nice, friendly guy to full-on defensive mode.'

'It was pretty hard to miss. I think we might need to bring him in for a more formal chat.'

'What about Heather? He said she's not well, what kind of meds do you think she's on? What if she saw those photos and they tipped her over the edge?'

'Let's see if she comes in of her own free will, but if she doesn't turn up today then we will see about bringing them both in.'

'He's a computer guy, Ben, he teaches it, he would know all about the Dark Web and gaming.'

'Heather worked in a butchers, she would have no problem using a meat cleaver to chop off the Lawsons' hands. But we've got nothing else on them.'

'What are you saying?'

'That circumstantial evidence against them is wonderful, but the fact that he knows computers and she is capable of using a meat cleaver to dismember a hand doesn't prove either of them actually killed the Lawsons.'

Morgan sighed. 'We need more evidence; we always need more evidence, it's so bloody difficult. We also need to know what his relationship with Sally was and whether Heather knew about any of it. Let's hope she comes into the station to speak with us; or do you think he won't even tell her we've been and spoken with him?'

'Who knows, he seems like a clever guy. Would you ignore the police requesting you to tell your wife to come to the station?'

'Erm no, not over something so serious.'

'Did you mean what you said, that you'd like to have been a computer geek?'

She laughed. 'You're so gullible at times, not at all. I mean it would be good to know how to fix stuff but I'm not really into computers. How often do you see me on one except for when I'm at work?'

Ben laughed. 'Ah, I see. You know, you could always consider a career in acting if this gets too much.'

She winked at him, and he grinned at her.

'Should we go grab something to eat?'

Morgan nodded, just as her work phone began to ring.

'Morgan Brookes.'

'Hi, Morgan, this is Annie Ashworth, are you free to talk?'

'Hello, Annie, yes, I am, how can I help?'

'I hope you don't mind me contacting you, I tried to ring 101 but it was a nightmare getting through, so I phoned Will and he gave me your number. It's a bit difficult to explain over the phone. Would you be free to come for a coffee at some point? It's easier in person.'

'I'd love that, yes, in fact we were just thinking of grabbing a bite to eat.'

'Perfect, I'll see you soon then.'

'You will.'

Annie ended the call.

'Who's Annie?'

'Will's wife, she owns this amazing café and shop in Bowness. She wants to have a word with me about something, so let's go there for lunch. Sally paid her a visit the week before she died, she thought she was being haunted.'

'Did I know this, and for real? How about I drive us to the station, you take the car and go grab some lunch from the café, speak to Annie, and I'll speak to Marc about the Riggs. I'm pretty sure a ghost didn't kill her.'

'Perfect, neither do I, but I'm following every line of enquiry, like my boss would want me to.'

She felt a bit bad she'd forgotten to update them on Sally's visit to Annie, or maybe she'd been waiting for it to become a more solid lead, because it was a little bit out there and she could just hear Amy taking the piss if she brought it up. It was much better for her to go on her own. When she'd spoken with Annie, she'd give the team a full brief on Sally's visit to Practical Magic and Annie's suggestion that she may have had a stalker, even though Sally hadn't believed so, or reported it.

TWENTY-NINE

At the station entrance Ben jumped out of the car and Morgan walked around to get in the driver's seat. As she began driving towards Bowness, she wondered why Annie had been at work today. She was sure she told her that she didn't work Sundays or Mondays. Whatever her reason, Morgan was glad of the chance to go and speak to her again.

Bowness was busy, full of crowds of tourists, which was brilliant for the area but annoying when you wanted to get parked. A car in a parking bay a little ahead of her indicated to pull out and she flashed it, waiting patiently and smiling to herself. Talk about perfect timing. Divine intervention or whatever it was. Morgan parked the white Corsa effortlessly and got out. It was a short walk down to the café, past the quirky row of shops selling clothes, teapots, pet accessories, a sweet shop, charity shop and confectionery. Morgan glanced in all of their windows, but nothing took her eye. The next row was bakeries with cafés, then a Domino's of all things; she expected the local restaurants hadn't been too happy with that opening up.

Finally she came to Annie's café. It was busy when she walked in, and she couldn't see Annie behind the counter, so she turned to go into the little shop and there she saw Annie serving a customer. Morgan waited until the teenage girl left, clutching her paper bag of assorted crystals along with a pack of tarot cards. Annie smiled at her.

'Come through to the office, I'll get Magda to keep an eye on the shop.'

Morgan followed her through to the compact office, full of neatly stacked boxes.

'Busy day.'

'Yes, typical, when I could have done with a bit of a breather to process everything as well.'

'I thought you didn't work Mondays?'

'I don't as a rule unless it's a bank holiday or Magda lets me know I'm needed, but see how busy it is and I'm a staff member down too, so I thought I'd better come in. Lily, my mother-in-law, should be here any minute to help out too. Can I get you a drink?'

'When we're done, I'll get some takeaway coffees and sandwiches if that's okay.'

'Of course, it is, thank you for coming at such short notice, Morgan, I really appreciate it. You've just missed Natalie, but I'm worried about her. I got a really strong vibe from her.'

Morgan perched on the corner of the sturdy pine desk. 'What sort of vibe?'

'That she's in trouble, the perfect way to describe it is haunted. She looked so different today than I've ever seen her. She's usually so put together, you know the type, those women who are fit, fabulous and never seem to age a day.' Annie paused, and Morgan nodded for her to continue. 'Well today she came in looking kind of bedraggled, I mean I look like that most days, but it was out of character for her. Even when she's been out fell walking or to yoga, she doesn't look like that. I asked her if she was okay, and she said that things were a bit weird at home. She feels as if she's always being watched but there's never anyone there. It's the same as Sally said she felt. She scoffed when I told her she might have a stalker, but what if she did and now that person is watching Natalie?'

'Did Sally know Natalie?'

'I couldn't say, but they're both of a similar age – in their late forties. Although it's hard to tell because they look so good, both well-off to a degree, both have families.'

Morgan was thinking it through. 'Families, how many kids does Natalie have?'

'One, a daughter, I think she's about fourteen.'

There it was, that icy trickle of cold water running down Morgan's spine as she connected the two women; maybe it went deeper than them both having children, but she had that gut feeling: what if Annie was right and whoever killed the Lawsons had a new family to concentrate on?

'Do you think Natalie would be up for me visiting her? Today, well now, would be great?'

'I already suggested to her I could come see her at five when the café closed, but I don't suppose she'd mind us calling now though. I hope you don't mind, but I presumed you'd want to speak to her, so she knows you're coming too, though I didn't tell her you were a detective in case it scared her.'

'Annie, you're brilliant. I think we need to go and have a chat with her as soon as we can, I don't want to leave it.'

'Give me a couple of minutes, to sort things out here.'

'I'll go grab the car, be waiting outside for you.'

THIRTY

Ben's desk phone was ringing as he entered the office. Amy and Cain were nowhere to be seen. He rushed in, just in time to pick it up.

'Matthews.'

'About time, what took so long?'

'I've just come back, afternoon to you too, Declan.'

'Good afternoon, I have some news. I've matched those two hands with Tim and David Lawson. They fit like a glove. Oh that was terribly bad taste, sorry.'

Ben smiled. 'That's good news, I wish we had Sally's hand. It doesn't seem right that she's missing it. I can't get my head around why someone would want to chop their hands off in the first place, it's so bizarre.'

'Has your girl, Morgan, not got a theory about it?'

'She has, how did you know?'

'A wild guess, she's very good at this stuff. Too good to be wasting her time in Rydal Falls that's for sure. Although I suppose we should be thankful she's happy enough or we'd never get any criminals caught.'

'That's true, though I think you're being a bit mean about

my department, we can catch criminals with or without Morgan's help.'

'*Mmm, really. Well, put me out of my misery anyway, what does she think this hand stuff means?*'

'She thinks the killer is acting as if he's the hand of God and passing judgement on the victims.'

'*That's certainly different, but interesting for sure.*'

'It's better than anything I've come up with. We also think that Tim was involved in some secretive computer game he was playing on the Dark Web, and that the neighbour may have had a crush on Sally. As to how they're connected though, not a clue.'

'*Blimey, I have a headache listening to that, good luck trying to figure it out. I have some news that might help. There is matter under Tim's fingernails, now it could just be the usual teenage grungy dirt, or it could be that he tried to stop his attacker and managed to get us some fabulous DNA samples that would lead us right to the killer's front door.*'

'Declan, you are brilliant.'

'*Ach, I know but it will take some time to process, we're just thawing out the hand now so we can get it collected and fast tracked.*'

'Thank you, I owe you a pint.'

'*You owe me more than that, but it will do for now. Catch you later.*'

Declan hung up. Amy was knocking on the window. Ben smiled at her, waving her in.

'There's a Heather Rigg at the front desk, she said you asked her to come in?'

Ben nodded. 'I did, well Morgan did. Wow that's brilliant, first Declan thinks he may have some DNA under Tim's nails and now Heather's turned up. Are you busy? I could do with you sitting in whilst I talk to her.'

'Not busy, where's Morgan?'

'Thank you, she's gone to a café in Bowness and is bringing back coffee and food.'

'From Bowness? It must be good.'

He shrugged. 'She thinks so.'

They went downstairs to the front desk and spoke to Brenda who was in the small office behind it.

'Heather Rigg?'

'That woman on her own near the doors. It's a good job you haven't taken ages to come down, she looks as if she might make a run for it at any moment.'

'Thanks, Brenda.'

'Anytime. The first room is empty if you want to take her in there.'

Ben was already opening the doors that led into the waiting area and crossing the floor towards Heather. Amy went into the empty interview room and held the door open so Ben could bring her in.

Heather's eyes were wide as she looked at the table with a single chair on one side and two opposite. Amy was smiling at her instead of wearing her usual frown and Ben realised that she was trying to put Heather at ease. Amy trying out charm, he never thought he'd see the day, perhaps Des's death had got to her even more than he'd realised. He pointed to the lonely chair.

'Please take a seat, thank you so much for coming to see us so fast, Heather. I'm Detective Sergeant Ben Matthews and this is my colleague, Detective Constable Amy Smith.'

Heather nodded. She took the offered seat, and he noticed she kept her hands folded under the table.

'I've never been in a police station.'

Amy nodded. 'Lucky you, we seem to live here.'

Heather side-eyed Amy, unsure of whether she was being serious or not.

'Luke is very angry with you. Was it you two that came to the house?'

Amy glanced at Ben, and he knew she would be wondering what was going on but she kept quiet.

'I'm sorry about that, I came with another colleague, Morgan.'

'He said I shouldn't come here, that I needed a lawyer if I was going to speak to you.'

'Have you got a lawyer?'

She shook her head. 'No, why would I need one? I haven't done anything wrong.'

'We only wanted to ask you some questions. I think Luke got offended, does he normally get so upset or lose his temper so easily?'

Heather looked down at her hands, then lifted her head.

'Sometimes, it depends on what he's being asked.'

'Did he tell you what we asked him about?'

She nodded. 'He said you accused him of having an affair with Sally Lawson, that your colleague was presumptuous.'

Ben was surprised that Luke had told his wife this. Maybe he wasn't having an affair.

'I'm sorry he felt that way, it's hard working any investigation, but a triple homicide is difficult from all angles. Do you think he was having an affair with Sally?'

Heather let out a long sigh. 'In my head, I would say no he would never do anything like that especially not with a neighbour but...'

Ben nodded in encouragement.

'I know that he liked her, a lot. He talked about her all the time, and he always wanted to invite them over for drinks, go out for dinner with them, then he'd always want to sit next to Sally. I think he has, or had, a huge crush on her. I don't think she felt the same way about him though, and I don't believe anything happened between them or at least I hope it didn't.'

'How do you know?'

'She told me. She said that she was sorry but she couldn't be around Luke because he was too touchy-feely, and it made her feel uncomfortable. He'd invited them around for drinks that night – I had no idea – but she'd said no. I was mortified, and Sally said she couldn't cope, especially when he did it in front of me and David. She said it was embarrassing, and she didn't want to upset me but thought I should know that was the reason they wouldn't be accepting any more invitations.'

Amy was the one sitting with her mouth open now. She closed it quickly then asked. 'How were you with this? I mean that's disrespectful to you, as his wife, and to David, did you have it out with him?'

Heather shook her head. 'I wanted to, I wanted to tell him he was a disgrace, that he should pack his bags and get out, that he had gone too far this time.'

'But you didn't?'

'I went for a walk to clear my head, when I got home; I'd been to get my hair cut and blow dried that day at Sally's salon. She told me when she was washing my hair and I just wanted to die of shame. To be told by someone you consider a friend that they don't want to see you any more because your husband is the world's biggest creep is humiliating. I was fuming with him and wanted to have it out with him, but I wanted to think clearly about the whole situation. I have Ava to think about. I don't work – it's Luke that brings in the money – so I went out. By the time I came home it was time to pick Ava up from her friends, and Luke insisted on coming with me. I have no idea why, he doesn't usually bother, but I think he could tell something was wrong. We walked out of the house, and I noticed the flames in the window of Sally's house and well, you know the rest.'

Ben was frantically scribbling down what Heather had told them. He looked up.

'So Luke was alone that evening? What time did you go out?'

'He was, I came back from the salon around four, then I went straight out again. I couldn't look at him.'

'Ava wasn't there?'

'No, she went straight to her friend's after school that day.'

'Heather, does Luke have a bad temper, do you think he's capable of hurting someone?'

'I think I've said enough, he's going to be furious when he finds out what I've told you. Is he going to find out what I've said?'

'Heather, has Luke ever hurt you or Ava in the past?'

She bowed her head. 'What's going to happen now?'

'We need to bring him in for an interview. Meantime, if you think that you or Ava may be in danger of domestic violence, you could obtain an occupation order, which would mean he wasn't allowed into the family home.'

Heather began to cry, loud, hitching sobs.

Ben crouched down next to her. 'We want to keep you and Ava safe; we have to, it's our job. If you want us to arrest Luke and seek bail conditions to keep away from you then we can do that, but you're going to have to give Amy a statement, so we have the power to do that.'

She stood up. 'I have to go; I need to get home; I don't want to leave Ava with him. He'll be angry if I'm here too long and I don't want him to take it out on her. Am I free to go?'

'Of course, you are. If you're worried about anything then ring 101, and if Luke gets violent towards either of you, ring 999 straight away, Heather, don't hesitate. We are going to have to bring him in for interview, I wouldn't be doing my job if I didn't.'

She nodded.

Ben pressed his key fob against the wall to let her out.

'Do you have a safe place you can take Ava to?'

'I could go to my friend's.'

'It might be best, for a couple of nights.'

Heather turned and walked towards the sliding doors, her head bowed, and Ben felt terrible.

He closed the door; Amy was standing up. 'Should we get a warrant sorted out?'

'Yeah, I'll go speak to Marc and we'll get an arrest team together.'

'Is there enough to arrest him?'

'I hope so, there's lots of circumstantial evidence. Feelings for Sally, computer knowledge. At least if we bring him in it will give Heather a chance to change the locks or pack some things to go to her friend's. Declan said that Tim may have scratched his killer. We will get Luke photographed and swabbed whilst he's here.'

Ben went to Marc's office hoping that he would agree with the need to bring Luke Rigg in for questioning.

THIRTY-ONE

Morgan parked on the double-yellow lines outside the café with the hazards on, waiting for Annie to come out. Moments later she rushed out of the door, a paper bag in one hand, a piece of paper in the other, and clambered in the front seat.

'Have you phoned Natalie to warn her we're coming now?'

'Yes, there was no reply, so I left a voice message. I hope she's in. Sorry, this might be a wasted journey.'

'We can only try, where are we going?'

'Hellsfield Road, it's one of those big old mansions that time forgot. I remember getting called out there when I was covering this area. It used to break my heart going around there looking for teenagers and seeing the state those houses were in. Now of course you'd need to be a millionaire to live there.'

'I love old houses, that's so sad. Would you have lived there, if you could, Annie?'

'I've never really thought about it, probably, but some of them needed a lot of work and even more money to bring them back to life. Natalie's husband is a property developer, he has the resources, builders and money to invest.'

Annie directed Morgan to Hellsfield Road. The name was

enough to give Morgan the creeps. She slowed the car along the narrow, overgrown, winding country road until just past the bend, when a pair of huge limestone gateposts appeared, and a plaque on one read 'Hellsfield Hall'. The ornate rusted gates were pushed open, so Morgan drove in slowly along the narrow drive.

If Morgan had garden envy at the Lawsons', she didn't know what she felt now. Imagine owning your own woodland. That would be unbelievable, she'd build Ettie a house inside of them so she could be near to her and... the car rounded a bend, stopping all thoughts in her tracks as the house appeared from nowhere, looming in the background. It was... how would Morgan describe it? Creepy, monstrous, something that would look right at home in a season of *American Horror Story*.

'Wow.'

Annie laughed. 'Wow indeed, it takes some getting used to, doesn't it?'

Morgan turned off the engine and jumped out of the car. It was like all her nightmares and bad dreams rolled into one. No wonder Natalie didn't feel comfortable in here on her own. Annie pressed the video doorbell that looked out of place on the wall next to the huge arched wooden door.

'*Annie, you're early.*'

'Sorry, my friend, Morgan, could only come now, is it okay?'

'*Yes, on my way.*'

It seemed like forever as they waited for Natalie to open the front door, and when she finally did she stared at Morgan.

Annie smiled. 'This is—'

'Detective Constable Morgan Brookes, why are you here? I don't need a police officer.'

Annie looked confused. 'Do you two know each other?'

Morgan shook her head. She'd never seen this woman before.

'I read the papers; I've followed some of your cases. Why are you here?'

Annie smiled at Natalie. 'It might be better if we come in and have a chat.'

'Of course, forgive me, where are my manners? Sorry, I'm a bit out of sorts today, it's not like me.'

They followed her inside, to the entrance hall. Morgan was last, turning to close the door behind them. It was surprisingly light and airy inside. She'd been expecting it to be all dark wood, panelling, rich coloured carpets, but everything was the complete opposite.

Natalie led them into a lounge with sofas big enough to hold at least eight people on each.

'Take a seat, would you like a drink?'

Both Annie and Morgan shook their heads.

'Natalie, why don't you tell Morgan what you were telling me earlier.'

Natalie looked as if she'd rather not speak another word, but she nodded.

'You're going to think I'm mad and please don't tell anyone. Jasper would be furious if he heard me talking like this.'

'I wouldn't tell a soul, what you say here is between the three of us.'

'Good, that's good. I appreciate that, Morgan, I really do. It's so stupid really but you can see how big this place is, and more often than not I'm rattling around in here on my own. Jasper is never here; my daughter, Lexie, would rather be anywhere else, and I can't say that I blame her. The internet is crap and I think it drives her mad. You know what kids are like, they can't live without bloody TikTok these days.'

'This is a big house for one person to spend their time in, it's beautiful though.'

'Oh, downstairs is gorgeous, I love it. Jasper, despite all his faults, did a wonderful job with it. The problem is when you go upstairs to the first and second floors, actually I don't even go up to the second floor, it scares the shit out of me.'

It was Annie who asked. 'How does it scare you, the feel of the place, sounds, smells?'

'The second floor hasn't been touched. It's the old servant's quarters, lots of small, dark rooms. The first floor, where we sleep, that's had a lick of paint to brighten up the bedrooms and a new bathroom, but it's still too... I don't know what's the right word, out of date, old-fashioned, creepy. I suppose all of them would do. When I'm in the house on my own I hear noises, creaking floorboards upstairs. I feel as if I'm being watched. Like, the hairs on the back of my neck prickle, as if there is someone staring at me from behind, yet whenever I turn around there's no one there. I go up and investigate the sounds, same again, it's quiet as a mouse when I'm up there. The only explanation is that it's haunted; a house this old with its history is going to have some dodgy owners that died here and haven't wanted to leave.'

Morgan smiled at her.

Annie stood up. 'Can we look around? Will you show us where you hear the noises and feel like you're being watched?'

Natalie stood up. 'Yes, I suppose you need to see it for yourself, although nothing will happen when you're here, it's only ever when I'm on my own.'

Natalie gave them a guided tour of the downstairs, four lounges, a dining room, library which Morgan fell in love with despite the severe lack of books on the many shelves, then there was the kitchen, it was the size of her old primary school dining room.

'Sometimes when I'm in here with my back to that door I feel like I'm being watched. It's horrible, I turn around and no one is there but it's just a weird feeling, you know.'

Morgan walked over to where she pointed, in front of the worktop, and slowly turned around – from here she could see out into the hallway and the foot of the stairs. As she stared every hair on the back of her neck began to prickle as a cold chill settled over her. She didn't know what was wrong, but something was, and she needed to figure it out before anything happened to Natalie and her family.

'Can we look upstairs?'

Natalie led them to the sweeping staircase. Annie reached out her fingers, trailing them along the wooden banister. Morgan noticed that Natalie didn't touch it; she kept her hands by her side as she led them up to the first floor.

THIRTY-TWO

Marc listened to what Ben had to say about Luke Rigg, and from the expression on his face he didn't look too interested in him as the main suspect, not until Ben told him that he'd been alone for a couple of hours before the fire began, and that his wife was convinced he had a thing for Sally Lawson.

'It sounds good, it does, but what about the CCTV footage of the boy walking home with someone? Where are we with that, has the person of interest been identified? If not, we're going to have to release the image to the press and see if any member of the public can name them.'

Ben had to stop himself from swearing out loud, he'd bloody forgot all about that. He nodded, gave himself a couple of seconds to recover then continued, 'Boss, we might be barking up the wrong tree with the CCTV. Rigg has a motive, I think we have to at least rule him out. His wife seemed very genuine when she gave a statement. She said she was so embarrassed by his behaviour, and I got the impression that he has a violent temper, too, only she wouldn't officially disclose that.'

'I'm not convinced, all we have is a statement from his wife about all of this and you know as well as I do how bitter women can get.'

'We also have the photographs on his phone that back up his wife's statement, and also that he discovered the fire and took the photographs of them all dead. If the fire had taken hold of the house like it was supposed to, we'd be struggling to get much from the crime scene. He had no choice but to show us the photographs he'd taken otherwise it would have been incriminating anyway.'

'Damned if he did, damned if he didn't. You really feel as though he could be a viable suspect, Ben?'

'I do, at least we can get him in then bail him under condition of not going near the family home, so his wife and daughter are safe for the time being. Whilst he's in custody we can get CSI to go through his house, we're still missing Sally Lawson's hand after all; he might have it in his freezer.'

Marc grimaced. 'Christ, I hope not. Okay, let's get a search team together, do you think he's going to come in without any bother or are we going to need backup from section?'

'If Cain and I go to arrest him, Amy and Morgan along with Wendy can sweep the house for evidence. I don't think he'll argue when he sees the size of Cain, but it won't hurt to have a couple of officers there to back us up, and we're going to need a van to transport him here anyway.'

Ben jumped out of the chair and made his way back to the office before Marc could change his mind.

Cain was eating a bacon bun; Amy was staring down into a plastic container filled with rice and chicken.

'Where's Morgan?'

'To be honest, boss, I think she's done a runner.' Amy didn't look up at him to gauge his reaction.

'Don't be stupid, where's she going to run to and why?'

'I don't know, because she's fed up with this job maybe, fed up with the bloody shite food the canteen has.'

Cain laughed. 'She's mad because I got the last bacon bun, aren't you, Amy?'

'Piss off.'

'Seriously has she not been back?'

'Not seen her, why?'

'She only went to get some lunch.'

'Yeah, but you let her go to Bowness for it, I mean the roads are busy, you can't get parked, the café will be heaving, she'll have to queue forever. It was never going to be a ten-minute lunch run.'

Ben took out his phone and dialled Morgan's number; it went straight to voicemail. The familiar, unwanted sense of panic that sometimes accompanied his worries about Morgan began to make his stomach clench. He left her a voicemail.

'Hey, soon as you get this give me a ring. I need you back at the station. We're going to make an arrest.'

Amy looked up from her unappetising lunch. 'We are?'

'Yes, we are, I want you and Morgan to be the ones to go in and search the house whilst Cain and I bring him in.'

'Who are we arresting, boss?' Cain said through the last mouthful of his lunch.

'Luke Rigg.'

'The neighbour, the guy who rang it in and went to see if he could get them out?'

'Yeah, that's him.'

Amy nodded. 'Sounds about right, always the good Samaritans.'

'No, it's not but there is a lot going on with him and Sally Lawson that we weren't aware of. There's too much for it to be ignored. Morgan and I went to talk to him, but he got angry and threw us out, which is why I think, Cain, that you'll be very useful in case he kicks off. Take your CS, cuffs and maybe your baton just in case you need them.'

'I thought this was a move up from all the fighting on a regular shift?'

Amy laughed so loud both men turned to look at her.

'Yeah right, this is where you've upgraded from drunken tourists and abusive spouses. You're fighting with the big boys now, Cain. Welcome to killer club where one wrong move could see you as the one who dies on duty.'

Ben stared at her. 'Amy, are you okay?'

'Fine, but it's true, isn't it? Look at how many times Morgan's had her run-ins with psychopaths, and Des. They should be paying us danger money on top of our shift allowance.'

Cain walked across and ruffled her hair. 'As long as you're with me you won't be fighting anyone, I promise.'

Amy smiled at him. 'Ah, you're such a big softie, Cain, but I fear even you can't keep us safe.'

He shrugged. 'Soft but deadly if I need to be.' He winked at her and grabbed his utility belt from the drawer with everything he needed on it, then headed out the door.

Before Amy could follow, Ben grabbed hold of her arm, tugging her back to him.

'If you need to take a break from all of this it's not a problem, Amy. It's been difficult, and no one would blame you if you wanted to go away for a few weeks, forget about this place. Maybe get Jack to take you somewhere hot where you can drink cocktails and relax.'

She smiled at him. 'You're a good boss, Ben, thank you. I'm okay, I think I just get a bit edgy; you know what I'm like. I think it's when I get worried, I get all defensive. Cain is great, he's not Des, but then again there wasn't anyone like him, was there? I think I just feel guilty that I couldn't help him when he needed us, you know.'

Ben nodded. 'Me too, I lie in bed wishing to God that I'd gone with Morgan to that church fete and not Des. I feel as if it's all my fault.'

'That's the two of us then, come on, enough feeling sorry for Des. He wouldn't have given a shit if it had been one of us who had been murdered, not as long as he was okay.'

Ben laughed. 'You're probably right, we should stop beating ourselves up so much over him; it wasn't me or you that killed him.'

'Not in the end, although come on, admit it how many times did he wind you up enough that you thought about it?'

She was laughing, and Ben joined in. 'No comment.'

They went to find Cain, who was talking to the two response officers who were going to follow behind with an arrest vehicle to put Luke Rigg in, if he kicked off.

THIRTY-THREE

The house was huge, upstairs was very gloomy, dark panelling, dark wood furniture, huge flowery wallpaper and velvet drapes in each bedroom. Natalie led them from room to room. Annie didn't say much, looking around, reaching out and touching things. Morgan thought it was creepy as hell because it was so dark.

'Whereabouts up here do you feel weird?' asked Annie.

'Everywhere, especially the kitchen and my bedroom, we're going to go into that one next.'

She pushed open the heavy door to a room that was painted white, everything was white, curtains, furniture, it was the nicest room they'd been in so far.

'This is lovely and bright.'

'It is and Jasper hates it, but I did it when he was away one weekend. Dragged all that awful depressing furniture into the room across the hall and had a ball at Ikea. Even Lexie managed to smile that weekend. We did the same with her room, only it's green instead. Jasper was so mad he threatened to put everything back, and I told him if he did, we were leaving. It calmed him down a little; he needs a wife and daughter to look good at his business functions.'

'Do you and Jasper not get on?' Annie asked.

'We do, I guess we're more friends than lovers now. It was different in the early days, he was infatuated with me, and I wanted to marry a rich man to take care of me, so I had no worries. My childhood and teenage years were not the best, I made some terrible mistakes. I know how shallow I sound but it was what I wanted.'

Morgan was staring at Natalie. 'What do you want now, do you still feel the same way?'

'God knows, I want an easy life, but I also want a husband who pays attention to me at least some of the time. It's like I'm his bloody housekeeper not his wife.'

'Have you told him this?'

'Yes, he said as soon as this big development is finished, he'll have more time.'

Natalie showed them the rest of the first floor, stopping at the narrow stairs to the second floor. 'If you want to go up there, you're on your own, I hate it.'

Annie smiled. 'Of course, you wait in the kitchen, put the kettle on and we'll go take a look.'

Natalie's eyes shone with unshed tears of gratitude, and she turned, leaving Morgan staring at Annie who leaned forward and whispered, 'It's okay, nothing bad up to now just a lot of residual energy.'

Morgan followed Annie up the narrow twisting stairs that were the complete opposite of the grand staircase that led up to the first floor. At the top Annie shone her phone torch around – it was even darker up here. There were lots of smaller rooms, most of them empty except for some rusted iron bed frames, small chests of drawers and lots of dust.

'Wow, no wonder she doesn't want to come up here, it's creepy as hell. I think I'd put a door across and seal the stairs off so I didn't have to think about it.'

Annie laughed. 'I didn't take you as the kind of person who is scared easily.'

'I'm not, but this is too spooky for me. What do you think, have you picked anything up?'

'I'm not sure, I don't feel as if anything of the unearthly kind is haunting Natalie or this house though.'

Morgan was beginning to wonder if she was wasting her time. What kind of mad link was it, to be considering Natalie as a target because Annie had got a bad vibe off her? Ben would be horrified listening to this. Oh God, Ben! She pulled her phone out of her pocket; he was going to be worried sick – she'd been gone nearly two hours. There were no bars at the top of her screen, no 5G signal.

'Annie, I'm sorry I need to get back to work. I completely lost myself and forgot I was on shift.'

'Of course, yes, that's no problem, thanks for coming with me. What do you think about Natalie? If she's not being haunted by something scary enough to make its presence known, do you think it could be a person who is watching her?'

'Like a stalker?'

'Yes, I'm convinced that Sally had someone watching her, too, which was why she felt so uncomfortable.'

'I need to just ask her before I leave.'

They went back downstairs to the kitchen where Natalie was standing with a mug under the tap.

'No kettle, sorry, we have one of these taps that boils the water.'

'I have to go, so don't worry about me. Annie, are you stay-ing? Natalie, do you think there is a chance that someone is watching you, not a ghost, a human being?'

'Why would they? I don't think so, if they could get past the security system, they'd have to be good. Annie, I can give you a lift back to the café if you'd like.'

'Perfect, thanks, Natalie.'

Morgan turned the conversation back to her. 'Is there any reason that someone would want to watch you?'

'Blimey, they'd have to be desperate, my life is pants at the moment.'

'You can't think of anyone who would have a reason?'

She shook her head, but her eyes betrayed her slightly by looking up to the right, and the smile on her lips didn't reach her eyes. Morgan got the impression that Natalie White was hiding something from them, but she had no idea what.

THIRTY-FOUR

Morgan still had no signal when she got outside to the car. She drove along the drive much faster than she'd driven up it. She needed to let Ben know she was okay before he sent patrols out looking for her; she couldn't cope with the shame of that happening again. Once she was out onto the road she glanced down and saw a single bar appear in the corner. Pulling over she dialled Ben's number.

'Where are you?'

'Sorry, long story, I'll tell you when I get back.'

'As long as you're okay. We've got an arrest warrant for Luke Rigg, can you meet us there? When we get him in the van, I need you and Amy to go in and search his house.'

'How long was I gone, what's happened?'

He laughed. 'I'll tell you when I get back.'

'Ha ha, okay I get it. I'll drive there now.'

'Morgan, hang back a little while, I don't want you going anywhere near his house, in case he kicks off. He's not going to be happy about this, and he was particularly angry at you this morning when we interviewed him.'

The line went dead, and she realised that he must be in the

middle of something. What had happened in the last two hours? She felt bad that she'd got sidetracked by visiting Natalie White. Something was going on with Natalie, she was sure, but she didn't know what, or whether it had any relation to the case. And then she realised that she should have asked her if she knew Sally Lawson. They were a similar age, if they were both local then it was more than possible. Damn she could kick herself; she was going to have to go back at some point and speak with her. For now though, she should be okay, she had the security system and CCTV and hadn't given Morgan a reason to suggest that she was in any kind of trouble. Morgan realised that Ben was going to be disappointed that she hadn't even managed to grab him a sandwich whilst she'd been AWOL, she wasn't going to live that down, but at least he was too busy to think about food for the time being.

She reached Hest Bank Road in time to see Cain escorting an angry Luke Rigg to the waiting van. She parked up behind the other two white Corsas, one containing Amy, the other empty. Maggie was out on her front doorstep watching, her dog Roley by her feet, his lead attached. She waved at Morgan who got out to go and talk to her.

'What's happening? Why on earth have they arrested him?'

'You're guess at this moment is as good as mine, I don't know.'

'They don't think he killed Sally, David and Tim, do they? I mean they were good friends; he must be devastated by their loss and now for this to happen. I have your pie inside; it will need to be eaten today, Morgan, though or it won't taste as good.'

Morgan smiled. 'I'm starving.'

'Well come inside and I'll warm it up for you, then I'll walk the dog.'

'I can't but thank you. Maybe when we've finished over at the Riggs' house I can nip over for it.'

'Well make sure you do, flower, you can't work on an empty stomach, and I can hear yours growling from over here.'

Smiling, Morgan crossed the road to where Amy was now leaning against the bonnet of the car. Maggie turned around, locked her door then set off on one of her many daily dog walks.

'You like her, don't you?'

'She's lovely, and lonely.'

'I never thought you'd have a soft spot for the old dears, but you really do, it's quite sweet really. You're like one of those eclairs – tough on the outside and all chocolatey and soft on the inside.'

'Shh, don't you go telling everyone. I like them to think I'm a moody cow, how did it come to this?'

'I'll tell you when you give up the goods.'

'What goods?'

Amy's mouth opened. 'You're kidding me, you took two hours to go on a sandwich run and never got any. What the hell have you been doing, Morgan? Did you even get any coffees?'

She shrugged. 'You wouldn't believe me if I told you where I've just been and no, sorry. I was supposed to go back to the café, but I got sidetracked and then panicked, driving straight here.'

Cain helped Luke into the back of the van, then slammed the cage doors so loud the noise echoed around the quiet cul-de-sac. The van left, and Ben came out of the house, passing where Heather Rigg was standing on the step watching everyone. He crossed towards where Morgan and Amy stood.

'That went better than I expected. Heather said you're good to go in. If you find anything that looks the slightest bit evidential, then show it to Wendy when she gets here. She's on her way from Kendal. Ava is still at school; I'd like the search completed before she's due home at four, if possible.'

Morgan looked at her watch, it was just gone two. 'No problem, we'll get on with that now.'

Amy passed Morgan some gloves and she tugged them on.

'Cain is going to assist me in questioning Luke whilst you two do the searching.'

'Boss, how did this happen?'

Morgan hadn't been gone long enough for such an important break to have happened.

Ben leaned closer, lowering his voice. 'His wife came in to give a statement as soon as I got back to the station, and she said that Sally had told her she couldn't be friends any more because Luke's attention was embarrassing. She also told me and Amy that she wasn't home at the time of the murders, but Luke was. We have motive, he was obsessed with Sally, and she didn't want anything to do with him, and he had the opportunity. It's circumstantial but it's better than nothing, I have to try. Make sure to seize his laptop or computer too – there might be a link on there to Tim.'

She nodded. 'Of course you do.'

He jogged back to the car where Cain was waiting for him. Morgan watched them drive away.

'Do you think he did it?' she asked Amy.

'That's for us to find out. I did Heather's interview with Ben though, and I tell you something isn't right with that family. She was very open and honest about him, said she was humiliated by his behaviour.'

Morgan looked across at the small woman standing on the doorstep, her arms wrapped around her stomach as if she was hugging herself. She didn't say it out loud, but the thought was there inside her head. *But were you so humiliated that you decided to teach him a lesson, Heather? You could have killed the*

Lawsons and set him up. Who is going to take his word over yours when there are those photos on his phone?

She followed Amy to the house, where Heather greeted them warily and stepped to one side to let them in.

'He's going to be so angry when he's released. I'm worried he's going to come back here and kick off.'

'We're going to give him bail conditions not to come back. Why don't you pack some things for him in a suitcase that we can give to him until this is all sorted out? It will save someone having to escort him here,' said Amy.

Heather nodded.

'Let us have a look around first and then we'll give you the okay. Does he have a home office?'

'I'll show you. It's the spare room, not much of a room to be honest. I wanted a guest bedroom, but because of Covid and working from home he needed an office, and what Luke wants he gets.'

She walked upstairs, and they followed her. This house wasn't as big as the Lawsons', but it was a nice size for a newish build. Heather pointed to the door furthest away.

'We had to swap rooms to accommodate him. He wouldn't have an office next to Ava because he said her stupid music, Facetime calls and TikTok video making would drive him mad. So we moved Ava down the other end, to our master bedroom, and now we're in Ava's; she got a good deal out of it with her own en suite.'

'She certainly did, I'm thirty-five and haven't got my own bathroom yet,' replied Amy, smiling kindly.

'What shall I do?'

'You can watch to make sure we don't make too much mess, or you can go downstairs and make yourself a coffee. We'll shout you when we've finished, if that's okay?'

'Fine, I don't want to know what he's got in that office.'

She left them to it. Morgan waited until they could hear her downstairs in the kitchen and whispered, 'Don't you think this is all a bit convenient?'

Amy shrugged. 'It doesn't always have to be hard.'

'I suppose not, it's the perfect excuse for her to get rid of her husband though, isn't it? What if she's the killer and setting him up?'

'Christ, Morgan, for once can we just focus on the evidence we do have? I'm starving, therefore I'm hangry because you failed to bring back even one half of a sandwich. So yes, it is very convenient, but right now I want it like that. I want it to be just as Ben said, that Luke's ego got the better of him, so he took his revenge out on her whole family.'

'But what about Isaiah and the person who came home on the CCTV with Tim? They were much smaller than Luke; in fact they were around the same size as Heather. Maybe she was the one who went home with him.'

Amy turned around holding her hand in the air. 'Morgan, stop it, please, for the love of God let's do what we've been sent here to do. Let's play nice, do what the boss has asked, tick some boxes and then if it doesn't work out, we can all look into your theory.'

Morgan nodded; she was annoyed with Amy, but she knew she was right. They would either find more evidence to incriminate Luke or to prove his innocence. She wasn't giving up on her theory though; she wasn't convinced that Heather Rigg was as innocent as she was making out.

THIRTY-FIVE

The search wielded nothing useful. No meat cleaver, no more photographs of Sally Lawson. Unless Luke had them stored on his laptop, which was a possibility. Morgan had expected Luke to have a desktop computer, he didn't, just a laptop, which they seized and bagged up to be sent off to the tech unit. They'd finished the office and bedroom when Wendy arrived. Now that she had arrived, they could look in the most important place – the freezer.

Morgan smiled at her, then turned to Heather. 'Is it okay if we search your freezer?'

Heather looked confused. 'Why on earth do you want to search that?'

'We found some vital evidence inside the Lawsons' freezer, and we need to check to see if there is anything similar inside yours.'

'Help yourself.'

All four women walked into the kitchen. Wendy photographed the kitchen, then the fridge freezer. It wasn't as huge as the one in the Lawsons' kitchen. Tugging open the door with her gloved hand she opened each drawer, removing the contents and looking inside bags that were open, feeling the ones that were closed.

'What the hell are you looking for? Human body parts?' Heather began to laugh, then realised no one else was and her face became serious. 'Jesus Christ, you think that the Lawsons' hands are in my freezer.'

Amy glanced at Morgan, who nodded. 'How did you know about the missing hands?'

'How do you think? Luke, he couldn't stop talking about how awful it was and why someone would want to chop off a person's hand. Oh, you think that he did it, he chopped off their hands and put them in the freezer. I'm going to be sick.' She was shaking her head. 'He's too much of a wimp to do something like that, he really is, he doesn't even like chopping up the chicken breasts when it's his turn to cook.'

Morgan stared at Heather. 'You don't mind doing that though, do you?'

'What do you mean by that? I don't particularly enjoy it, but no, it doesn't bother me especially if we want to eat a wholesome meal.'

'Luke said that you worked in the butchers on the high street.'

'Oh, he did, did he? Seems like he was as keen to talk about me as I am about him. Yes, I did but I didn't even last a month, I couldn't stand it, the smell was just awful.'

Wendy continued checking every item in the freezer, then turned to Morgan and shook her head.

'Well, thanks for letting us in, Heather, we haven't taken much, just his laptop. Do you want to go and pack him a suitcase?'

Heather didn't speak, her face solemn, her eyes downcast. She nodded and left them whilst she went upstairs to pack him some clothes.

Wendy whispered, 'Well, that was awkward, she's a bit of a weird woman, isn't she?'

Amy whispered back, 'It takes all sorts.'

They heard her opening and slamming drawers, banging wardrobe doors then the sound of her footsteps stomping along the hallway and down the stairs. She appeared red-faced and out of breath.

'Just so you know, I'd never hurt a fly let alone do something like that. In case you're wondering, I couldn't even if I wanted to, and I didn't want to not one little bit. Sally was my friend until he ruined it.'

She thrust the cabin-sized suitcase at Morgan, who grabbed it from her.

'Thank you, we'll pass this on to Luke.'

All three women walked out of the Riggs' house, breathing a sigh of relief to be out of the awkward atmosphere and into the fresh air.

THIRTY-SIX

By the time Luke Rigg had been booked into custody, had his DNA and fingerprints taken, and his upper body checked for any scratches, his solicitor had arrived. He was taken into an interview room where Lucy O'Gara was waiting for him. She looked at Ben and smiled. 'Thank you, but I'd like to speak with my client alone first.'

Ben nodded and left them to it, going to stand at the custody desk with Jo, the on-duty sergeant. Cain was already there sitting on a chair, feet up looking comfortable.

'He's gone very quiet after all that effort to get him in here.'

'Probably realised that it's better to be compliant and get it over with. Do you think he's going to cough?' asked Jo. Cough was police speak for a confession.

Ben shrugged. 'Be nice if he did, we could get this thing put to bed. Somehow, I don't see Luke Rigg as the confessing type though, I think he'll believe he's far cleverer than us and play the game.'

'Lucy won't let him anyway, will she?'

'Probably not, but it depends on how good the story he tells her is. If he's in there playing the victim, she might believe everything he tells her.'

Ben sat down next to Jo, all three of them waiting for Lucy to give them a shout.

It didn't take long before she was at the door beckoning them in. Ben went in, followed by Cain who towered over him. They sat down and Lucy smiled at them.

'My client maintains his innocence in all of this, and he is going to use his right to remain silent. You may present your evidence and we'll take it from there.'

'Very well, but these are serious crimes and it would be in your client's best interests to help us with our enquiries.'

Ben looked at Luke Rigg who was sitting tight-lipped, fury shining out of his eyes at the indignity of the situation. Ben sat up straight and stared Luke Rigg in the eyes as he introduced everyone for the benefit of the tape and then began to ask the questions he'd carefully put together, the frustration as Luke replied no comment to each one giving him heartburn.

Lucy smiled at Ben. 'I believe you have evidence of Timothy Lawson coming home from school that day accompanied by an unidentified person. We'd like to see that, please.'

Ben knew that Lucy was going to ask to see it, and he had it ready to play on the station laptop. As Luke and Lucy watched, Luke began to laugh, Ben pushed his hands underneath the table so that neither Lucy nor Luke could see his fingers curling into tight fists.

'What's so funny about that clip, Luke? Tim is walking home and unbeknown to him, about to be brutally murdered. His entire family were killed in cold blood, executed as if they were nothing, and you are finding this hilarious. It could have been Ava and Heather, it could have been you.'

He stopped laughing. 'I'm not laughing at Tim, I'm laughing at whoever is behind him, because there is no way that's me. Is that the best you have?'

Ben glanced at Cain, asking Luke, 'Do you know who the person with Tim is?'

Luke leaned closer. 'Play it again.'

Ben did, twice.

Luke leaned back in his chair, his fingers clasped together on the table in front of him. 'I can tell you one thing, have you asked Heather about this? It looks suspiciously like her. She was out walking at the time or so she said, maybe you should be bringing her in, taking her prints and DNA.' He smiled at Ben.

Lucy looked up from her notes. 'Is that all the evidence you have, DS Matthews?'

'No, we have the photographs from Luke's phone of Sally Lawson, and we believe that you, Luke, were desperate to start a relationship with her, but she turned you away, didn't she? Were you so annoyed that she didn't want to start an affair with you that you thought you'd take your revenge by killing her entire family?'

Luke stared into Ben's eyes, not blinking until he finally smiled and spoke. 'No comment.'

Ben wanted to lean across the table and punch Luke Rigg right between the eyes; instead he looked down at the clipboard with his notes, breathing slowly to calm himself down.

'Tell me about Isaiah.'

'Who is he?'

Ben felt every last piece of the confidence he'd had about bringing Luke Rigg in drain away.

'We believe it's an online game that Tim Lawson was playing on the Dark Web, did Tim ever ask you about the Dark Web?'

He shrugged. 'I barely knew Tim except to say hello to. How would I know what games he was playing and no, we never talked about gaming or the Dark Web?'

Lucy looked at Ben. 'From what I can see everything you have is circumstantial, DS Matthews. Do you have anything that would forensically link my client to the scene? And let's not forget that my client spent a lot of time at the Lawsons' house, they were neighbours as well as friends. If you have nothing substantial, then I'm going to suggest that we close this interview here, and I wouldn't suggest bringing my client back unless you have concrete evidence of his involvement.'

Ben said, 'For the benefit of the tape, interview stopped at sixteen forty-two.' He looked at Luke. 'You will now be taken to be pre-charge bailed. Do you have an alternative address you can go to?'

Luke looked confused. 'Why would I need that when I have my own home?'

'For your family's safety you're not allowed to stay there or have any contact with your wife or daughter while we carry out further enquiries.'

'You're having a laugh; I haven't done anything, what has Heather said?'

'I'm not at liberty to discuss what your wife has disclosed.'

Luke's cheeks flushed a deep red. 'I don't understand, what the hell could she say that would cause all of this? I told you she's off her Sertraline; it's been causing her to have significant mood swings and feeling depressed even more so than before she started to take it.' Seeing that Ben wasn't going to answer, he said, 'I can stop at my mother's, she lives at Derwent Avenue.'

Ben looked at Cain. 'Could you please bail Mr Rigg?'

'Yes, sarge.' Cain turned to Luke. 'Come on then, let's get your bail date from the custody sergeant and then you're free to go.'

Ben thanked Lucy, then left. He had to get away from Luke Rigg before his head exploded.

As he walked out of the custody suite, Cathy waved him over to the small room they were using to view the CCTV footage which had been seized from the houses in Hest Bank Road.

'I have something to show you, sorry we missed it the first time around. It was on a pen drive that we thought had been viewed but it hadn't.'

'Please tell me it's good, and that it involves Luke Rigg leaving the Lawsons' house carrying a bloodied meat cleaver.'

'Erm, no, but it shows a clearer picture of the person who came home with Tim. You better just watch it. So this is a different pen drive, it shows the door about thirty minutes after we saw Tim and the guy going inside. I've forwarded through the half hour of the door being closed.'

She pressed play as Ben sat down on the chair to watch. Soon enough, the front door opened and the person they had seen entering walked out of the hallway and down the drive, hood down. Whoever it was looked around the same age as Tim, now they had a better image of him. He turned to wave as Tim closed the front door.

'Sorry, I can't believe we missed this. Sam took a still to the school and the head of year, Mr Mackintosh, identified him as Ryan Cross, who is in the year above Tim. He's been off school with appendicitis; he got taken into hospital the same night the Lawsons were murdered and is at home now, recovering from his operation.'

Ben scrubbed his hand across his face. 'It's okay, thank you, that's some excellent work there by you and Sam, do you fancy joining CID?' He smiled at her while she shook her head.

'Erm, no thanks, you lot are busier than section. We're after an easier working life not harder.'

He laughed. 'I don't blame you, but thanks, at least we know that when Ryan left Tim, he was still alive and breathing. We can cross Ryan off the most-wanted list, though I think we need to have a chat with him. He might know about the game and also could have noticed anyone hanging around when he left.'

Ben left Cathy and headed straight for the gents. He needed to take a minute to calm down, he was so tightly wound, and the only place he wouldn't be disturbed was sitting on the toilet lid, in a cubicle with the door locked, whilst trying to breathe deeply in and out like Morgan taught him, to slow his heart rate and blood pressure.

THIRTY-SEVEN

Natalie dropped Annie off at Practical Magic. She loved the place; it gave her such happy vibes and being here saved her from rattling around that house on her own. She had never wanted a drink so badly in her life; her hands were shaking just thinking about how good it would be to open the bottle of icy cold vodka Jasper kept in their freezer, and to just chug it down right out of the bottle. Or one of the cold bottles of white wine or rosé he kept in the wine chiller. She had never told Jasper she was a recovering alcoholic when they met; she hadn't told Jasper a lot of things and he'd never asked. Whenever the subject of alcohol came up, she always told him she hated the taste of the stuff and the way it made her feel. It was probably one of the biggest lies she'd ever told him, because in actual fact she loved it, craved it daily. He'd put the huge wine chiller in the kitchen, and kept a well-stocked bar of every spirit under the sun in one of the downstairs lounges. She avoided that room at all costs unless they were socialising. The kitchen though, that was impossible to keep out of, so she tried her best to ignore the bottles of wine, telling herself this was her punishment, it was what she deserved, and that God was tempting her to make her stronger. Of course, she didn't believe any of that bullshit, but she had to tell herself something as she stared longingly at the bottles of wine that seemed to call her name every time she walked into the kitchen.

She eyed the salon opposite the shop. Maybe she could go in and ask if they could squeeze her in for a massage, to take her mind off getting mind-numbingly drunk. Annie was lovely and her detective friend was nice, but it had unsettled her even more having them look around her home. She'd thought they'd be able to come out with it and tell her she was living in a haunted house. But there had only been, what had Annie called it? 'Residual energy,' something like that. But if there was no ghost, why did she feel as if there was something terrible waiting in the shadows for her? She pushed the thought from her mind, she was being ridiculous. That night, that drunken night she had pushed to the far depths of her mind never to think about it ever again, was that what this was? A horn blared behind her, and she realised she was holding up the traffic on the narrow, busy road. Pulling out from the kerb she stuck her hand out of the window to wave an apology to the bus driver who was shaking her head at her. What was she going to do? She could go and see Harry, he'd calm her down, yes that was a good idea, why didn't she go and see him? Who else was there? If Harry wasn't available, she could go and see that nice new vicar at St Martha's, maybe it was time to confess her sins. It might make her feel better and, if she was being haunted, then it might be what they needed her to do. Harry worked at the Mere Hotel, a small boutique establishment with themed rooms that in Natalie's opinion were horribly bad taste, but it was popular with couples. He managed it and lived in. She'd only ever been there once before, to meet him for coffee when he was short-staffed and couldn't make their usual Friday lunchtime meetup at the café.

She parked in the small car park, squeezing her Porsche 4x4

in, not caring that she was blocking two cars in – if they needed her to move, she'd do it. Right now, she needed to speak to Harry because if she didn't, she was afraid she'd go straight to the nearest pub and get drunk.

Inside, the hotel was busy with couples checking in and out. Harry waved at her from behind the reception desk, looking flustered, and she felt bad. This was a bad time for him, but still he waved her over. She walked behind the desk as if she belonged there. Waiting for him to finish checking in the Spanish couple, who were giving daggers to each other. Harry kept on smiling and passed them the room keys. As they walked away, he whispered to her, 'What's wrong?'

The next couple stepped up to the desk, and she smiled at them and whispered, 'Nothing, I'm sorry, I didn't know this was your busy time, I'll come back later.'

She walked away as Harry greeted the customers, hearing him call after her.

'Natalie, call me if you need to speak about anything, I mean it.'

Waving her hand at him she went back to her car, feeling awful for putting him on the spot. He was one of the good guys. She was a bad person; she wasn't deserving of the time and effort that he put into being her sponsor.

THIRTY-EIGHT

Maggie was sitting curled up on the sofa reading, which was her favourite pastime. Her new Kindle meant she didn't even need her reading glasses because the font was big enough to read without them. She was thoroughly enjoying *Malibu Rising* by Taylor Jenkins Reid, a new author to her, but she knew she was going to have to read every other book she had written. There was an almighty crash from outside somewhere, so loud it set Roley off barking, and Maggie dropped her Kindle as she scrambled off the sofa to see what it was. Across the road at the Riggs' house there was a gaping hole in the front window, and the blinds were flapping in and out with the breeze. Maggie felt her heart begin to race, who had done such a thing? This was turning into the kind of terrible street that you heard about on the news, where all the neighbours hated each other and had those ASBOs to try and make them keep the peace. She heard shouting coming from across the road, picked up her phone and dialled 999, then pushing her feet into her slippers she rushed as fast as she could over there. She had never heard poor Sally or Tim or David crying for help, she certainly wasn't going to ignore whatever was happening here.

The front door was wide open. Ava was standing in the hallway her eyes wide, staring into the front lounge where the shouting was coming from. Maggie stepped in, took one look at the girl and whispered, 'Go and wait in my house, dear, the police are on the way, we need to get you to safety.'

'Don't you fucking dare come in here and interfere.'

Luke's voice was loud and venomous as he turned to her. Maggie grabbed hold of Ava's arm, pushing her out of the door.

'Go now, lock the door when you get there.'

Ava nodded, her eyes fixed on the huge knife that Luke was brandishing as he waved it around. Then she turned and ran across the road to Maggie's bungalow, slamming the door shut. Maggie heard Roley bark in surprise, but she also heard the key turn in the lock and thought *good girl* to herself. She turned to look at Luke, who was pacing up and down. He looked wild. Heather was crouched in the corner, blood running down her cheek, but it wasn't too bad.

'Luke, what's the matter? You need to calm down.'

'Don't tell me to calm down.'

His eyes were wide, and spittle flew from the corner of his mouth as he shouted in Maggie's direction. He took a couple of steps towards her. The blade of the knife glinted under the bright white lighting, and she could see a couple of drips of blood running down the blade.

'Whatever is going on I'm sure we can talk it through, Luke, there's no need for this. Heather is bleeding and you've scared Ava.'

'Heather can bleed to death for all I care, the traitorous bitch. She tried to set me up. She told the police I killed them, the crazy, lying cow.'

Maggie felt her stomach begin to knot up. The knife was huge, and he was suddenly standing right in front of her. She glanced to her bungalow where Ava was watching from the front window, then turning her back to Ava she faced Luke.

'Well, they didn't believe her otherwise you wouldn't be standing here now, would you? Give me the knife, Luke, you don't want to hurt anyone, do you?'

Heather was no longer crouching in the corner; she had pulled herself up and picked up a large brass poker off the fireplace.

'I want to hurt Heather. She's a liar, a devious sneaky little bitch and a cheat. She doesn't deserve to live when Sally is dead.'

Sirens cut through the early evening air just as Heather lifted the poker and brought it down hard against the back of Luke's head. He fell forwards, towards Maggie who instinctively reached out her arms to catch him. As he toppled towards the old woman the knife blade pierced the paper-thin skin on her chest as it sank deep inside of her. Maggie let out a surprised 'Oh' as her legs gave out under her, and she slid against the wall to the floor. Luke fell to his knees as Heather hit him again, and this time he blacked out and hit the wooden flooring with a loud thud.

Morgan heard the call come in over the airwaves radio, and as she wasn't far from Hest Bank Road, she straight away turned the car around. She arrived before the first patrol van and went running into the Riggs' house without even thinking about her own safety. The hallway was absolute carnage but the only thing she cared about was Maggie, who was on the floor, her face ashen, with a large knife sticking out of her chest.

'Maggie.' She knelt down next to her. 'It's okay, don't worry, you'll be okay, we'll get this out of you in no time.' Morgan knew that she couldn't pull the knife out because at the moment it was like a plug keeping the blood suctioned in. She glanced at Heather, who was holding a bloodied brass poker, and the unconscious Luke, who was lying on the floor.

'Control, we need an ambulance now to Hest Bank Road, number thirteen. One unconscious, one severe stab wound.' She looked at Heather. 'It's okay, Heather, put the poker down, officers will be here any second.'

The sirens were so close they were deafening. Maggie closed her eyes.

'Maggie, Maggie, I need you to keep looking at me.' Morgan gently took hold of her hand, sitting next to her and leaning her back against the wall. Her Doc Marten boots were near enough to Luke's head that if he so much as moved an inch she would kick him as hard as she could.

Maggie looked at Morgan and she smiled at the woman. 'You're doing great, the ambulance won't be long.'

Maggie coughed and a trickle of blood ran down her lips. 'I don't feel so great, please will you look after Roley for me?'

She nodded. 'Of course, I will, but you'll be home in no time to look after him yourself.'

The slamming of van doors outside signalled the arrival of backup. Finally. It always amazed Morgan how in situations so desperately serious, every second felt like an hour, yet it had probably been three minutes tops. Al, who was the only taser officer on duty, ran in and his mouth dropped open as he surveyed the scene.

'Are you okay, Morgan?'

She looked down and saw that she had blood on her hands.

'I'm fine, any update on the ambulance?'

More sirens in the distance was her answer and she felt a rush of relief. Luke let out a groan. Morgan pointed in his direction.

'He's going to need to go to the hospital, head wound, but Maggie is priority. I don't care if his skull is sticking out of his head, Maggie goes first.'

Al nodded. 'Does he need cuffing?'

'Probably, I got here afterwards. Heather what happened?'

'He was going crazy; he smashed the window then climbed in through it. I'd had the locks changed whilst he was at the police station. He had a knife, Maggie came over and sent Ava to her house, then he just turned on her. She was only trying to help, so I hit him over the head with the first thing I could grab. I didn't mean to hit him that hard. But he fell, and he stabbed Maggie.'

'Ava is okay, she's not injured?'

'No, she's in Maggie's house over the road.'

'Good, that's good.'

Al looked at the two officers behind him. 'I think we're going to have to bring Heather in for a statement, but he's going to need you two to babysit him at the hospital in case he kicks off.'

Footsteps outside and van doors slamming signalled the paramedics who came rushing in then stopped dead.

'Oh.'

Morgan smiled at Nick who had attended her quite a few times in the past. 'This is nothing to do with me.'

He nodded, then bent down to start working on Maggie. His colleague checked Luke out, but soon turned his attention to Nick and began to assist him.

'He's got a nasty cut on the back of his head, but he's starting to regain consciousness.'

Morgan moved away from Maggie to let them work on her, just as Ben arrived with Cain.

'What the hell happened?' he demanded.

'Luke lost it with Heather, by all accounts, for changing the locks.'

'Morgan, are you bleeding?' The concern on Ben's face mirrored hers as she watched Nick working on Maggie. 'No, it's not mine.' She knew he wanted to grab her and hug her, but he wouldn't; he would wait until they were alone. She also knew he was going to be furious with her for running into this without waiting for backup to arrive.

He looked around. Heather was standing staring down at Luke. Al pointed to Heather.

'I'll take Heather to the station and get her booked in. Col and Lisa are going to accompany Luke here to the hospital, in case he's still as angry when he regains consciousness.'

Morgan looked at Ben. 'I'll go with Maggie, see if I can get a statement from her and check on her injury.'

Ben looked unsure. She knew he was judging whether he wanted her anywhere near Luke Rigg, injured or not. 'I'll be fine, I have to go with her, Ben, she has no one.'

'Okay, but as soon as you have an update on her condition, I want you out of there, Morgan.'

'Oh God, Ava is in Maggie's house, someone is going to have to go and tell her what's happened and check on Maggie's dog.'

'We'll go and get Ava, but really, we have to sort the dog out?'

She nodded. 'I promised Maggie we would make sure he was okay. When you lock up take the key to the front door to the station, and I'll get it from you so I can check on him later on.'

Ben rolled his eyes at her, and she knew what he was thinking: they already had Des's cat, Kevin, to take care of, she wasn't sure he would let her bring Maggie's dog home with her too. But they couldn't leave him in the house on his own.

Al escorted Heather out of the house to the back of his van and helped her inside. Ava came running out of Maggie's house screaming, 'Mum, Mum.'

It was Ben who intervened; he rushed towards her and gently took hold of her arm.

'She's okay, Ava, we just need to get a statement off her, to find out what's happened.'

'She didn't do anything; we were eating our tea, watching

the TV, when one of the stones out of the garden crashed through the living room window, covering us in glass.'

'I'll take you in my car back to the station to wait for your mum or until we can find someone to come and collect you. Amy will write down what happened, so we have it on file. Is that okay?'

'I'll wait for my mum; I'm not leaving without her. Is Maggie okay, where's my dad?'

'Maggie is in good hands and your dad is still inside, let's just get you back to the station.'

Al had already driven away; Morgan was getting into the back of the ambulance with Nick and Maggie. Another was on its way to transport Luke to A&E, to get his head looked at, and two PCSOs were on their way to scene guard the house until it had been documented by CSI. Then a joiner would be called out to board up the broken window.

THIRTY-NINE

Natalie had looked different today, almost like every other forty-something woman should. No tight sportswear, no neat hair or perfect make-up, she'd looked a little frazzled, one could almost say haunted. This made the person watching her smile. They'd looked on as she sat at her usual seat chatting to the woman who owned the café, no yoga friend today which was a first.

'What's eating you, Natalie?' they whispered to themselves.

'What did you just say, are you talking to me?' the supervisor had asked.

They had snapped their gaze away from the café across the road, not realising they'd spoken out loud.

'No, just singing along to the radio.'

The supervisor had frowned but didn't ask anything else, and went back to gossiping with a customer. That had been careless, and they had been lucky to get away with it. Now it kept replaying on their mind; they realised they were getting sloppy, and it wouldn't do.

They didn't know what was wrong with Natalie, but she wasn't her usual self. For all her being the wife of a rich guy she looked more miserable than they did waiting for payday. Still, it was what she deserved, wasn't it? Somehow, they didn't think that killing her husband would upset her that much. He was hardly home; the kid was almost as bad as he was, she was rarely there either. Such a big house for poor Natalie to wander around in. Still, she wouldn't have to do it for much longer. Soon she'd be dead. They could just kill her quickly, but where was the fun in that? And it would be over way too fast, whereas they liked to make things last. If they killed Jasper though, then Lexie, and saved Natalie until the end, would she know that this was all her fault? Just like with Sally Lawson, would she realise that she was the reason her family had been killed?

They smiled in happy anticipation. The police had no idea what was going on, the plan was working perfectly. The only worry was the visitor from today. They had seen her photograph in the local paper many times, had even met her, and they were hoping that Detective Constable Morgan Brookes wasn't as good as her reputation. If she figured out what was happening that could ruin everything, and they really didn't want to have to deal with her as well, when she had never been a part of the original plan.

FORTY

It was chaos at the hospital; Maggie had been first to arrive and had been rushed down for surgery to remove the knife and deal with her internal injuries. The doctor had been lovely, mistaking Morgan for her granddaughter and telling her she may as well go home because she might be some time yet, and then Maggie would be going into Intensive Care to recover. Morgan had kissed Maggie's cheek before they whisked her away, and promised her she would take care of Roley. Big, wet tears slid down Morgan's cheeks and she realised that she was definitely too involved, but she liked Maggie and the woman had no one else. As she was walking out the next ambulance to arrive had Luke Rigg in the back, and she hung back to see what kind of mood he was in and if the two officers with him needed a hand. When the doors opened and he was brought down on the tail lift, he was lying there staring into the distance. Morgan looked at the officer in the back of the ambulance who had accompanied him.

'He's a lot calmer now, aren't you, Luke? Got a bit of a headache too I should imagine.'

There was a gauze bandage wrapped around his head. He

looked at Morgan and whispered, 'How's Maggie? It was an accident. I didn't mean to hurt her.'

'She's gone down to surgery.'

He closed his eyes. 'I'm sorry, it's all such a mess.'

She didn't answer him because yes, it was a complete mess, and she didn't know how his family were going to recover from this. They would, of course they would, but she couldn't shake the feeling Heather had set Luke up from the minute she got a chance, and she wanted to know why. What was it about the man that had made her want to frame him for murder and then almost kill him as soon as she got the chance?

'Do you need me at all?' Morgan asked the officers.

Col shook his head. 'Me and Luke made a pinkie promise in the back of the ambulance, we have an agreement, don't we? No more angry outbursts; he's going to try some deep breathing instead and hopefully the docs will give him something to ease the pain and chill him the fuck out. Isn't that right, Stu?'

Morgan had to turn away to stifle the laughter threatening to explode out of her mouth. Col had a way with words, but it always seemed to work with the angry guys and girls. Sometimes a bit of plain talking was what a person needed to bring them back down to earth, and it looked as if Luke had come down fast when he'd realised just how much trouble he was in.

'I'm going back to the station. If you get an update on Maggie when she's out of surgery, can you ring me, Col? I'm desperate to know that she's okay and made it.'

He gave her a thumbs up as the paramedics began to wheel Luke through the automatic doors. Nick glanced back at her and gave her a smile, and she smiled back. They'd come close to going out a couple of times, she liked him but not as much as she loved Ben. What a day, she was exhausted just trying to get her head around the last hour. Instead of solving the Lawsons' murder, now they had to investigate Maggie's attempted murder, providing she made it through surgery, as well as Luke's criminal damage and Heather's assault on Luke. Morgan squeezed her eyes shut then opened them again. To top all of this off, everyone was starving because she'd totally screwed up the lunch run by getting sidetracked and going off with Annie to visit Natalie White. She walked towards the car park then stopped dead in her tracks, she didn't even have a vehicle to go back because she'd accompanied Maggie. There was a broken wooden fence running along one side of the car park, and Morgan sat down on it and phoned the office. It was Cain who answered.

'CID.'

'Hey, are you busy?'

'Well, I'd have to ask the boss if I am or not. He's about to interview Heather Rigg and I'm not sure if he needs me, why?'

'I'm stranded at the Royal Lancaster Infirmary.'

Morgan spotted a familiar face, crossing the road, and stood up. 'Actually, it might be okay. I'll see if Declan can drop me off.'

She hung up and waved her arms in the air. 'Declan.' Her voice was so loud everyone in the car park turned to stare at her.

Declan stopped, then waved at her.

She crossed to where he was standing. 'Are you busy?'

'Not for you, my sweet, what's up, has lover boy dumped you here?'

She grinned. 'I came here with a serious stabbing victim, but she's gone into surgery and might be hours yet. Could you give me a lift back to the station?'

'Rydal Falls, Lord that place is like a hotbed of violence. Yes, my love, but only because it's you and I would hate to see you stranded here. You know Lancaster is a busy city, with a thriving university, and somehow we don't have half the number of violent attacks you get in that quaint beauty spot.'

'Tell me about it, I'm fed up with it.'

She walked with him until they reached his pristine white Audi.

'And I'm hungry too, with a blinding headache. It's been the longest day.'

'That's not good, if you want my advice. I can stop off at the McDonald's drive-thru on the way and you can fill your boots.'

'That might be a good idea, thanks, Declan.'

As he smiled at her, she realised that she might just be able to redeem herself, if she brought back everyone a Maccies. There were no fried chicken or burger restaurants in Rydal Falls, and they would be so hungry they wouldn't care if it was cold by the time she got back.

FORTY-ONE

Morgan walked into the office with bags of cold, greasy Maccies in one hand and a tray of colas in the other. Both Amy and Cain fell to their knees, their hands offered up to the sky in prayer, bowing their heads.

'Hahaha, aren't you two the perfect comedy duo. Get up, you pair of idiots, I got Big Macs and large fries all round.'

'I'm forgiving you for messing up lunchtime, Saint Morgan.'

'Thanks, Amy, that's great to hear.'

Cain had pried one of the bags from Morgan's hands and was shoving a handful of lukewarm fries into his mouth. Amy took her burger and sat at the desk sniffing it before lifting it to her mouth and taking a huge bite.

'You two are animals, don't you want to at least warm them up in the microwave?'

'Nah, we're good and too hungry.'

She shrugged. 'Where's Ben?'

'Probably passed out in the corridor somewhere of starvation.'

'Amy.'

'All right, he's with the boss discussing what to do with the lovely Heather Rigg.'

'Where's Ava?'

'With Sam and Tina, they're waiting with her until Heather is released. Ava won't go anywhere without her mum apparently, even though her mum is as deranged as her dad, poor kid.'

Amy relayed this information through a mouthful of burger and lettuce, as Ben walked in the door and stared at her in disgust.

'Didn't your mother teach you it was rude to speak with your mouth full?'

She nodded, then carried on eating. Ben looked longingly at the burger she was munching on.

'I got you one too, it's a bit cold though.'

'I don't care, thank you. How's Maggie, and was Luke behaving himself when you left?'

'Maggie is in surgery; I'm praying she'll be okay, bless her. Thanks to Col, Luke has seen the error of his ways; he said it was an accident and he didn't mean to hurt Maggie, and he was sorry.'

'Blimey, we better get Col to attend all our raging, angry offenders.'

She smiled. 'What's happening with Heather?'

'Tricky because she can claim it was self-defence, after all he broke through the window and was waving a knife around. What I don't like is the fact that she hit him hard twice across the back of the head when once was enough. If he hadn't fallen forwards, Maggie wouldn't have been stabbed. He's a tall guy, he went down heavy with the knife in his hand.'

'How do you know she hit him twice?'

'All the way back she kept saying what a mess it was, and she didn't mean to hit him twice. The DI thinks we need to charge her with GBH, so we can keep an eye on her.'

'But isn't she the victim?'

'It's complicated. Yes, she is but the only reason we brought Luke in earlier was because of her coming here and practically accusing him of killing the Lawsons. We have to take into account that she might have been setting him up, with an ulterior motive, which I should have thought about earlier. This is kind of my fault.'

'Hardly your fault, you weren't to know how he was going to react.'

Ben took his bag of food out to the small kitchen area down the corridor and warmed it up before coming back. He sat at Des's empty desk, muttering, 'Sorry, Des.'

Morgan was trying to figure it all out. She'd eaten her food in Declan's car whilst it was still warm and he was catching her up on his latest love life news.

Ben looked at her. 'How did you get back here so fast?'

'Declan. He was finishing work and he kindly dropped me off.'

Ben smiled. 'He's a good one, oh here's the key for Maggie's house.'

She nodded, taking the key from him. 'Have you spoken with Ava yet?'

'No, I think it might be better for you to speak with her. She's seen you a couple of times now, so she might feel more comfortable talking to you than me.'

'Where is she?'

'In the canteen with Tina and Sam. I don't know how long we're going to keep Heather for, so we might need to find someone to come and collect Ava. Can you ask if there's someone who she'll go with instead of sitting here for hours?'

'Of course.'

Morgan left them to it. She'd much rather speak with Ava than Heather, because if she went into an interview with Ben she'd have to turn her phone off, and she was waiting for a call from either Col or the hospital with an update on Maggie.

The canteen was empty apart from Tina, Sam and Ava. They were all watching *Love Island*, although it was clear Ava was distracted. Morgan shook her head; she'd rather poke her own eyes out but each to their own.

'Ava, is it okay to have a chat about earlier?'

Ava turned to look at her, then nodded.

Sam turned the television off. 'Are we okay to go get a brew?'

'Of course.'

Both PCSOs left Morgan and Ava alone. The girl looked tired; she was sipping a can of Vimto.

'Rough couple of days for you, how are you?'

She shrugged. 'Tired, is Maggie okay? I feel awful. She came over and pushed me out of the door, told me to go and wait in her bungalow until everything calmed down. Last week everything was normal, and now it's a complete mess.'

Morgan felt tired too, everything felt too heavy. 'She's in surgery. I'm just waiting on an update, but I'm sure she'll be fine.' Morgan had her fingers crossed under the table as she said it. 'Does your dad normally lose his temper like that?'

Ava shook her head. 'I've never seen him like that, him and Mum argue but it's usually her that starts them. He always tries to keep the peace with her, because she doesn't speak to him for days when they fall out and he hates the atmosphere. Did she tell you she hasn't been taking her meds? She said they made her worse, but clearly they didn't because she's far worse now without them.'

'Ava, I know you're not stupid and you must know what this is all about, so I'm not going to insult you by pretending that you don't. Was your dad having an affair with Sally?'

'No, I think he might have wanted to, but Sally definitely didn't.'

'How do you know that?'

'Tim, he told me he heard his mum telling my dad that she wasn't interested in him. That he was ruining their friendship. He said he was so embarrassed listening to it.'

'How did your dad react; did Tim tell you that?'

'He said he cried.'

'He wasn't angry?'

'No, he was crying and apologising.'

'Did your mum know about this?'

Ava rolled her eyes. 'Of course, she knows everything. She was furious with him, told him he had to sleep in the spare room or move out.'

'Does your mum have a bad temper?'

'What, you think my mum was so angry that she went and killed them all? Are you mad?'

'We have to look at every possibility or we wouldn't be doing our job.'

'No, she didn't kill them. She wouldn't do that even without her tablets.'

'Thanks. Look, we don't know how long your mum is going to be here. She has to be interviewed and it can take a while for the solicitor to turn up. Is there anyone I can contact to pick you up? What about your grandparents?'

'They're all dead.'

'Have you got any friends' houses you could go to?'

'I could phone Lexie, I suppose, she usually comes to my house, but I could go to hers for a change.'

'Lexie?'

'Lexie White, her mum will probably pick me up.'

Another cog in Morgan's brain slid into place, it was such a shame there were so many whizzing around in there, but Ava,

Tim and Lexie were all friends. Sally thought she was being haunted; Natalie thinks she's being watched or haunted.

'Morgan, do you want me to message her?'

'What?'

'Lexie, to see if her mum can pick me up?'

'Oh yes, please, that would be great I just need to check with your mum that she's happy for you to go there.'

Tina came back carrying two mugs. 'Did you want a brew, Morgan?'

'No thanks, I'm going to ask Heather if it's okay for Ava's friend's mum to pick her up. When she gets here can you let me know so I can have a word with her?'

Tina mouthed, 'Thank God,' to Morgan, who nodded.

'Ava, I just have to go and file some paperwork, but I'll come and see you before you go.'

She left Tina talking to Ava and rushed down to the custody suite to speak to Heather who had agreed that her daughter could go to Lexie's house. Morgan went upstairs, back to her office. Somehow these three teenagers were connected, and she needed to figure out what connected them.

Back upstairs she rang the tech unit, to see if anyone was still around.

'Evening, tech unit, Bev speaking.'

'Amazing, it's Morgan Brookes from—'

'Hello, Morgan, it's funny you're phoning me, I've just emailed you with a bit of an update about Isaiah.'

'You did? Bev, you're a saint, thank you. I was phoning to see if you had anything yet.'

'It's not a lot but it's definitely some kind of game where the players have to complete challenges to go up a level. It's all very basic at the moment. I couldn't get any further than the first chal-

lenge on Tim's computer. I'll keep at it though and let you know.'

'Thank you.'

'You're welcome, it's the most exciting thing I've had for a long time to be honest. It beats retrieving vile images off paedophiles' computers. Bye, Morgan.'

She hung up, and Morgan felt relieved they were getting somewhere at last.

FORTY-TWO

Morgan needed to speak to Lexie, to find out if she had heard of the game, *Isaiah*. She had a terrible feeling that all three teens may have been involved in it. Ava had denied it, though, when asked, saying she knew Tim played it; but now Morgan wondered, what if she hadn't admitted it because she hadn't wanted to get in trouble? She opened the file on her computer containing all the information from the Lawsons' crime scene. Things were getting too confusing, she wanted to start at the beginning again, to see if they had missed something. First, she looked at the photographs, at the pictures of the fire crew tackling the blaze on first arrival, and she caught her breath. They had been so busy with everything that had happened after that they hadn't really focused on why the killer had started a fire in the first place. She knew the investigator from the fire service was investigating the arson side of it and made a note to speak to Nigel. Had the killer wanted to get rid of all the evidence, or had they wanted someone to phone it in, so the bodies were discovered sooner? The more she thought about it the more she realised that they may have been overlooking vital clues. She sent all the photos to the printer. It was late but she knew Wendy was prob-

ably still at the Riggs' house. She would have a contact number
for Nigel, she thought, deciding she would call in and check on
Roley after she'd spoken to Natalie White. Her desk phone began
to ring, and she answered it, hearing Brenda's familiar voice.

*'Morgan, there's a Natalie White at the front desk to collect
Ava Rigg. Tina said you wanted a word with her.'*

'Be right down, thanks, Brenda.'

Morgan locked her computer, grabbed her laptop bag and
called at the printer to collect the copies of the photos before
stuffing them inside her bag.

She made it to the ground floor in record time, bursting through
the double doors into the reception area, making Natalie White
jump and let out a small screech.

'Sorry, can I have a quick word?'

Natalie nodded; Morgan opened the door to one of the
interview rooms.

'Thank you for coming to collect Ava, I really appreciate it.'

'What the hell has happened? I got some garbled message
from Lexie saying we had to come here for her. Is Ava in trouble? What has she done and where are her parents, shouldn't
they be the ones picking her up?'

'Ava hasn't done anything, it's her parents who have, but
you'd be better getting the full story from her. I wanted to ask
you something else while you're here. Has Lexie mentioned
playing an online game called *Isaiah*?'

Natalie looked blankly at Morgan. 'Not that I recall, should
she have, what is it?'

'I don't know, that's what I'm trying to find out. Did you
know Sally Lawson, Natalie?'

'Well I knew who she was, I sometimes go to her salon for a
fresh cut and blow dry but only occasionally. I wasn't friends

with her, she's just someone I said hello to. I don't know anything about her or her life. Look, I need to get going, I've left the dinner in the oven.'

'What about Tim? He was friends with Ava and she's best friends with Lexie, surely they all knew each other? Are you sure you didn't really know Sally that well?'

Natalie looked at her. 'I haven't really spoken to her since we were teenagers, some stupid drama. She took my boyfriend off me back then, and we fell out and never really spoke since. I'm sorry that she's dead, that they're all dead, but I can't help you.'

'Oh, I guess that must have been difficult.'

'It was a long time ago, I got over it and I didn't hold a burning grudge against her, if that's what you're wondering.'

Morgan shook her head. 'Of course not, thanks again, maybe you could ask Lexie about the game and see what she says?'

'Haha, you're kidding right. My daughter doesn't tell me what she needs for her cooking lessons, so she's barely going to tell me about some online game, but I'll ask her and let you know.'

'Thanks, I'll send Ava down now.'

Morgan opened the door so Natalie could go back into the reception area.

Swiping her ID card to let herself back into the station, she went up to the canteen. Was Natalie hiding something? She had a feeling deep down inside her stomach that she was.

'Ava, Lexie's mum is here for you. I'll let your mum know where you are when she's allowed to go home. Have you ever played a game called *Isaiah*?'

Ava shrugged. 'I don't think so. How's my dad?'

'He's okay, probably got an awful headache, but he's awake and talking.'

Ava nodded; Sam led her down to the front office so she could get out of the building. Morgan watched the pair of them go down the stairs, thinking that at least Ava had a best friend she could confide in about the downward spiral her life had just taken, and she wasn't alone.

Morgan's radio began to vibrate signalling a private call. She had no idea who it was.

'Hello.'

'Hi, it's Lisa, Col said to let you know the old lady who got stabbed earlier is out of surgery and in Intensive Care.'

'How is she?'

'Okay I think, they didn't say anything bad at least.'

'Amazing, thanks, Lisa, tell Col thanks too.'

The line went dead, and she felt a tiny spark of relief that at least something was looking up. If Maggie had survived the surgery there was a good chance she was going to be okay. She would go and speak to Wendy now, then feed the dog and take him for a quick walk. Once Heather was home, she could let Roley stop with them until Maggie was out of hospital, it was the least, she could do.

FORTY-THREE

Morgan was glad to see the CSI van still parked outside of the Riggs' house. Cathy was standing talking to the joiner who was waiting for the all clear to board up the front window. She joined them and asked, 'How's Wendy getting on?'

'Not long now I think, it's only the broken window and the hallway to document and she's almost finished in the hall.'

As if on cue Wendy appeared at the front door. She took one look at Morgan and pulled down her hood and mask.

'I'm bloody sick of this street. If I have to come back again, I'll scream. I thought this was the nice part of Rydal Falls; it's got a worse crime rate than Barrow.'

Morgan grinned. 'You're right, have you had a full report yet from the fire department about the arson at the Lawsons'?'

'Everything takes time, Morgan, not every emergency service has a Wendy or a Claire to jump to it and work God knows what hours to make sure everything is rushed through.'

'I know, aren't we the lucky ones? Thank you, Wendy, I love you.'

Her stern face broke into a wide grin as she laughed. 'Cain

is a bad influence on you, next you'll be walking around hugging people.'

'Only the people I like, I'm not really the hugging kind.'

'I can give you Nigel's number, if you want to speak to him. He might not be on duty or on call though, so don't expect a miracle.'

'That would be amazing, thank you. I have a couple of questions that's all.'

She turned to Cathy. 'Do we still have a key for the Lawsons' house?'

Cathy patted the pocket on her body armour. 'Aren't you in luck? I forgot to hand it over to the duty sergeant before I came down here. You can have it and sign it back in. I'm as fed up with this place as Wendy. I've spent the last three days of my shift down here and each time I come back it's worse than the day before.'

Rooting around in the pocket she pulled out around fifteen pens, a half-eaten packet of soft mints and finally a small, red plastic keyring. 'There you go, knock yourself out.'

Morgan took it from her and smiled. 'You're a lifesaver too, thanks, Cathy. Make sure Ben buys you guys a takeaway as a thank you for all your hard work.'

Cathy laughed. 'He's going to kill you for suggesting that because now that you have, I won't be able to let it go.'

She shrugged. 'It's the least he can do, a bit of appreciation and all that.'

Wendy, who was on the front lawn photographing the broken window, turned to look at her. 'He can bloody buy me a pizza too after this week.'

'He will, and if he doesn't then I definitely will.'

She winked at them and began to walk the short distance to the Lawsons' house.

. . .

Because of the fire damage by the front door and in the hall, they had been using the bifold doors at the rear of the house to go in and out. At least until they got the all clear from Fire. The front was smoky and sooty, so at least going in this way saved her boots and clothes from getting all blackened and smelly. The garden was lit up, well placed lights around it including solar lights, fairy lights and lights built into the side of the decking gave it a lovely warm glow. Enough to make sitting out here on a chilly autumn night, in a big woolly jumper, with a mug of hot chocolate, the perfect place to be. Something about this space really spoke to Morgan on some deep level, and she thought it was so sad that the Lawsons could no longer make use of it.

Opening the doors, she stepped inside and for a brief moment was taken back to the night of the murders. She would never forget the first time she set eyes on the Lawsons. It was horrific and also terribly sad. The smell of burned wood lingered in the air, which to Morgan was better than the smell of blood, although she could still smell the underlying coppery tang, but the competing smell of the smoke damage was stronger. The table was still a mess of dried blood that had soaked into the wood. She didn't look at it, not wanting to see the Lawsons' slumped bodies staring back at her. As she walked out of the kitchen into the hallway, where the worst of the smoke damage was, her phone beeped. It was a message from Wendy, with a phone number and a fire emoji next to it. She was no fire investigator, but she could tell that the fire had been started in front of the door, blocking anyone from getting out or in. The killer set the fire, then left through the back door, escaping through a gap in the garden hedging and keeping out of sight. Everywhere was still damp from the fire hoses and she wanted to sit down and think about things, but not in here.

Morgan made her way to the outdoor sofa where she sat down, still thinking about the reason for the fire. She dialled the number Wendy had sent her, expecting it to go straight to answerphone and was shocked to hear a voice answer.

'*Evening, Nigel Adams, how can I help?*'

'Hi, Nigel, it's DC Morgan Brookes. I'm sorry to disturb you so late, but I'm at the Lawsons' house and wondered if you had any updates. I'm trying to figure out why the killer set the fire in the first place.'

Nigel's voice was warm and friendly. '*That's a million-dollar question, isn't it? I still haven't finished my official report, Morgan, but there's a few things I can tell you that might help you make sense of it all.*'

'That would be brilliant and very much appreciated.'

'*Well then, I'll start at the beginning, the seat of the fire was on the rug at the front door. Arsonists like to choose their target area to make sure it's in the right place; the point of origin must be in a place that is going to ensure the flames can reach fresh fuel, enabling the spread of flames. I think that whoever set this fire knew enough about fires to make them more than likely a serial arsonist, however they're not the brightest.*'

'Why?'

'*It's a relatively new house and new houses are built with all sorts of flame retardant materials. The base of the walls for instance would be a great location for the point of origin because fire spreads fastest across the underside of a ceiling. If this had been an older, terraced house built in the 1950s, the fire would have spread up the wall and across the ceiling, and the house would have been engulfed quickly. However, the plasterboard that covers most new builds suppresses a fire; once the paint and wallpaper have burned off the fire will die rapidly. Which is why the fire was contained mainly by the front door and hallway.*'

'Oh, wow, I had no idea.'

'*There are two ways to look at this, one is that your killer knew this would happen and planned it, so the fire caught the attention of the neighbours who called the fire service, who were able to put it out before it caught hold. Or, they didn't know the fire would be suppressed so quickly, and it didn't go to plan. They either wanted the bodies to be found and quickly or they wanted to destroy the evidence.'*

'I kind of came to that conclusion too.'

'You know, statistically, a lot of arsonists will walk to the scene of the fire; they usually know the area well and live within a two-mile radius. But the problem we have with that is what the fire was used for. Most serial arsonists will target bins, skips, empty buildings, those kinds of things.'

Morgan sighed; this wasn't helping; she was as confused as before.

'That's not what you wanted to hear, was it?'

She laughed. 'No, I wanted you to be able to tell me which one it was. Thank you for your help though.'

'Just a thought, Morgan, the majority of arsonists like to return to the scene of the fire to watch it. Did anyone notice if there was someone hanging around who didn't live on the street?'

'I knew that, or at least I'd read it in one of my true crime books, but this is the first time I've had any experience of arson to this degree. I've only dealt with one bin fire, and once when someone didn't put out one of those disposable barbecues and it got a little out of hand. As for someone loitering in the area there isn't anyone we're aware of, the whole street has been canvassed for house-to-house enquiries and no one mentioned anyone weird hanging around.'

'Then it might be worth looking closer at the neighbours. And I hate to say this because it's kind of like going against my own, but the fire crew that attended, they won't have been full-time, they're retained firefighters. It could be worthwhile sending you a list of the names of the crew that attended for you to check out.'

'Thank you, that would be great. It would be good to get

them ticked off the list. You've been very helpful, I appreciate it.'

'Anytime, sorry I couldn't be more use. Goodnight, Morgan, and good luck, I'll email those names over to you in the morning.'

Morgan put her phone away and went back inside the house one last time. Sally thought she was being haunted, what had made her feel that way? Taking out her phone she began to take her own photos of the crime scene to compare with the ones she'd printed out. Making her way from room to room she looked for hiding spaces, opening cupboards and wardrobes to see if anyone could have been in them. There was a large hatch to the attic above the stairs, but it was bolted from the outside. No one could have gone in and out of there, so who was watching Sally, and how?

FORTY-FOUR

Natalie tried to make polite conversation with Ava and Lexie, who gave her one-word answers all the way home, yet were driving her mad constantly whispering into each other's ears.

'Girls, I hate to be rude and interrupt your even ruder whispering, but just what the hell is going on? I think I have a right to know why I've had to pick you up from the police station, Ava, and why your parents are nowhere to be found.'

'Mum, don't be so rude or nosy.'

Natalie glared at her daughter in the rear-view mirror. 'It's not being rude, it's a basic need to know what is going on.'

Ava elbowed Lexie then spoke. 'I'm sorry, Mrs White, it's all been a bit horrible to be honest, I don't really know how to explain it.'

'I don't care what's happened, but I need to know how long you'll be stopping with us. I'm not here to judge anyone, Ava, but it seems obvious that your parents are in police custody and it is more than a bit worrying. Are they going to be let out, or is a social worker going to get involved and take you into foster care?'

Both girls yelped in horror, and Natalie felt bad scaring

Ava, but damn it she wasn't going to get herself into some almighty mess and not have a clue what it was.

'They wouldn't do that, would they?'

She shrugged. 'They might, technically they could, you're not old enough to be left alone.'

'My dad got taken to the police station earlier and asked questions about Sally, the woman who was killed. Then the police spoke to my mum, who said he was on his own when it happened and basically tried to blame him for it. When my dad was released, he wasn't supposed to come to our house, but he was pissed off and raging with my mum. She also had the locks changed while he wasn't there.'

Natalie's eyes were so wide they were almost popping out of their sockets, and she had to force herself to keep watching the road and not Ava.

'Then what happened?'

'He stabbed Maggie, the old lady across the street, with a big knife after my mum smashed him across the back of the head with a poker.'

'Holy fuck.'

'Lexie, do not use language like that.' Natalie admonished her daughter, but had been thinking exactly the same thing.

'Where is your dad now?'

'The hospital, she knocked him out cold. He was so mad at her, he smashed the front window and climbed through it to get inside. Honestly it was terrifying.'

Natalie was wondering just how something could go so wrong. 'Is the old lady okay?'

'I don't know, she got rushed to hospital and taken to surgery.'

'Your mum is still at the police station?'

'Yep, they are taking a statement from her.'

'Are you happy now, Mother, anything else you want to know, like if Ava has a boyfriend or girlfriend?'

'Lexie, I'm warning you stop the attitude, or you're grounded, young lady.'

She drove the rest of the way to her house in silence, trying to get her head around the mess that Ava's parents had caused. The girls didn't speak another word. When they reached the house, they ran straight upstairs to Lexie's bedroom, leaving her still shocked about the turn of events. She didn't mind Ava stopping a couple of nights, but she wasn't going to be able to let her stay here indefinitely. Lexie was an absolute nightmare at the moment, and the thought of two moody, hormonal teenage girls in her house would send her over the edge in no time at all. As per usual, Jasper wasn't home.

She didn't know if Ava had eaten or if she was hungry, but she grabbed a couple of frozen pizzas out of the freezer. She'd feel better if she kept herself busy and made her something to eat; at least the house wasn't so quiet with the two girls upstairs.

Music began to filter down the stairs, that heavy thud, thudding beat that Natalie hated, but if it made Ava happy, she could put up with it for a couple of hours. Tonight had been a tough night for the poor kid, the least she could do was feed her and hope that by tomorrow something had been sorted out so she could go home. As she began slicing open the pizza boxes, she felt the familiar chill settle across the back of her neck – someone was watching her. Spinning around she stood in the huge kitchen, a knife in one hand, staring out into the hallway expecting to see the boogey man standing there, or a ghost. There wasn't even a dark shadow because Lexie had left every light on in the hallway, and on the stairs. If there was no one there, why did she feel as if there was? Why was the skin on her arms raised in little goosebumps, and why did she have the unsettled feeling that something wasn't right?

FORTY-FIVE

Morgan had dropped the key back at the station, then gone home after walking the dog for Maggie. She'd been tempted to bring him back with her, but Kevin was strutting around the kitchen as if he owned the place and she didn't know if he liked dogs. Not to mention that Ben didn't really like either animal, although she suspected it was because he was too soft and didn't want to get attached to them. He clearly liked them because whenever she came in Kevin was usually curled up near to Ben and neither of them seemed to mind. She'd promised Roley she'd be there first thing to let him out and find him somewhere to stop until Maggie was able to come home, making sure he had fresh water and a bowl of dog biscuits. He didn't seem bothered and had padded down to Maggie's bedroom, using a little set of plastic steps to climb onto her bed. Morgan ordered pizza because since she'd mentioned it earlier, she hadn't been able to stop thinking about it, and there was no way she was starting to cook now.

Ben still wasn't home, so she sat at the kitchen table and spread out the pictures of the Lawsons' house, then she down-loaded the photos she'd taken onto her laptop so she could enlarge them to study them. Annie had thought that Sally may have had a stalker, which was the most plausible considering what had happened. If so, though, how were they able to hide and watch her? Or Natalie for that matter? She'd checked her house herself and although there were cupboards and walk-in wardrobes to hide in, it just didn't seem possible. She tucked the photos of the Lawsons' dead bodies away from view, not before glancing at a close-up of Tim though. She shuddered, just thinking about his awful death; pointless death made her so sad.

A loud knock at the front door signalled the arrival of her piping hot pizza, as well as making her jump out of her skin. As she opened the door and took hold of the box, she looked around Ben's hallway. This was a big house, a Victorian house probably built around the same time as Natalie's. Did this have places someone could hide in and watch you? God, she hoped not, she was scaring herself now and she didn't scare easily.

Taking the pizza to the kitchen she grabbed a few slices and sat down to stare at the photos again. How could you watch someone and not be there? She looked up at the discreet security camera in the corner of the room. Ben had installed a top-of-the-range system when she'd agreed to live here. A camera, of course, she could have slapped her own forehead. Why had it taken her so long to figure that out? Someone could have hidden tiny cameras in Sally's house that she didn't know about, and watched her whenever they wanted to. How would they get them inside though? She looked at the freshly painted walls, the new bathrooms, the beautiful open-plan kitchen. There were a multitude of places you could hide one of those tiny spy cameras. When she'd been a response officer, she had gone to a house where the husband had reported that he'd found a camera in the smoke alarm in the bedroom that his ex-wife must have put in, so she could still watch him to see if he brought anyone around. None of the crime scene photos showed any smoke alarms, but the house must have them, she decided. She would check tomorrow.

As she finished her pizza, Kevin was pushing against her legs, and she bent down to scratch his ears. 'I don't know about you but I'm having a shower and going to bed. I'm knackered, Kev.' He miaowed loudly which she took as his agreeing with her.

Ben should have been home ages ago, she hoped he wouldn't be long. Tomorrow she would get started on the list of names that Nigel would be sending her, and look them up to see if any of them were on the intelligence system, not that they would be, she thought because she was pretty sure that whether retained firefighter or full-time, they would still have to go through all the usual DBS checks. It was possible they'd slipped through the net, though, it happened, or maybe they could have given false details, she would also cross-reference their addresses to see if anyone lived in close proximity to the Lawsons'. She'd tell Ben when he got home, but by the time she'd showered and got into bed he still wasn't home, and she couldn't keep her eyes open. A loud thud as the mattress at the end of her bed went down signalled that Kevin was about to make himself comfortable whilst Ben wasn't here, and it made her smile to herself; at least he was good company.

FORTY-SIX

Morgan found herself there, at the Lawsons' house, watching them all going about their business. David grabbing a slice of toast before kissing his wife on the cheek and rushing out of the door. Tim in his bedroom, hunched over his laptop playing a game on it. He was so absorbed he didn't hear his mum shouting for him until she hammered on his door, making him jump up, slamming down the lid so she couldn't peek at what he was doing. Morgan whispered *what are you doing? Why are you being so secretive?* He grabbed his school bag from the bed and rushed downstairs, taking a packet of chocolate fudge pop tarts from the cupboard before running out of the door, shouting, 'Bye, Mum.' Sally was left on her own. She had her back to Morgan as she was rinsing cups, using her left hand to put them in the dishwasher. As if sensing she was being watched, Sally began to turn slowly to face Morgan. Her lips were parted in a wide o shape, but the worst thing of all was the bloodied stump where her right hand had been cut off, rivers of blood running down Sally's arm, huge, fat drops hitting the pristine marble tiled floor. There was so much blood and Morgan couldn't do a thing to help her because she was frozen to the spot. Finally, a scream burst through her lips, and she began to shake.

'Morgan, Morgan.'

Her eyes opened to see Ben next to her in bed, shaking her gently.

'Oh my God that was horrible.'

'Really, you scared the crap out of me. I was flat out, and you screamed down my eardrum. I thought something terrible had happened.'

Throwing off the duvet she sat up, turning on the bedside lamp, scared that Sally Lawson was going to be standing in the shadows in the corner of the bedroom, waving that stump at her. Wild-eyed she looked to Ben as she tried to slow her breathing down.

'I'm sorry, it was so real.'

He was sitting next to her rubbing her back. 'You're telling me, you were thrashing around as if you were possessed.'

'Just a bad dream, that's all, about the Lawsons.'

He leaned his head on her shoulder and kissed her neck. 'It's been a rough couple of days.'

She glanced at her phone on the bedside table to see what time it was: almost time to get up. She didn't think she could go back to sleep after that.

Ben yawned. 'Let's have half an hour.'

She kissed his cheek. 'You have half an hour, I'm awake now.'

Standing up as he lay back down, she saw Kevin sitting by the bedroom door staring at her in disgust, and she shrugged.

'Sorry, cat, I scared myself just as much.'

He turned and walked out of the bedroom.

She followed him downstairs, where he disappeared out through the cat flap they'd had installed, and she began to fill the coffee machine with fresh water. She'd put the photos of the crime scene away, but they'd stayed fresh in her mind as she'd fallen asleep. There was a lot to do today, and she wanted an early start. After her coffee had brewed and the milk had been warmed and frothed, Morgan opened the back door and took her mug outside. It was going to be a lovely day; she could already feel the heat of the sun as it burned through the clouds. She looked at Ben's garden, it was much bigger than the Lawsons' and need a lot of TLC but suddenly she was glad it didn't look anything like theirs. She sat down on one of the white cast-iron chairs, putting her mug on the table and enjoying a few minutes' peace before she bombarded her mind with the to-do list she had to tick off as well as find the Lawsons' killer. She was getting close; she could feel it in the pit of her stomach, and she'd learned a while ago not to ignore those gut feelings.

Coffee drunk, she stood up and stretched then went back inside the kitchen. Phoning the hospital switchboard she asked for the Intensive Care Unit.

'Hello, I'm a close friend of Maggie Wilkes, please could you tell me how she is this morning?'

Morgan had her fingers crossed that they would tell her and that it was good news.

'Hang on, I'll just grab the nurse who's looking after her.'

Moments later she heard a soft voice ask who she was.

'I'm, Morgan, she's a very good friend, she also has no family.'

'Yes, she said she was on her own.'

'She's awake and talking?'

'She most certainly is, she's doing amazing and by all accounts will be home later today to check on her dog.'

Morgan laughed, a huge grin on her face as the relief that Maggie was made of as tough a stuff as she was filled her with hope.

'Will she be home today?'

'I don't think so, but she's off the ventilator. She's a bit sore but breathing fine considering one of her lungs was perforated. I'd let you speak to her, but she's drifted off with the painkillers. We are moving her onto a ward soon though, which is good news.'

'That's amazing, please tell her that Roley is fine and I'm looking after him. I'll pop to see her after I finish work.'

'I will, bye.'

Morgan punched the air, so happy to have good news for a change. Today was going to be a great day. She went upstairs to get dressed then wrote a note for Ben.

Gone to sort Maggie's dog out, will meet you at the station. She's doing great off the ventilator!

XX

Opening the cupboard where they kept the cereal she grabbed a breakfast bar, relieved there was no packet of chocolate fudge pop tarts in there after that terrible nightmare. She had no idea if Heather Rigg was home or not, but she would soon find out.

FORTY-SEVEN

Hest Bank Road was silent, there was no one around and considering the last few days of non-stop police activity, she bet the residents were relieved. Morgan could see the Riggs' smashed window had been boarded up, and there was a light on in the hallway. She had no idea if it was on an automatic timer or if Heather was home, but she would give her a knock. First, going inside Maggie's she was greeted by Roley who was waiting by the front door, his tail wagging, and she felt bad. Crouching down she rubbed behind his ears and stroked him.

'I'm sorry, were you lonely? Your mum is okay though, she'll be back soon to look after you.'

She went in the kitchen and noticed his bowl had been licked clean, and smiled, glad that despite being on his own he hadn't gone off his food. She fed him, changed his water and waited for him to eat his breakfast before clipping his lead on. Despite the grey hairs on his face betraying his age he jumped all over her like a puppy, making her laugh.

'Come on, you've been promoted to a detective dog, we're going to check the streets out around here and see if there are any in walking distance where our suspect could live.'

She knew it was pointless, Nigel had said a two-mile radius and she didn't think the dog could walk that far, but at least they could look at the surrounding streets. Then if any names and addresses came up that matched a name on Nigel's list, she'd already know if they were from this part of Rydal Falls. Roley walked further than she'd given him credit for and when they returned, he was ready for a drink.

After putting him inside, she crossed the road to see if anyone was in at the Riggs'. Before she could knock on the door it opened and Heather stood there, swollen, bleary-eyed, her hair mussed and a pair of mismatched pyjamas on.

'How's Maggie, any news?'

'She's okay, they're moving her out of Intensive Care later today.'

'Oh, thank God. I don't suppose you know how Luke is, do you?'

'I don't, sorry. I've come to ask a favour.'

'Yes, I'll have the dog. I've been worrying about him all night on his own, but I didn't have a key to get inside to go grab him.'

'Thank you, Maggie will appreciate that.'

'It's the least I can do, it's my fault she's in there. God, what an absolute mess this all is.'

Morgan nodded. She had no idea what had happened with Heather last night, if she'd been charged or bailed pending further investigation. She hadn't spoken to Ben to find out what he or the CPS had decided, and she didn't want to sour Heather's mood by reminding her of that particular dark cloud hanging over her head. But whatever was happening with Heather, she didn't think she'd harm Roley.

'I'll go grab him for you, and let Maggie know where he is.'

'Yes, please, give her my love if you speak to her and tell her I'll take very good care of Roley. I've got a doctor's appointment this afternoon to sort out my medication.'

Morgan smiled at her. 'That's good and thanks, I will.' Finally turning back to the Lawsons' house she cursed under her breath, the scene must have been released because there were no PCSOs guarding it, she wouldn't be able to get inside without a key. It was time to get to work, she would have to grab a key and check later on. She hoped that Nigel had sent the list of on-call firefighters over for her to cross-check against their records.

Morgan was the first one in the office. She relished the peace, not that it ever got overly busy with just the four full-time detectives. Cain was like a breath of fresh air and seemed to be able to handle Amy just fine, which she knew had been a big relief for Ben. As she fired her computer up, she couldn't help glancing at Des's desk. It was always going to be strange knowing what had happened to him. It was like he'd wished it on himself with all the worrying that something bad was going to happen. She had twenty-eight new emails since she'd last been logged on last night, but only one of them was any use to her for the investigation. She saw Nigel's name and double clicked on it, waiting for it to load. Attached to the message was a list of names of the on-call fire officers who attended the night of the Lawsons' fire, their addresses and their places of work, which was very handy. In his email, Nigel explained that not only did they have to live within a five-minute travel time of the station they also had to carry a pager when on shift. She checked the names and addresses, but none of them rang any bells or brought up information when she typed their names into the computer. She sat back, relieved in a way that it wasn't one of the good guys, that was all they needed. Her inbox pinged and she saw another email from Nigel.

Sorry, there were two fire engines that night one from Rydal and one from Windermere. I've attached the crew list for the Windermere one.

She opened it and did the same as previously. One name stood out immediately. Jackie Thorpe. She was the woman Morgan had spoken to outside Sally's salon. She frowned slightly, wondering if she had time to nip there before the others arrived, to speak to her. Deciding that she did, Morgan grabbed her coat and was on her way to the salon in a matter of minutes, eager to find out if Jackie had realised it was her boss's house she'd saved from burning down, and why she hadn't mentioned it last week.

The salon door was propped open and there were a few customers having their hair cut and styled. The woman standing behind the small reception desk smiled at her.

'Have you got an appointment?'

'No, I'm Detective Constable Morgan Brookes, I'm investigating Sally's death and have a couple of questions.'

She nodded seriously. 'Come up to the staff room, it's a bit noisy in here.'

Morgan followed her upstairs and into a room that smelled of fresh coffee.

'We're just so saddened by it all, none of us know what to do. I guess keeping the salon going is the only thing we can do for Sally at the moment. It's horrible though, who would want to do something like that to her entire family for no reason at all?'

'It's very tragic and that's why I'm here. I'm investigating every line of enquiry that comes up. I wondered if Jackie is around, I'd like to have a word with her.'

'Who?'

'Jackie Thorpe.'

The woman looked confused. 'I'm sorry, you've had a wasted journey, there's no Jackie Thorpe working here.'

Now it was Morgan's turn to look confused. 'There's not? She told me she lives above the salon?' Something wasn't right here. 'Have you ever employed a Jackie Thorpe?'

She shook her head. 'Never and no one called Jackie lives above us, it's empty.'

'Oh, right.' Morgan looked around to give herself a minute to compose herself. 'Does anyone here work as an on-call fire-fighter?'

The woman laughed loudly. 'You must be joking, no one here would risk breaking a nail, that's not happening this side of the millennium. Are you sure you have the right place?'

Morgan's cheeks were burning, she felt stupid. Just who had she spoken to a few days ago about Sally outside of the salon?

'Does anyone here have a sibling that might work as a fire-fighter?' Morgan knew she was clutching at straws, but if an employee had a sibling that might have a dodgy criminal record, they may have used this as their work address.

'Not that I'm aware of, actually I have a client that comes in now and again who is one of those retained firefighters.'

'You do? What's her name?'

The woman laughed. 'Jacqueline, I've never called her Jackie. She's a little bit strange at times.'

'Do you have her address to hand?'

'Look, I want to help you, I really do, but you're wasting your time. She didn't know Sally; she only ever came in when Sally wasn't here.'

Morgan couldn't let it go and knew any moment she was probably going to get thrown out of the salon, but until it happened, she was going to keep asking questions.

'Does this Jacqueline have a family, what about parents, children, does she live with them?'

'No, as far as I know, she's single, she's an only child. She has no family; her parents were killed a long time ago when she was a kid. Some drunk driver crashed into them, killed them both, it's very sad.'

Morgan nodded; she could feel something begin to click into place in her mind. But what?

'Okay, thanks for the information. Have you got her address all the same?'

She blew out her lips, a long sigh of resignation. 'We got a new computer system and all the addresses got wiped out. She hasn't been in since to update it. She used to live near the fire station though, the end house nearest to it. No idea what number it is though.'

'Thank you so much for being so helpful, I really appreciate it.'

Morgan left the shop, Jacqueline was an orphan, like her. Bless her, that must have been a terrible accident, what an awful thing to have to live with. In her car she took out her phone and logged on to the British Newspaper Archive, where she would be able to hopefully search old drink-driving accidents in the area. Her heart broke a little at just how many came up. Narrowing down the search she typed in 'couple killed by drink-driving Rydal Falls'. A headline in the results read, 'Couple Mown Down by Drunk Teenager'.

Clicking on that link she was taken to a newspaper article covering the court case. There were no photographs, but the article named eighteen-year-old Erica James, who was arrested at the scene of the horrific crash for drink-driving. She fully admitted it, and was given five years for death by dangerous driving. Morgan shook her head, five years for killing two people and ruining their only child's life. It was nothing, that was no sentence at all. She typed in the name 'Erica James' and a few grainy pictures came up of some kids on an outdoor camping trip, another of a young girl in a school assembly, the next a teenage girl being led into court, her hair much longer, her head down. She peered at the pictures, thinking she looked vaguely familiar, could Erica James be Natalie White? It was hard to tell, it was so long ago, and Natalie White had plenty of money now to change her looks, her hair. Both Sally Lawson and Natalie White were around the same age, in fact she'd admitted to knowing her as a teenager. The only thing that made no sense whatsoever was where the hell did Jackie Thorpe come into all of this? And that was assuming Jackie was Jacqueline. Morgan squeezed her eyes shut; she was getting a headache. She had to go back and tell Ben; she could look up Erica James on their system and see if she could connect her to anyone in the investigation. As she drove back to the station she thought about Sally, *where do you come into this, Sally? If I'm even on the right level? I need someone to listen to all of this and tell me whether I'm clutching at straws or have something we can work with.*

FORTY-EIGHT

Morgan opened the office door for the second time this morning, only this time she was greeted by the sight of Cain, Amy and Ben sitting chatting.

'Where did you get to, you set off way before me?'

'I had some information about a possible lead, so I went to follow it up.'

'Any good?'

'Not really, well kind of, I need to do some searches and double check some stuff. What happened with Heather?'

'Bailed pending further enquiries, or until we can figure out what the hell happened.'

Amy stood up. 'Come on then, Cain, let's get an early start.'

'Where are you two going?'

Cain stood up, crossed to Morgan's desk eyeing up her latte. 'I always thought we were good friends yet here you are, two days on the run getting a coffee without me. I'm hurt, Morgan.'

'I didn't know if anyone was in yet, I'm sorry. Anyway, I brought you McDonald's yesterday, so there you go.'

He bent down and pecked her cheek. 'My bad, yes you did. You're forgiven. Amy is taking me to the hospital to get statements from Luke Rigg and Maggie Wilkes, if they're up to it.'

'Say hi to Maggie for me and tell her Roley is fine and being looked after by Heather, please.'

He nodded. Morgan wished she was going to see Maggie, but she'd go after work.

Ben also stood up. 'I've got a morning meeting followed by the monthly command meeting, let me know if you need me for anything though, Morgan. I'll be glad of an excuse to not go to either.'

And then there was one, she was on her own before she'd even had chance to discuss her theories with Ben, or Amy and Cain. She logged on to the computer. She should have said something. If she found anything on here, she would go and get Ben out of his meetings.

After first searching for 'Jackie Thorpe', she got nothing, so she typed in 'Erica James'. It always surprised Morgan how many people shared the same name as the list of them appeared on the screen, with passport-sized photos next to the name. Erica James was there, sixth picture down, her face smudged with trails of mascara, glassy eyes swollen with tears and a deep cut above her right eyebrow that would probably have left a scar. She closed her eyes as she pictured Natalie, remembering that she had a small scar above her eyebrow. She'd noticed it when her hair was scraped back into a ponytail. Next to her name it said Vehicular Manslaughter and OPL – over the prescribed limit, police speak for drink-driving. She was so young, she looked nothing like Natalie White, with her short brown hair and hazel-coloured eyes. That didn't mean it wasn't her though, cosmetic surgery, expensive hair colour and extensions, coloured contacts, it was relatively easy to change your appearance especially for a woman. Morgan enlarged the photograph, sending it to the printer. She would ask Natalie later if she was Erica James. She began to read the information all about the tragic incident. It was truly horrific, the Thorpes didn't stand a chance. It had been a warm day and a glorious summer's evening according to the report. They had been out riding their bicycles when a drunken Erica James had left her friend's eighteenth birthday party and got into her car. She told the officer who was first on scene that she'd been upset because she'd caught her boyfriend cheating on her, and had been crying so much, she never even saw the couple on their bikes before she ploughed into them. Panicking she had pressed the accelerator instead of the brake and had mown them down. Morgan shuddered, it was too horrific to contemplate, what an awful, painful way to die. She opened another report where she found mention of the Thorpes's child – Jackie Thorpe, nine years old and with no living relatives to take care of her, was put into foster care with the Pearsons.

Morgan sat back, she needed to speak to the social worker who had dealt with the case. She smiled because at least she knew where to find Angela Hardy, as she'd been to her house before, when she'd been trying to figure out her own childhood. Morgan knew that Angela wouldn't answer her phone to an unknown number, so she would have to go and see her in person. She picked up the printout of Erica James's photo and old address. If she needed to, she could also try and speak to Erica's parents, if they were still living there, to confirm her identity. There was nothing else on file for Erica, so she must have kept out of trouble when she was released. She desperately wanted to confront Natalie White, but knew that she needed proof before doing so. Natalie could deny it as much as she wanted but if she had spoken with her parents first, they could confirm her identity. She was on the right track, she knew it.

Morgan drove to Brantfell Road, parking opposite the cottage with the pink front door, which now had a vibrant summer wreath on it. Morgan loved it. As much as black was her go-to colour, pink was her next favourite. She wondered if Ben would let her paint his front door pink. This made her smile; he'd probably say yes even if he hated it because he always tried to make her happy. She crossed the road, hoping that Angela was in, and knocked on the door with her fingers crossed behind her back. She heard footsteps and smiled as the door opened a little bit.

Angela peered over her glasses and proclaimed, 'Morgan, what a surprise, how are you? Come inside.'

The door wide open, she stepped into Angela's quaint cottage and gazed at her cropped, pastel pink hair.

'I'm good thanks, how are you, Angela? I love your hair, it's amazing.'

'Thank you, I'm pretty good, although is that about to change?'

Morgan laughed. 'I hope not, I'm just after some information about a child you placed with a family back in 1991.'

'Nineteen ninety-one, would that be Jackie Thorpe?'

'How did you know?'

'There weren't many kids that had to be put in foster care in 1991, and Jackie always stuck in my mind. It was tragic what happened to her parents, a terrible shame for everyone, so many lives ruined that night.'

Morgan took a seat on the sofa, a velvet fuchsia pink sofa; this house was full of pink and white, it gave off such a happy vibe. She would quite happily move in tomorrow, if Ben got fed up with her.

'I was reading the reports, it's so sad, the poor little girl must have been devastated.'

'She was, such a quiet thing as well. She never really spoke much after that; I can't even imagine how hard it was for her. She was placed with Mr and Mrs Pearson. They were an older couple who genuinely were lovely people and quite often stepped in at short notice when we had an emergency. No children of their own, but they had quite strong religious beliefs. They took a shine to Jackie, and she stayed with them. Nancy was a Sunday school teacher, and her husband was a vicar.'

Morgan felt everything slide into place in slow motion. Taking out her phone she found the screenshot she had of Sally, and passed the phone to Angela.

'Did you know Sally Lawson?'

'Is this Sally?' She took her phone from her and held it close to her face. 'Hard to say, she looks vaguely familiar but not enough that I can place her. Why?'

'She was murdered along with her entire family, and I'm trying to find out the motive.'

Angela gasped so loud it filled the room. 'Oh my God, that's the family that were killed. I saw the headlines, but I didn't read them. It's too sad and scary.'

'Did you know the girl who killed the Thorpes?'

'Erica James? Not really, I knew of her of course, and I followed the newspaper reports at the time. I felt a bit sorry for her. She never meant to kill the Thorpes, but all the same her actions destroyed Jackie's life, and the little girl was my priority. I often wonder what happened to Erica when she got out of prison, if she ever managed to put it behind her and move on. How do you do that though, when you have two deaths on your conscience?'

'Could this be her?' Morgan passed her phone back to her, this time showing a different woman on the screen, the ultra-gorgeous Natalie White. Angela stared at it for some time.

'I'm sorry, I'm rubbish. It was so long ago. I suppose that could be her, who is she?'

'Natalie White, lives in a big old Victorian mansion with her property developer husband, Jasper.'

'I know the names; I've heard Jasper mentioned a lot. But I'd have thought Erica James would have upped sticks and got away from Rydal Falls when she was released. I'd be surprised to hear she's still hanging around.'

Morgan stood up. 'Thanks, Angela, you've been very helpful.'

'Have I?' She laughed. 'I'm not sure I have, but you're always so polite, Morgan, it's a pleasure to chat with you.'

Morgan left Angela, and once she was inside the car, she took out her notebook.

Jackie Thorpe placed in foster care with the Pearsons, both religious people.

Sunday school teacher and vicar, the hand of God – passing judgement on others, retribution, taking revenge but how are you involved in this, Sally, what happened?

Erica James, if she's Natalie White then she is in danger, her family are too

Morgan needed to find Jacqueline, the retained firefighter who used Sally's salon, and talk to her. If Jacqueline was Jackie Thorpe then this might just be the final piece of the puzzle.

She drove to the fire station situated on the outskirts of Windermere. There were three houses a short distance away from it. Two of them were boarded up and hadn't been lived in for as long as she could remember, as well as one that wasn't quite in the same state of disrepair, but it was getting there. The front curtains were drawn, the wooden front door was faded and cracked. *At least we can get in with a whammer should we need to put the door through*, she thought to herself. There was no car parked on the paved drive and hadn't been for a long time, judging by the weeds poking through the gaps in the paving. Morgan felt a sense of foreboding just looking at the house, and wondered if she should be here, doing this alone. But before she could do anything about it her feet walked up the drive, and she found herself hammering on the front door with a closed fist. She wanted to find out what the hell was going on and hovering around outside wouldn't give her any answers. She listened carefully, there wasn't a single sound from inside the house. Turning she glanced across at the fire station, to see if anyone was over there, but it was all in darkness; it looked almost as desolate as this house.

Walking around the side of the house she looked into the small garden, with knee-high grass and dandelions. The back of the house looked as sad as the front, but at least the curtains were open, along with a kitchen window that she registered she might just be able to climb through. Pressing her face as close to the glass as she could, she cupped a hand over her eyes. She just wanted to find a photograph of Jacqueline, to see if she recognised her as the woman who called herself Jackie Thorpe. Inside was immaculate, the kitchen cupboards were old, but it was spotlessly clean. There wasn't a single thing out of place, no dirty pots in the sink waiting to be washed. No washing lying around, it was cleaner than Ben's kitchen. She hadn't been expecting that and she took a step back. There was no sign of anyone being home. Morgan looked around; she knew she shouldn't do this without a warrant, because if she found something it would not be admissible in court. But she couldn't bring herself to walk away now. She let out a sigh, and tugging down her sleeve, she knocked on the kitchen door and waited a couple of minutes. And there was always another scenario: what if Jackie needed help? She could be inside, injured. That would be a good enough reason to go inside. Morgan's hand reached for the door handle, expecting it to be locked, but pushing down on it the door opened, and she was standing on the threshold of the kitchen.

'Hello, are you there? It's the police.'

She was greeted by the sound of the fridge freezer humming in the corner and nothing else. She knew that she should speak to Ben, get a warrant and come back, but if Jackie Thorpe was involved it would give her time to destroy any evidence.

'Do you need help?'

Morgan stepped inside, telling herself just a cursory look around and then she would get out of there. There was a small hallway leading off the kitchen where the door to the living room was wide open. Inside was a small leather sofa and a television. There was another door that was closed next to the bottom of the staircase. Morgan paused at the bottom of the stairs to listen for any noise. Her heart was racing but she'd come this far. She twisted the door knob, pushing the door open. It was dark in this room; the curtains were closed. Taking out her phone she pressed the torchlight and shone it around the room, gasping as she did. There was a huge desktop computer with three monitors on a large table that filled one side of the room, and behind it was a wall of newspaper clippings, photos and what looked like photocopied reports. She stepped closer to read them and felt her heart beat even faster. She had been right, Jackie Thorpe was involved. There were photos of the scene of the accident her parents had been killed in, twisted bicycles lying in pools of dark liquid. Another of a car with its bonnet so badly crushed it was amazing the driver walked away with only a small cut to her head. There were pictures of a young Erica James plastered on the wall, pictures of Natalie White along with pictures of Sally Lawson, and another man Morgan didn't recognise. She leaned closer to read the highlighted print on a report that read, 'I never would have gotten in the car if that bitch Sally hadn't been giving Jason a blow job in the alleyway.'

Morgan paused, oh God was this Sally Lawson? Had that single dreadful event that night all those years ago caused this catastrophe of death and destruction? A cold shiver ran the full length of Morgan's spine as she snapped a couple of photos of the wall. Her thigh knocked the corner of the table, and the monitors came to life. Each one had small squares, each showed different angles of the Lawsons' burned shell of a house, and Natalie White's house. Morgan could see Natalie on the screen now, moving about in the kitchen. She felt the nerves in her stomach begin to knot themselves and a wave of sickness washed over her. *Oh God, I sent Ava Rigg there, thinking it was a place of safety, when I might have sent her to her death.* Snapping a couple of photos of the room with her phone, she turned and rushed back into the kitchen, she needed to get out of here. As she did she looked across at the freezer. They hadn't found Sally Lawson's hand yet. She couldn't stop herself, and she crossed the floor. Tugging open the door the freezer was as sparse as the rest of the kitchen, but she could see a pale, flesh-coloured hand resting on the top shelf. Stifling a scream, she pushed the door shut and ran. Slamming the back door shut behind her, she had to get to the White's house now.

Back in the car she phoned Ben; it went to voicemail.

'I'm going to Hellsfield Hall, where Natalie White lives, on Hellsfield Road, Windermere. I think that the killer is, no, I know that the killer is going to go after Natalie White next. I'm going to get her to a place of safety. Ring me as soon as you get this. I'll let you know what happens.'

Then she phoned the control room and asked them to send an officer to watch the house.

Morgan began to drive towards the Whites' mansion, hoping that she wasn't too late and that she could put a stop to this. If she got the slightest hint she was too late and anything was wrong, she'd call for backup, but she needed to see if she could get them out of there.

FORTY-NINE

Natalie was making breakfast pancakes for Lexie and Ava because what else was there to do? Jasper had left early for work, and she was furious with him; just once it would be nice to have him here with her, co-parenting and doing his bit. She was sick of being a single parent; she was also sick with worry about the past catching up with her after all this time. She was hand-whisking the eggs and milk so hard the mixture was flying all over the kitchen worktop, but she didn't care. Ever since those horrible murders she'd been on edge, then the feeling that someone was watching her was just too scary. She felt as if she was constantly on high alert, on show, that someone was in her home. And what if they were, what if the person that murdered the Lawsons was going to do the same to them?

Maybe it was time to confess, tell Jasper, Morgan, Annie who she really was and what she'd done, tell them that she'd known Sally Lawson but hadn't spoken to her since the night of the accident because of what had happened. The people she'd killed. Tears began to fall down her cheeks, not for herself but for the teenage girl who had recklessly got into that car drunk, for the poor couple who were out enjoying a summer's night cycle ride, most of all for the kid whose parents she had taken away from them, whom she had never got the chance to even say sorry to. So many lives ruined in one night, yet here she was living a life where she could have anything she desired. She was getting her punishment sure enough though, since the only things she really wanted – a loving, attentive husband and a kid who liked her – were non-existent.

The tiny hairs on the back of her neck began to stand on end, the all-too-familiar sensation of being watched made her feel uneasy. A creak behind her made her spin around and scream. She managed to knock the glass mixing bowl off the counter and it smashed into a million shards as it hit the floor, but there was nobody there. Natalie looked at the mess and began to cry, not because she'd broken the expensive glass bowl but because it signified her entire life. That batter mix, congealed with the broken glass, just about summed her up. To top it all off it had flown everywhere, covering all the cupboards, the tiles, the ceiling and one of the drop down lights behind her. So concerned was her teenage daughter that she hadn't even called down to see if she was okay. Running the tap, she filled the sink with hot soapy water and kept whispering *this is what you deserve, it's what you deserve*, over and over as she began to scrub at the tiles. The smell of sizzling pancake mixture came from the industrial light bulb, and she realised if she didn't turn the light off and clean that first, every time she turned the light on the kitchen would stink. Marching to the switch she knocked the lights off, then grabbed a tea towel from the rail, to unscrew the bulb with so she didn't burn herself. As she unscrewed the light, she noticed the tiniest square thing attached to the fitting. That shouldn't be there, she was sure it hadn't been there when she'd bought it. Grabbing it with her fingers she pulled it and stared into the smallest lens she'd ever seen, a feeling of horror washing over her. Someone *was* watching her? How many of these were there around the house? Her first thought was Jasper, and she was furious he was never here, yet he was spying on her? The absolute arsehole. Picking up her mobile she phoned the number Morgan had given her, and it went to voicemail.

'Hey, Morgan, it's Natalie, can you come over? I've found a spy camera in the light fitting, and I don't know what to do.'

She stared at the thing, then shuddered and dropped the tea towel on top of it. Moments later she lifted it off and spoke into it.

'Jasper, you're a creep and the worst husband there ever was. I want a divorce.'

Throwing it back down she dropped the tea towel on top of it, so he couldn't watch her, and began to search for any more. The broken glass and mess were forgotten about whilst she hunted high and low, in all the places she could think there might be more of them hidden.

Lexie and Ava were upstairs on the computer – Lexie was on her huge Apple iMac; Ava was using her MacBook – and they were both trying to log on to the game called *Isaiah* they'd been playing with Tim. Neither of them had admitted to their parents that they played it, because then they'd have known that they had been accessing the Dark Web and had installed cameras in their own homes to watch their families, and they would be furious with them.

Lexie stood up. 'I'm going to get something to eat. I think the game's been taken down. Whoever was running it might have heard the police were asking questions and removed it.'

Ava shrugged. 'Why though, isn't that the whole point of the Dark Web, so you can do stuff without getting caught? It was only a game. I quite liked being able to go inside other people's houses and watch what they were doing. It made mine seem not so boring, and my next level prize was supposed to be the new iPhone.'

Lexie laughed. 'You think your life is boring, I watched my mum once and it was so painful. All she did was stare at the wine fridge for ages. I literally felt like messaging her and telling her to have a glass or two, I'd get the bus home or walk. Poor cow, she never drinks anything because she says it doesn't agree with her, yet she spends more time watching the wine fridge than the TV.'

Lexie walked out onto the first-floor landing, laughing. She didn't notice the figure in the shadows watching her, their gloved hands holding a plastic bag, with a piece of rope dangling from their pocket along with some cable ties.

FIFTY

The whole drive, Morgan couldn't shake the feeling of complete and utter fear that was lodged in the back of her throat. Turning onto the driveway for the big house she decided to go on up; hopefully Ben would get her message and be here soon, if she needed help. The house was so huge and forlorn standing against the backdrop of the mountains. Morgan didn't knock on the door, instead she turned the handle to see if it opened. It didn't, it was locked, which was good for security, not so good for her. She rushed around the perimeter of the building to get to the back door; she ran up the steps that led to the kitchen door and peered into the kitchen, her heart almost stopping instantly. At the table were Lexie and Natalie White, both of them red-faced, struggling to breathe, with plastic bags over their heads. Pulling out her police radio Morgan pressed the small orange button on the top of it. Once the button was pressed it vibrated loudly and transmitted every word spoken until it was turned off.

'Hellsfield Hall, Hellsfield Road. Urgent assistance, crime in progress, attempted murder.'

The door was locked, and Morgan had no choice but to

break a pane of glass. Smashing the small window with a rockery stone, she put her hand through to turn the key and let herself in. Natalie was no longer struggling against the bag pulled tight over her head. There was a cable tie keeping it in place. Morgan looked around saw the broken glass everywhere and instead of wasting time looking for a pair of scissors, she picked up a large shard and began sawing through the plastic. It snapped, and she tugged the bag off Natalie's face. She was unconscious but still breathing. Morgan pushed her forwards, so she was leaning on the table, then ran to Lexie whose eyes were bulging out of their sockets as she desperately tried to suck in air that wasn't there. Morgan did the same, sawing with the sharp glass until the plastic snapped, and then she dragged the bag off her head. Lexie was gulping for air. She pointed to the stairs and croaked, 'Ava.'

Morgan nodded. She had nothing to defend herself with against a killer, except the sharp piece of glass she clenched in her hand. Wrapping her fingers around it she didn't notice that it had sliced the skin of her fingers. Blood was dripping down from her hand, but she couldn't feel it, the adrenalin was pumping so fast around her body. She ran for the stairs, heading straight for Lexie's room. Standing inside the open doorway with her back to her was a blonde-haired woman, the same woman she'd spoken to outside of Sally's salon on Friday, who called herself Jackie Thorpe. She was struggling to control the teenage girl in her grip who was fighting for her life.

'Let her go, it's over.'

The woman's head shook from side to side, but she didn't turn to face Morgan. Instead, she tugged the plastic bag down over Ava's head, holding it tight so she couldn't breathe.

Morgan pressed the orange button on her radio again, and it started to vibrate against her trouser leg, so the control room could hear everything that was happening. Then she ran at her, hitting her hard from behind with her shoulder to knock her off balance, so hard that she let go of Ava who scrambled away from her, pulling the bag off her head.

'Run, Ava, the police are coming, let them in the front door.'

The woman turned to Morgan, her face a mask of fury.

It was her eyes that scared Morgan the most. They were so dark and showed not the slightest bit of fear. She took a gamble, and spoke, 'It's over, Jackie, you aren't the hand of God, you never were. I'm sorry for what you went through, no one should have to lose their parents like that, but you can't go around deciding who lives and who dies.'

Jackie smiled at her, but it didn't reach those cold, dead eyes. It merely lingered a little on her lips then died.

'I think you'll find that I can, and I have. They deserve to die, every single one of them. An eye for an eye, isn't that what the Bible teaches us? When a person causes another to suffer then they should suffer an equal amount. I have no use for eyes, but hands, well they mean something more to me.'

Morgan shook her head. 'Tim was a fourteen-year-old boy, he did nothing to you, neither has Lexie or Ava, yet you were willing to kill them, for what?'

'I don't care about their ages; my life was torn to pieces when I was only nine years old, and no one gave a fuck about me. Perfect Sally, who everyone loved, was a vile, horrible slut who instigated the events that night. But I got her back. Now it's Erica's turn.'

Morgan had to keep her talking. 'What about Jason, where does he fit in, he was involved too that night? Don't you see how it will never end? Trying to place blame won't bring your parents back.'

'Oh I'll get him, too, he would have been first, except he moved away years ago. I haven't found him yet, but it's only a matter of time.'

'Ava and Lexie don't deserve this, Jackie; you can't blame a child for the sins of their parents.'

She began to laugh. 'I suppose not, but you can torture that parent by killing the child. That bitch Erica ruined my life. She killed my parents and didn't care one little bit about me. It's only fair that she sees me kill her family before she dies too.'

Morgan hoped that backup was coming, as she didn't know how long she could keep Jackie talking. She caught a glimpse of flashing blue reflecting in the large picture window behind her, and turned her head. But she went a little too far, taking her attention away from Jackie. In that split second she rushed towards her, and Morgan saw the meat cleaver raised in the air. She froze as she was almost on her. Remembering the glass in her hand she turned away just enough so the cleaver whooshed through the air, narrowly missing her head, then turned back to ram the glass into her chest. At the final second she heard Cain shout, 'Morgan, get down.'

She dropped, just as he pulled the trigger on the taser and the two barbs shot out of it, embedding themselves into Jackie's chest. Jackie paused, her arm raised, her mouth open in anger, and then her entire body began to jerk as she fell to the floor, twitching, almost landing on Morgan.

Morgan scrabbled to get away from her, then Cain was there, his big hands pulling her to her feet. His face ashen as he shook his head, 'Too bloody close, Morgan, that was too bloody close.' Then he hugged her briefly before updating the control room that they needed an ambulance and that the suspect was on the ground.

Amy had Jackie's arms behind her back, and Cain passed her the handcuffs from his belt, and she expertly had them cuffed before Jackie could even move. The pounding of boots running up the stairs filled the air, and Morgan released the breath she'd been holding. Cain was right, it had been too close. The appearance of the response officers was a sight to behold as they filed in ready to deal with Jackie.

'Who's doing the honours?' Cain asked.

Morgan couldn't even find her voice and pointed at him.

'Me? Cool, thanks.' He bent down and began to read Jackie Thorpe her rights. 'You do not have to say anything. But it may harm your defence if you do not mention when questioned something which you later rely on in court. Anything you do say may be given in evidence.' Then he stood up. 'Come on, let's leave this piece of shit with our colleagues.'

They went downstairs, where they found Ava and Lexie were huddling together in the corner, and Nick, the paramedic, was bending over Natalie, who had an oxygen mask on, but her eyes were open, and she was okay.

Ben ran through the door, took one look at the scene then turned his attention to Morgan.

'You're bleeding.'

'I am?'

She looked down and realised that her fingers were bleeding. Uncurling them she let the huge shard of bloodied glass drop to the floor. 'Ouch, they are and they're stinging like mad.'

Nick rushed over, packets of gauze in his hand. He began to rip them open and pressed them into the palm of Morgan's hand.

'Try and press your fingers against it and raise your hand. They're not too bad, maybe need a couple of stitches.'

Morgan felt her knees begin to wobble, but before she could pass out Ben was there, his arm around her waist, guiding her to a chair.

Natalie lowered the mask and whispered, 'You saved our lives, thank you, Morgan.'

Cain patted her on the back. 'You did it again, super cop Brookes, don't you go and pass out on us because of a bit of blood.'

She laughed. 'I'm good, thanks.'

He winked at her. 'You know Amy drove like a madwoman to get to you.'

Morgan smiled at Amy, who nodded. 'We're not losing anyone else from this team.'

A second ambulance arrived, the paramedics glancing over the mess in the kitchen before being sent upstairs to transport Jackie to hospital with her escort of four burly police officers, to keep her from hurting anyone else.

FIFTY-ONE

Morgan thought Cain was right, it had been too close, for Ava, Lexie and Natalie not to mention herself. She looked across at the trio who were sitting on the sofa, all three of them getting the all clear from the paramedics. They'd probably have flashbacks for a very long time, but nothing a bit of counselling couldn't help with, she hoped.

Nick smiled at them. 'I think you're all good, but if you want to go to the hospital for a check-up then we can take you there.'

Natalie shook her head. 'No, we're all okay or as okay as we can be. I don't want to waste anyone's time.' Natalie looked pale, but she was breathing okay.

Nick shrugged. 'Your call, if you feel unwell then call an ambulance.'

'We will, thank you so much.'

Natalie turned to look at Ben who was standing alongside Cain. 'What happens now?'

'We'll take statements when you feel up to it. Is there anywhere you can go, or are you happy to stay here whilst we document the crime scene?'

'I'd rather be here, as much as possible. This place is big enough, we can keep out of your way. I don't feel like going to a hotel or anywhere else at the moment. I need to talk to you about my past.'

Morgan shook her head. 'I know all about it.'

Tears began to fall down Natalie's cheeks. 'You do? Then there are a lot of things I need to tell my husband and Lexie. It's time they knew the truth about who I am and what I did.'

Lexie, who was sitting with her arms around her mum, didn't let go, and Morgan smiled, their close calls with death had made them realise how lucky they were to be alive and to have each other.

Morgan nodded. 'That's good, what happened was a long time ago and a dreadful accident.'

'I can never change what I did that night. I've spent so many years wishing that I could. I'll find some way to make things better. Do you think I'll be able to talk to Jackie when all of this has died down?'

'I'm sure you will, if that's what you want.'

'I do, I was never allowed to tell her how sorry I was, how I wished that it had been me and not her parents who died.'

Natalie was crying. She bowed her head, and Lexie hugged her even tighter. Morgan knew that Natalie could never put right the destruction and heartbreak she'd caused that fateful night, but admitting it and speaking to Jackie might be a start.

Nick turned to Morgan. 'Do you want to go to hospital, or would you like me to sort those cuts out for you?'

'Could you do it?'

He smiled and took hold of her elbow, walking her outside to the ambulance.

'I don't know what happened here, but I think you had a close call, Morgan.'

She laughed. 'You think right.'

She held out her hands as he began to clean up the blood

from her fingers. Lifting them up he examined them carefully
and smiled. 'One bit of good news, they're not as deep as I
thought. I can glue them for you, if you want, and wrap them
up. Keep them dry and they'll be as good as new in a few days.'

'Amazing, thank you.'

Nick began to work on the cuts as her phone began to
vibrate in her pocket. She took it out and answered it to a now-
familiar voice.

*'Hey, it's Bev from the high-tech unit. Is now a good time to
talk?'*

Morgan laughed. 'Not really but go on.'

*'I found some stuff on Tim Lawson's computer, bless him.
He'd also been visiting a site called Stonewall, which is a coming
out advice site that gives support to young gay, lesbian, bi and
trans people about their sexual orientation. I wish I could have
met him and given him a bloody big hug; I remember what it was
like when I was his age. I was terrified about telling my mum I
didn't like boys, anyway, just thought I'd let you know.'*

'Oh, that's so sad, bless him it's such a tough age. Thanks,
Bev, bye.'

Morgan felt another piece of her heart break for Tim
Lawson, and she too wished she could give him a hug. Wished
she could have saved him from everything, and she felt hot tears
well up in the back of her eyes. The boy who had come home
with Tim, Ryan Cross, the person she'd never got around to
speaking to, she wondered if they had been in a relationship. He
must be devastated. She made up her mind to go and pay him a
visit. She would offer him what support she could; it was the
least she could do for him and for Tim.

A LETTER FROM HELEN

Dear reader,

I want to say a huge thank you for choosing to read *Their Burning Graves*. If you did enjoy it, and want to keep up-to-date with all my latest releases, just sign up at the following link. Your email address will never be shared and you can unsubscribe at any time.

www.bookouture.com/helen-phifer

I'd like to take a moment to thank you from the bottom of my heart for choosing to read this book. I'm so grateful to all my amazing readers for your support and for loving Morgan Brookes and taking her into your hearts. People often ask where I get my ideas for these stories, and I have to say just like Morgan I do love a true crime podcast and documentary. Sometimes I take little bits and pieces from them and turn them into my own or should I say Morgan's own nightmares.

In this story the Lawson family are brutally murdered, I had never heard of a Lawson family being murdered. Then my daughter, Jeorgia, told me I should watch 28 *Days Haunted* on Netflix because I love a good ghost adventure. Imagine my surprise when it showed an old black and white photograph of the Lawson family who were violently murdered in 1929 and no one was ever caught for it. It left me gawping at the TV for quite some time, it's a strange old world at times.

I hope you loved *Their Burning Graves* and if you did I would be very grateful if you could write a review. I'd love to hear what you think, and it makes such a difference helping new readers to discover one of my books for the first time.

I love hearing from my readers – you can get in touch on my Facebook page, through Twitter, Goodreads or my website.

Thanks,

Helen xxxx

www.helenphifer.com

 facebook.com/Helenphifer1
twitter.com/helenphifer1

ACKNOWLEDGEMENTS

For Emily, I can't believe this is our last book together. Thank you so much for your help in making Morgan Brookes what she is today. It's been quite a journey and I'm so thankful I got to take it with you. I will miss working with you more than you could ever imagine, you have literally changed my life and I will forever be indebted to you. I wish you all the luck in the world in your new role, you will be fabulous because you are one of those special humans that literally sparkle and shine their way through life. However, it's not goodbye because you owe me coffee, or do I owe it to you? Hahaha, I actually owe you much more than coffee but it's a start.

To the fabulous team Bookouture, thank you for all your hard work. It takes a whole team to turn a rough draft of a story into a gorgeous, shiny book and I couldn't do it without you all. Huge thanks to Jenny Geras for believing in my stories and being one of the most amazing, inspirational women I know. A huge thanks to Janette Currie for her tireless work on the copy edit front. Thank you to the amazing design team who always blow my socks off with the gorgeous covers. A huge thank you to the marketing team and everyone else who are so amazing to work with, there are just too many of you to thank individually but you are so deeply appreciated.

A massive thank you to my publicity gal, Noelle Holten, who works so hard on cover release and publication days. You have had my back more times than I can remember and you're such an amazing wing gal. Huge thanks also go to Kim Nash,

Sarah Hardy and Jess Readett for all their hard work too, it's very much appreciated.

As always, a huge thanks to my fellow Bookouture authors who are always so wonderfully supportive and just downright amazing. It still blows my mind to know that I get to mix with such a talented bunch of bestselling writers, but my favourite is drinking Prosecco with you all at the summer parties. There is no party like a summer, Prosecco filled party!

A huge thanks goes to Alison Campbell who brings Morgan to life so brilliantly and the rest of the Audio Factory team.

Thank you to Paul O'Neill for being my favourite surveyor of all time and his super-fast reports. You literally make my life so much better, Paul, and I'm so grateful to you for your support.

Thank you to all the friends whose names I steal for my characters, I hope you'll forgive me one day.

A massive thank you goes to Nigel Adams for his wealth of knowledge when it comes to the fire service and forensic investigation. If I have got anything wrong, I'm sorry and I hope you can forgive me. You were so kind and helpful I can't thank you enough for sharing everything with me and answering questions.

As always, a huge thank you to all my gorgeous, supportive readers. I wouldn't be writing these stories without your support. I'm so lucky to have the most amazing readers and friends who are always so kind and generous with your love for my stories. I wish I could hug you all, you mean the world to me. That you read my books when there are so many to choose from absolutely blows my socks off, I honestly can't thank you enough.

Thank you to my home gals, Sam Thomas and Tina Sykes, who are always there for coffee and a chat to talk about real life. You really do keep me sane, and I love seeing you both.

A massive thank you to Jessica Silvester-Yeo for her brilliant, ingenious ideas and help with all the stuff I'm rubbish at. You keep my Instagram alive and my newsletter worthy of opening.

I'm so grateful to all the amazing book bloggers out there who are so lovely and supportive. You're all wonderful, special and so very much appreciated. It honestly means the world to me that you choose to read my books and are so generous telling others about them. You are the rock stars of the book world.

A massive thank you to the absolutely wonderful Selina Smith for all her help looking after Jaimea who adores you. You have no idea how much you've changed our lives and eased the pressure; you are literally a saint and we all can't ever thank you enough.

As always thanks to my husband, Steve, who is there to push me out of the door and into my office to write on the days I say I can't be bothered. He's also my number one bag carrier on all of our little road trips.

Thank you to my gorgeous kids Jess, Josh, Jerusha, Jaimea and Jeorgia for growing up into pretty amazing humans.

A huge thank you also to Tom, Danielle and Deji for being so lovely and putting up with my kids ☺

Lastly, thank you to my adorable grandkids Gracie, Donny, Lolly, Tilda, Bonnie, Sonny and Sienna who I love more than life itself. You all bring me so much joy and pleasure not to mention the best cuddles a Nanna could ask for.